DARK VANITY

Not your typical Hollywood murder...

Gregory E. Seller

ISBN 978-1-7371682-0-1 (paperback)
ISBN 978-1-7371682-1-8 (hardback)
Library of Congress Control Number: 2021910018

Hardback
Paperback
Ebook

Published by Gregory Seller Consulting, LLC
Palm Springs, California

Author: Gregory E. Seller

Editor: Lynn Jones Green

Cover concept created by Oscar Lievano, Adkins & Associates

Cover/interior design and layout:
Mark E. Anderson, www.aquazebra.com

AquaZebra™
Web, Book & Print Design

Printed in the United States of America

Dedication

For my muses, Blade & Penny

Table of Contents

Freefall

Blair screams as she sees the body falling from the tenth floor of a corner balcony in the building next door. She jumps up from her chair, martini still in hand. It seems to happen in slow motion. This beautiful male body dressed in a tuxedo executes a perfect swan dive off his balcony and holds form all the way down until he vanishes behind the tall trees ten floors below.

Blair peers over the railing of her balcony in disbelief. Feeling like all the air has left her lungs leaving her unable to inhale, Blair falls backward, her martini glass smashing under her. She hits her head on the balcony floor and loses consciousness. Her hand and back are bleeding from the shattered martini glass as she lies motionless on her balcony. A stream of blood flows around her.

Just moments earlier, Blair had made her usual evening cocktail before stepping out onto her balcony. Nolet's gin, taken from the freezer, poured into a Baccarat martini shaker with a few shards of ice. Not cubes, but shards, pounded by hand. She slowly shakes this concoction with her beautiful hands for just a few seconds. It sits for a minute, then she gently pours it into a very tall, frozen martini glass. To finish, a sole olive, pimento removed, speared with a silver toothpick, dipped in vermouth, then drowned immediately in the waiting gin. The ice shards rise to the top.

Blair hoists her martini glass and whispers, "Perfect." Then, a slow sip. Her head rolls back. A glance in the mirror above the bar, a wink and a smile back. For Blair, this is the blissful end to each day, whether it has been dreadful or utterly perfect. This day would end dreadfully in just a few minutes.

With her perfect gin martini in hand, Blair steps out onto her balcony, eight floors above the pool and lush gardens below. It is a warm and very breezy September evening in Los Angeles. The sun has just set, and the breeze is getting stronger. Blair sits in her favorite chair near the balcony railing, her martini placed in the center of the high-top table at the corner of the balcony. The tall buildings to the west in Santa Monica are visible in the distance, and a low bank of fog rolls in at the coast. The setting sun dips into the fog, making for an early twilight, that magical time between night and day.

And then she sees him. A stunning figure in the building next door, standing on his corner balcony on the tenth floor, gazing back at Blair with steel-blue eyes. Though too far away to see the color of his eyes, she knew them to be steel-blue. In fact, she knew them well. Closing her eyes, she takes a deep breath to slow her racing heart. When her eyes open, this handsome figure draws closer to the railing, leaning over to gaze at her.

He is fabulous, even at a distance. Tall, thin, but with a muscular upper body. And that smile, so alluring even from afar.

Wearing a white tuxedo shirt and black bow tie, blonde hair blowing in the breeze, he hoists his martini glass to her and smiles. She nods, smiles back, and they both take a sip from their martinis. She gazes at him as he licks the rim of his martini glass, slowly and deliberately, while staring down at her from his balcony. Aroused by his attention, her breathing intensifies when he finishes licking the rim of his glass and smiles at her. She imagines his embrace and how he smelled when they first kissed. That smile, the steely gaze of his blue eyes. Even from afar, she knows how intense they are.

Lifting his arms up from the railing, he finishes his martini in one gulp and blows her a kiss. He hoists himself up on a table at the edge of his balcony, an empty martini glass still in hand. He winks and blows another kiss to Blair. Turning to face the back of the building from his corner balcony, Blair can now only see his profile as he stands on the table with his eyes fixed on something far below. It startles Blair at first, but then she smiles, nods her head, and blows a kiss back at him. He continues to gaze down at the ground below for almost a minute, as if to calculate something in his head. At first, confused by his actions, the anticipation now arouses Blair. He quickly jumps off the table to the floor of his balcony, carrying his empty martini glass back inside the apartment. Seconds later, he emerges from his apartment without a martini glass, but now wearing his tuxedo jacket. He runs to the table at the corner of the balcony and again hoists himself up on top. Lifting his hands over his head, he looks like a diver preparing to jump. Hands together over his head, he arches back slightly, takes a deep breath, and springs off the table over the balcony railing. It's a perfect swan dive, as if he is diving into a pool, but in this case the pool is ten stories below. The tuxedo jacket fits so perfectly, it barely flutters as his beautiful body falls from the balcony and straight into the garden below.

In total disbelief, Blair jumps up and screams. She leans over her railing to see his falling body vanish behind the tall trees and hedges surrounding the pool and gardens in the building next door. She faints and falls backward onto her balcony with her martini glass smashing beneath her.

A View to Die For

He holds the binoculars close to his eyes. The sun has just dipped into the fog to the west, so it is now twilight and becoming more difficult to see. He's been waiting on the roof of this building for more than an hour.

Spotting his first target in the building next door, he whispers to himself, "Hmm. *Finally*. The rendezvous." Letting the binoculars drop from his eyes, he turns to a small television monitor beside him. The picture is wobbly, but he now fixes the drone camera on his *second* target. The second target is on a balcony several floors below him in the same building.

From his vantage point on top of the Wilshire Palms condominiums, he observes the sensual choreography of the handsome blonde man in the tuxedo on the tenth-floor balcony of the building next door called The Colonnade. Another whisper to himself: "Could he be any more handsome?"

The drone camera captures the *other* target several floors below him in the Wilshire Palms. She is beautiful. With a martini in hand, she's flirting with the handsome man in the tuxedo in the building next door. Focusing his binoculars on the man in the tuxedo, he also glances back to the monitor from the drone. It amuses him to witness the visual foreplay of the two balcony voyeurs.

"Here we go," he whispers to himself as the handsome man in the tuxedo shirt runs back into his apartment and emerges only seconds later wearing the tuxedo jacket over his shirt, neatly buttoned. The man runs to the corner of the balcony and hoists himself up on a table at the edge of the railing.

The drone camera shows the momentary shock on the face of the beautiful woman on the balcony below as the man in the tuxedo in the building next door strikes a diver pose and prepares to jump off the table.

Looking through the binoculars, he smiles at his target next door. "Okay, Casanova, here's your big move. Do you have the guts or not?"

The handsome target in the tuxedo arches back and makes a perfect swan dive off the balcony ten floors above the ground. The binoculars follow him all the way down until his body vanishes behind the trees in the back of the building next door. His form is perfect, but deadly.

Taking the binoculars from his neck, he smiles, then moves to stare intently at the drone monitor. Target number two is distressed and screams as she witnesses the perfect, ten-story swan dive.

The drone camera watches target number two fall to the floor of her balcony and pass out. As if on cue, a pool of blood forms around her body. He frowns and becomes concerned. *Should there be that much blood from a broken glass?*

After a few minutes, the woman in the pool of blood on the balcony moves. It is getting dark, so he has the drone camera zoom in closer. Her eyes are still closed, and her face shows she is in pain. He wonders, *Could she script this any better? If only her acting was as good as this performance. Such a bitch.*

The drone camera stays fixed on target number two until she fully regains consciousness and moves. She slowly gets up, gazes over the balcony in disbelief, then walks inside the open French door to her apartment.

He sighs in relief that target number two is not dead. He then moves the drone to the back side of the building next door to examine the resting spot of target number one, the swan-diving man in the tuxedo. As the drone moves closer, he is not happy with what he sees. The swan diver lies motionless next to, but not on, a large, inflated cushion. The diver missed a four-foot thick custom mattress used by stuntmen to cushion falls from high places. A tall, thin man in a black suit is leaning over the body, taking pictures. He recognizes this man almost instantly. *Crap, how'd this asshole get involved? Why is he there?* He moves the drone even closer so the camera can snap a few pictures. In a matter of seconds, another person appears on the pool deck and is noticing the drone. He quickly pulls the drone back and pushes a button on the control that says "Home." Within a minute, the drone lands a few feet from him on the roof of the Wilshire Palms.

Placing the drone in a case and the binoculars and drone controller in a bag, he dons his sunglasses and hat, and then he puts on a pair of leather gloves. Moving away from the cooling tower on the top of the Wilshire Palms, he quickly makes his way to the emergency stairwell.

As soon as he exits the stairwell in the parking garage of the Wilshire Palms, his cell phone rings.

"He fucked it up, damn it! Did you see it? I'm screwed. Screwed!" The caller is obviously frantic, and in a state of shock. "Did you hear me? Are you there? You've got to help me! Shit! It's all fucked."

"Calm down. I saw him miss the fall mat. Is he hurt? How badly? Or is he dead?"

"Well, of course he's dead! You don't fall ten stories and survive. He missed the fucking mat! How am I going to get out of this?"

Trailer Tryst

Blair regains consciousness, her head throbbing from the fall. With no idea how long she has been unconscious, Blair attempts to get up. Her hand is bleeding from the broken martini glass, and her dress is wet with perspiration and blood. Feeling sick to her stomach, Blair tries to stand up, feels dizzy, and falls back again. Reaching for the railing of the balcony, she pulls herself up.

Peering over the railing, Blair first looks down below. Nothing. No activity or noise. She then looks back up at the empty balcony on the tenth floor of the building next door. She hears nothing except for the hum of traffic on Wilshire Boulevard on the front side of her building. Her puzzled mind asks, *Why is there no commotion next door? Did no one see what happened?*

Rubbing her forehead, Blair turns away from the balcony, opens the French door to her living room, and steps inside. She reaches for her cell phone sitting on the cocktail bar, dials 911, but then disconnects before even hearing the first ring tone. Putting her phone down, she looks at herself in the mirror over the bar, whispering aloud, "Blair. Think this through. Did you see this happen?"

Blair knew the answer to her whisper was yes, it happened. If she saw it happen, then *someone else* did too. Two high-rise condominium buildings, with twenty floors each, sit right next to each other on Wilshire Boulevard. Someone else had to be on their balcony or down at the pool in the building next door when this beautiful body came crashing down from ten floors above. It was almost dark when it happened, but there had to be other witnesses. So why should she get involved? *But I'm already involved. How can I say I'm not?*

Witnessing this event cannot be helpful to her career. And for Blair, every decision, every move she makes depends on whether it helps her career. Blair is a successful British actress, thirty-three years old, with a major part in a popular TV mini-series in the U.S. She is also competing for a starring role in a major film and made it through the first three rounds of auditions. It is now down to her and two other women, both of whom are younger. While Blair has good acting credentials, she is a bit old for the part. She is also a buxom brunette, with dark olive skin, whereas the part calls for a sleek blonde with fair skin. No matter. Blair knows she can adjust her looks for the part and will do whatever she needs to do to get that role. This is a big part with a major Hollywood director, and at thirty-three years old, she won't get roles written for younger women much longer.

She goes back out to the balcony and looks down one more time. It's dark and still silent next door. *Is it a trick?* she wonders. *That beautiful body can't be just lying there in a pool of blood and nobody notices.* And she knows that he had a beautiful body.

It had happened only that afternoon at the studio commissary. He'd spotted her as she entered the dining room reserved for actors only. Blair had her tray of food from the commissary line and was walking toward the entrance to the dining room where a sign read "NO FILM CREW PERMITTED."

Seated by himself at a table for two, he lifted his head and smiled at her as she eyed the room for a place to sit. She smiled back and then proceeded to a solo table she spotted out on the patio. He was very handsome and looked familiar to her, but she couldn't place him. As she passed by, he stood up and pulled out a chair at his table. She stopped, and he waved for her to sit. "Please, join me. We're working together."

His statement confused Blair. "And where will we be working together?" she asked.

He winked at her. "Let me tell you all about it." He then motioned for her to sit. She paused for a moment, then took the chair being held out for her, noticing how striking he was up close. Tall, blonde, muscular upper body, steel-blue eyes, and a trim waistline. Something awfully familiar about him, but she didn't know why.

Blair frowned at him, "If you're part of the film crew, you know you shouldn't even be in here."

"Ouch. That hurt," he replied.

"Since you know who I am, may I ask who you are?"

"Excuse my manners. My name is Reid. Reid Garrett."

Blair hesitated for a moment. How could she not have recognized him? She felt embarrassed. "Ah. Episode six. We film next month. Funny, you don't look like your pictures." She felt stupid for saying that the moment it popped out of her mouth.

"Makes two of us."

Blair winces. "I'm not sure how to take that."

"Oh, come now. We'll have a steamy sexual affair for three episodes, so let's at least pretend we're attracted to each other."

"Three episodes? I don't think so. You're a guest star for one episode."

Reid leaned forward and whispered, "You haven't read your script."

"Never do. Not until the week before filming."

"Well, that's too bad, because we need to rehearse some difficult scenes."

"Oh? Difficult scenes? That would be a stretch for this dreadful little show. Everything has been so predictable."

"You're wrong."

"Well, we shall see."

"Let me show you after lunch."

"I won't have time. I need to be back on the set in less than an hour. Some other time, Mr. Garrett." It intrigued Blair, but she was wary of his motives.

Reid wiped his mouth with his napkin and stood up. He took Blair's napkin from her lap, wipes her mouth, and pushed her tray away. "If you've only an hour, I suggest we eat later."

Blair grabs at her tray and scowls at Reid. "And what do you think you're doing?"

"Taking you to my trailer. To show you the script. I promise I won't disappoint you." He takes Blair by the arm and she stands up from the table, taking one last gulp from her glass of iced tea.

"I'm not sure why I'm doing this, but . . ."

Blair, never one to pass up a dalliance, held Reid's arm as they left the commissary and proceeded to his trailer. Their joint exit from the actor's dining room didn't go unnoticed by the other diners, most of whom were gazing at handsome Reid dining alone before Blair joined him. They knew who he was, even if Blair had not.

Reid's trailer was behind the soundstage and not near most of the other dressing room trailers. Blair found that odd. "For such a big star, you only have a trailer out here in the crew parking lot?"

Reid smiled. "Not to worry, Ms. Kilian. My part doesn't start until next month. My trailer location will improve once I'm part of the show."

Blair glanced over her shoulder, happy to see that no one else was around as Reid escorted her into his trailer. Her heart raced as he waved her in, grinning from ear to ear. She realized it was a fancy star wagon, much nicer than Blair's. With no mention of a script, and neither one of them saying a word, they embraced and undressed each other.

Reid displayed his naked body, and Blair was all too eager to take advantage of it. He was tall, his body toned and muscular. The hair on his head was thick and blonde, but his pubic hairs were black. Drawing back the sheets on his bed, a wave of his hand invited Blair to join him. He winked at her and smiled as they embraced.

Reid and Blair became aroused so quickly, their sexual romp ended in exciting satisfaction for both, but more quickly than either would have liked. Reid knew his luncheon bet had paid off. He had Blair Kilian in his bed. Exactly as he had planned, and perfectly executed.

Less than thirty minutes later, Blair was putting her dress back on and fixing her hair. "You have a shabby make-up trailer, Mr. Garrett. No makeup and not even a comb."

Reid still lay in bed naked and aroused. He smiled at her and said, "Pardon my bad manners. I don't think the studio outfits my trailer until my role begins. While I don't have a comb or make-up, I've got some tasty wine and champagne in the fridge. Stay for another romp. Look, I'm ready to go!"

Blair smiled. "Bad enough I will be late on the set. I can't show up drunk as well!"

"How about later?"

Blair was quiet for a moment but wanted to say yes. She found him exhilarating in the sack and wanted more. "I've got dinner with my agent tonight."

"Too bad. How about a toast before you go out, and then I'll come over after dinner?"

"A toast? That's it? Just a toast? Where?"

"Well, we're neighbors, so that should be easy."

"You live in my building? You live in the Wilshire Palms?"

"Not quite. The building next door."

"The Icon?"

"No, other side. The Colonnade."

"Well, why didn't you say so? Where should we meet?" Blair desperately wanted to see him again. Their tryst aroused something in her she hadn't felt for a long time. His bed manners were sensual and on the rough side—exactly as she liked it.

"You'll see me," he assured her.

"I'll see you? Where?"

"Are you having your usual cocktail before you go out? Around 6:30?"

"I imagine so, why?" Blair was curious about how he would know her evening cocktail routine, and she was unnerved.

"Look for me," he said.

Blair glanced at him, confused. "Where?"

"Just . . . look for me."

And with that, Reid got out of bed, still naked and a bit aroused, and he opened his trailer door for Blair. As she headed out the door, Reid put his arms on her shoulders and pulled the back of her neck to his mouth. His long kiss on her neck gave her goose-bumps. Reid smiled and thought, *This couldn't have gone better.*

She sighed and started down the steps out of his trailer. As she walked away, she turned to Reid and shouted, "You still owe me lunch."

Reid smiled, blew her a kiss and replied, "Toast you tonight!"

4

A Very Successful Seduction

Alton Price is the best "fixer" in Hollywood. He takes care of trouble that celebrities, producers, business tycoons, and even prominent clergy get themselves into. Most commonly, it's a sexual indiscretion that needs to be covered up or a messy mishap that needs to "go away" and stay hidden from the public or paparazzi. Occasionally, it's a carnal adventure gone wrong that results in a death. Alton makes the death scene less gruesome before they call the cops. From time to time, he addresses a murder, committed either by mistake or intention. Those are the messiest, and most costly mistakes to "fix."

The Los Angeles Police Department detectives all know Alton. His perfection in concealing crimes and misbehavior frustrates them. They often recognize his handiwork in altering or hiding a crime but can't implicate him directly. Alton loves that part of his job the most.

Most often, the client hires Alton directly. Other times, the studio, a producer, or a lawyer hires him to take care of a problem for one of their clients. He's known for producing results, but the process is usually ugly and often skirts the law. No one else in town is as good at his craft as Alton Price. But then, none of the other "fixers" or private investigators in town used to be on foreign counter-intelligence assignment for the Central Intelligence Agency. While the terms under which he left the CIA have never been clear, his former colleagues revere him and fear him, all at the same time. Some of them still help him when he needs it.

Others can't wait for him to make a fatal mistake.

Standing at his bathroom sink, Alton is carefully trimming his beard, which he keeps closely cropped and tightly groomed. His jet-black hair is just beginning to turn gray at his temples and at the beard line under his chin. With a chiseled face and perfect smile, he is often more handsome than the celebrities who hire him. The blue eyes with the dark complexion and hair give him an exotic look, but he's just a boy from suburban Los Angeles County.

Putting his scissors away, Alton stands back from the sink and looks at his naked body in the mirror. Lots of dark chest hair, but not too thick, and a body that is tall and trim. He's toned but not muscular. The body of a yoga or athletic Pilates fanatic, of which he is both. But no yoga or Pilates today. He takes a deep breath, slides his hands from his chest down to his groin, rubs the hair around his penis and then reaches his long hands down to the floor for a deep stretch.

Hearing the ping of a cell phone text message, Alton rises from his stretch and glances at the screen on his phone. The text message says, "Calling you now." Seconds later, Alton Price picks up the call on the first ring. "Mission accomplished?"

The caller is extremely excited and replies, "Yes! It was perfect!"

"Perfect in bed or perfect completion of the assignment?"

"Both."

"Well, for being in L.A. for such a short time, you've quickly developed a Hollywood attitude."

"I like it here and I like her. Didn't think I would, but I do."

Alton replies, "Well, I'm not crazy about your liking her just yet."

"Why?"

"Not important. Are you sure she'll show up tonight? On time?"

"Yes, absolutely," the caller replies confidently.

"Oh, how I love that word, 'absolutely.'"

"What now?" the caller asks.

"Where are you?"

"In the studio parking lot."

"They recognized you, right?"

"Yes, front gate and in the commissary."

"How about her? Did she know you?"

"Funny, not at first, but when I said my name was Reid Garrett, it embarrassed her."

"She's not the brightest actress in Tinseltown."

"Very sexy, though. That's for sure. This thing we are setting her up for, it won't hurt her, will it?"

"No more questions," Alton responds. "That's a wrap on your performance. That's all you need to know. Lie low. Put on the hat and sunglasses, and drive to my place right now. No stops. Don't talk to anyone. Put the car in the garage and Jimmy will come for it later."

"That's it? I'm done?"

"Done for right now. I'll explain more tonight."

"Thank you, Alton."

Both men hang up.

Alton sends a text to someone else, "Call me."

Immediately, his cell phone rings. "She took the bait. Or should I say, she enjoyed the bait. She'll be there tonight."

The caller replies, "That's great. Blair will be on her balcony tonight for her usual cocktail? About 6:30?"

"That's what he tells me. She's smitten with him and will be on her balcony to toast him before she has dinner with her agent tonight. You *are* still her agent, aren't you, Cam?"

"Don't rub it in, Alton."

"So, let your star boy know that you accomplished your task, that you did what he wanted, and you set the bait."

"Yes. I'll let him know."

"Cam, are you ready for all of this to unfold? You know what he's up to, right?"

"Yes, I know what he's doing. You'll be there?"

"Taken care of."

"Oh God, Alton, I feel so terrible for her."

"You should feel sorrier for yourself. Bit of a mess you created with your psychotic star boy, wouldn't you say?"

Silence on the other end, then Cam muffles, "I know."

"I'll let you know how things go tonight. It won't be pretty, so you know what to expect."

"I do."

5

Swan Dive Becomes Swan Song

"Why are you calling me on your cell phone, you prick? I gave you a disposable phone to use for tonight."

"Yeah, well, you know what? At this point it won't matter."

"Well, it matters to me. I don't want my number on your cell phone tonight. Hang up and call me back on the disposable phone."

While waiting for the frantic caller to phone him from his disposable phone, the man with the drone looks at the pictures on the drone camera. He thinks, *That shit? He did it purposely. Damn him.* His cell phone rings again, and the caller ID says "Caller unknown."

"That you, Reid?" he asks.

"Shit, Tony, who do you think it is?"

"Hey, spoiled star boy, I wouldn't get snotty with me tonight. You're an accomplice in manslaughter."

"It's not my fault! He missed the fall mat, the fucking idiot!"

"Oh, he didn't miss it. They moved the mat."

Reid is stunned. "What? How? How does a huge, inflated fall mat just move ten feet? No, he fucked up. He miscalculated."

"Reid, he is one of . . . well, he *was* one of the best stuntmen in town. He's made ten-story leaps hundreds of times, so he knew what he was doing. They moved the mat as he jumped off the balcony, and he didn't have time to adjust his trajectory."

"Moved the mat? How?"

"Not 'how'. . . 'who.' I think the asshole is Alton Price; I saw him on the drone camera. He was right there at the edge of the mat after your little swan diver hit the flower bed. Looks like he had two guys dressed as caterers with him to assist."

Reid is furious. "Fuckin' Alton Price? Who's he working for? It can't be Blair Kilian; that bitch didn't know what would happen tonight. She couldn't have tipped him off." He stops to consider the horrific situation, then continues: "Oh shit, this is terrible! I hired the catering staff. So how did he slip in there? No one was to be there except my phony caterers, the photographer, and the models. Crap, what do we do?"

Tony shoots back, "First off, where the hell are the phony caterers you hired? Weren't they supposed to deflate the fall mat and sneak it, and your diver boy stuntman out of there? Wasn't that your plan?"

Reid's voice softens. "Yeah, that was the plan, but now it's all fucked up. When they saw Derek miss the mat and hit the flower bed, they called me in the apartment right away. I told them to deflate the fall mat, pack up the catering shit and put everything in the catering van. Then to get the hell out of there."

"Okay, but what about Derek's body?"

"I told them to tell the security guard a guest drank too much and passed out somewhere in the bushes by the pool. The guard told them he would check on the guest. I didn't want my guys carrying out a dead body."

"Shit, so you left the body there?"

Reid is crying. "Sorry, but yeah. I didn't know what else to do. Shit. I am *so* fucked."

"All right. All right. So, your five buddies posing as caterers got out, and they took the fall mat with them?"

"Yep. The catering shit and the deflated fall mat are all in the rental van. They're gone."

"What about your other guests?" Tony asks.

"Just two girls and a photographer. The girls and the photographer left before Derek's big performance. That's it, there's no one else."

"Ok, so Derek's body is laying down there in the bushes somewhere. That's where I saw Price. He snapped a couple pictures right after the fall. Looks like he left before your buddies deflated the fall mat. The models and photographer; did they see what happened?"

"No, they were on the other side of the pool in the rose garden. I told Bobby to keep them away from the fall mat and to be sure they didn't witness the fall. Turns out they left early because it bored them."

"Who's Bobby?"

"My friend. He's the photographer."

Tony asks Reid, "Do you trust him?"

"Hope so. I never told him what we were doing, and he left early with the models, anyway."

"Why were models there with a photographer?"

"A diversion. It had to look like an actual party and a photo shoot. That's what we told the building when we rented the pool deck for three hours."

"Ok, so Derek's body is lying there somewhere in the bushes, and your boys cleared everything else out?"

"Yup."

"Was there blood? On Derek's body?"

"Uh, yeah, there was some blood coming out of his nose," Reid replies. "He hit the bushes hard, but they said he wasn't bleeding anywhere but from his nostrils. At least, that's all they saw when they were deflating the fall mat."

"Are you sure he's dead?"

"Oh, fuck, Tony, are you kidding? You fall ten stories and only get a bruise? He's dead. They said he wasn't moving and wasn't breathing. I told them not to touch him or try to move him because a ten-story fall breaks every bone in your body. I told them to deflate the mat, get the catering stuff, and get out of there."

Tony clears his throat, "Okay. So where are you now?"

"Sitting in my car down the street."

"Go home. If anyone calls you, stick to the plan."

"Oh God, what about Derek? Shit! He's got a wife and a kid. Fuckin' Alton Price! He murdered Derek! But why?"

"I don't know why and don't know how he got involved in your little scheme. Do you think he's on to you? To us? Or does he have a grudge with Derek?"

"I don't know the answer to any of those questions, Tony. But you got Price's picture on the drone camera?"

Tony is silent for a moment. "Not quite. I saw him on the drone camera, but by the time I snapped the shot, he'd vanished. It was getting dark anyway. It was him, but I don't have a picture to prove it."

"Oh, fuck. Should I go see Derek's wife?"

"Does his wife know he was doing this little stunt for you tonight?"

"No, she doesn't. He retired from high dives and rough stunt work after their kid was born. He was doing double's stuff, stand-in work and light stunts. His wife wouldn't let him do any more of the high dives or film shoots with aggressive driving. He made an exception for me. Well, for the money. I would pay him fifteen thousand dollars for that dive."

"Did you give him the money?"

"No. I have it here in my car and would have given it to him when I took him home, but now that's not happening. Shit, now what?"

Tony uses a gentle voice: "You go home. Let the police contact his wife. Will there be anything on his body that would link him to you? Are you in his cell phone directory?"

"He was wearing a tuxedo I rented for him. Same size as mine. He carries nothing with him when he does high-diving stunts. I don't think he had anything in his pockets. And yes, I'm sure that I'm in his phone directory."

"What about his wallet, cell phone, keys and things like that?"

"Shit, I don't know," Reid cried.

"Did he give anything to you?"

"No. I picked him up a couple blocks from his house and drove him to the gig. I don't think he had anything with him, but I'm not sure."

"What about his clothes? What was he wearing when you

picked him up?"

"Gym clothes. I put them in my bag because I was to rendezvous with my guys after the party and Derek would change clothes in my car. I'd take the tuxedo he was wearing, then he'd put his clothes back on, and I'd drop him at his house. That was the plan."

"Check his clothes. If you find his cell phone, let me know. If you don't find it, then he must have left it at home. Will there be voicemails or text messages about this stunt?"

Reid is silent.

"I'll take that as a yes, you stupid ass."

"Well, what about . . . ?"

"Enough!" Tony cuts Reid off. "I've had enough for tonight. You have too. Go home. I'll call you tomorrow once I know what the police have found. You know who I have to tell about this, don't you?"

"Shit, yes. I'm sorry."

Reid hangs up, and Tony shakes his head while he dials another number. The man on the receiving end of the call answers, "Yes?"

"Problem. I've got a potential problem. Seems our Hollywood boy may have botched up recruiting our newest addition to the club."

The voice on the other end of the line sighs and then asks, "How so?"

"There may be a body in the bushes by the pool at the Colonnade Condominium. Or the body may turn up dumped somewhere. Stunt man, named Derek Christopher. I need to be sure I've got the cell phone when the police find the body."

"Shit, Campanelli, I'm supposed to do the setup, not the cleanup."

"I know," Tony assures him. "I'll try to handle it on my own, but if that phone turns up with the cops, I need it."

"Give me the address they'll use to report this to 911."

"Colonnade condominium building on Wilshire Boulevard. They should report finding a guest in the bushes after a party. It was a photo shoot."

"Shit, Campanelli. That sounds fishy just from the start. How much latitude you giving our star boy partner these days? I've always thought him to be a dope. Did you sign off on the newest victim being added to our club?"

"I did, sir. She's got lots of connections, and there's a personal relationship that links her to one of our current club members. A connection that will let us raise his fee to remain silent, if you know what I mean."

"Ok. I'll follow this one as soon as they call it in. It will probably be officers responding from the Brentwood station. Don't make this a habit, Campanelli." The man on the other end of the call hangs up.

A Double Agent

As she comes in from the balcony to her living room, Blair shakes her head, as if it will make the events of the day and this evening go away. She glances at her watch. It's nearly 8:00 p.m., and she is meeting her agent for dinner at 9:00 p.m. She makes one more visit to the balcony, leans over, and only hears the traffic on the other side of the building. The sharp pieces of crystal from her broken martini glass are still on the floor of the balcony, as is a sizable pool of her blood. She opts to deal with the clean-up after dinner. Her dress is blood-stained from her fall on the balcony, her hair a mess, and a gash on her arm is still bleeding.

Confused and distraught, Blair glances at herself in the mirror over the bar and concludes she's too upset to meet her agent for dinner. Then she hesitates. *If* something bad really happened to Reid Garrett next door, then deviating from her plans might look suspicious. And, if there was anyone looking for witnesses in her building, she'd rather be unavailable. She looks at her pained face in the mirror and thinks, *I really liked him. How could this happen?*

Then another thought fills her head. What if she just witnessed the suicide of a well-known actor? But why would he seduce her earlier that same day? Was he just wanting to be sure he had a witness to his suicide?

Blair opts to put that question out of her mind and stay on schedule for dinner with her agent. She changes her dress, cleans up the blood from her arm and back, and freshens up. After touching up her hair and makeup, she heads downstairs to the lobby. Her mother, who is a prominent British actress, often told Blair she was insensitive as a child, and even worse as an adult. "You act with empathy when you have an acting part that demands it, but you can't seem to find it within you for your own life."

As she summons the elevator, her stomach tightens up, and she feels faint again. Despite shrugging off what she just saw, the fact she likely saw Reid Garrett commit suicide torments her. Or did she see it? Could it be a joke? He had seduced her into his bed this afternoon and told her he would join her in a toast from the building next door. Was it just scripted as a joke? That is the option Blair can live with—at least through dinner with her agent.

Her agent has sent a car for her, which is waiting downstairs as she exits the lobby.

"Good Evening, Ms. Kilian."

Blair half-smiles at Jimmy, the usual driver her agent sends to retrieve her for social events. She finds him just too cheerful and familiar. Blair prefers strangers. No need for small talk with them. People like Jimmy are inconvenient, since they require her to feign interest or courtesy, both of which she views as insincere and therefore a waste of time. She prefers to be with people who can do something *for* her, not vice versa. Acting is a tough business, particularly for women. Blair's mother struggled for years to become a successful British actress, and she told Blair, "To get ahead in this business, it's better for a woman to be tough instead of nice. Don't forget that." Blair has her mother's words written on a piece of paper and taped to the make-up mirror wherever she works.

Jimmy cheerfully looks at Blair in the rearview mirror and asks, "We are on our way to join Mr. Haines for dinner at Spago, right?"

Blair ignores Jimmy's glance by staring out the side window. "No, *we* aren't having dinner with Mr. Haines, but I am. And yes, at Spago."

Jimmy clears his throat but says nothing.

She arrives at Spago in Beverly Hills just a few minutes late.

There are many newer, trendier restaurants nearby, but Blair loves Spago and dines there often. She loves being recognized, and as a well-known place for tourists to spot movie stars, Spago always boosts her ego—unless fans don't recognize her, or the restaurant staff doesn't fawn all over her. In that event, she throws a commotion on the way out to be sure they acknowledge her.

Dominic, the maître d' at the restaurant, greets Blair with a big hug. "Cam is at his usual table; follow me."

"No worries, Dom. I know my way there. Does anything ever change with Cameron?"

Dominic winks and waives his hand for Blair to pass into the dining room.

Before entering, she scans the main dining room for just a moment. Cameron's usual table sits tucked away in a corner, so if someone is going to notice Blair, it will be during her strut through the dining room. Once seated, she will be hard to find, let alone noticed.

As she crosses the dining room, someone snaps a picture from a cell phone, with the flash on. Then another at the same table. Blair does not recognize anyone, but she smiles and proceeds to Cameron's table. *Tourist cell phones, no doubt,* she thinks. *Not the paparazzi, unfortunately.*

Cameron Haines is an "A-list" Hollywood agent, and one of a very few who is African American. He's striking to look at, even for his age at fifty-eight. His hair is still black, with only a trace of gray around the temples. Educated in England, he speaks with a slight British accent. Cameron is experienced enough to represent his talent aggressively, though he's not as nimble as his younger counterparts.

All of Cameron's other clients are more well-known than Blair. She practically begged him to take her as a client when she first came to America from London. He eventually agreed to sign her. He told her she would be his "project," and that accurately describes their ongoing relationship. Cameron has guided her career for several years, and most recently, she has been quite successful. While Blair was a rather mediocre draw at the movie box office, she has done extremely well on TV. Her current mini-series is a hit and is a spin-off from a prior series that was equally successful. Blair has a leading role and an enormous fan base from the show.

Cameron only has a handful of major Hollywood talent as clients, but they are all big names—except for Blair. She is the least known, least paid, and the most frustrated. She's often overheard fellow actors or producers speculate that there must be something going on between Blair and Cameron; otherwise he'd never have taken her as his client. Even Blair isn't sure why Cameron agreed to take her as a client, but she is grateful. Cameron changed her life.

Dressed in a pale blue Dior suit, white shirt, and deep yellow tie, Cameron sits at the back of a small, padded banquette, with two chairs across the table from him. He's speaking on his cell phone, but he rises to greet Blair. Pulling her chair out with one hand, while he holds his cell phone with the other, he winks at her while he finishes his conversation. Blair notices that there are two chairs at the table facing Cameron's seat in the banquette, instead of just one for her. *Who else is he expecting?* she wonders.

He ends his call and looks up at Blair. "Don't say it."

Blair starts to speak, but Cameron holds up his hand.

"Just don't say it."

"It's rude to greet your guest with a cell phone glued to your ear. There. I said it."

Cameron smiles, shakes his head, gives her a wink. "How was your day? All good on the set?"

Blair hesitates for a moment, then answers, "Uneventful."

Cameron takes a sip from his wine. "Uneventful? I hardly thought this important day on the set would be uneventful."

Blair flinches, then clears her throat. "Oh? Why should a day on the set of that dreadful show be anything other than uneventful?"

Despite her quick answer, Blair was unnerved by what had happened earlier that evening. Does Cameron know what she witnessed? Or what happened at the studio with Reid during lunch? Reid Garrett is one of Cameron's most famous clients, and they speak daily.

Raising his eyebrows and smiling, he whispers, "Well, I guess he didn't take my advice. Sort of surprised, though."

Blair says nothing and reaches for her water glass. "You haven't even offered me a drink."

Cameron places his hand over his heart, pretending he's concerned. "What bad manners! I'll take care of that forthwith." He glances up to locate the waiter. Catching his eye, the waiter makes his way to the table.

"Yes, Mr. Haines?"

"My beautiful companion here would like to order a drink."

The waiter, recognizing Blair, beams. "What may I bring you, Ms. Kilian?"

"Gin martini, dry with two olives, raped. Nolet's gin."

"Nolet's dry martini, up, two olives, pimentos removed." The waiter smiles as he turns away.

Cameron rolls his eyes at the "raped" olive comment. "You're the only person I know who is allergic to pimentos."

Blair frowns. "Not 'allergic.' I just don't like them. It's a texture thing."

Cameron picks up his phone and scrolls through his recent call list. "You say Reid was a no-show at the studio?"

Blair is astonished at the question. She doesn't answer and pretends to be looking at the menu, startled that Cameron expected Reid to meet her at the studio earlier today.

Cameron sees another text message on his cell phone. "Excuse me for just a moment. I need to reply to this quickly."

Blair's relieved she has a moment to gather her thoughts. She is uneasy with Cameron's question about Reid.

Cameron puts his phone down and looks up at Blair. "So, you didn't meet him? He just never showed up. Did he try to call you?"

The waiter arrives with the martini just in time to give Blair another pause before answering Cameron. "That looks yummy!" She presses the glass to her lips so quickly that she nearly spills it. After taking two large gulps, Blair puts the glass down and wipes her mouth with a napkin. She says nothing but smiles at

Cameron. Her mind is racing with what her answer will be: *Did I meet Reid at the studio or not? Why is he asking anyway? And what about the balcony incident? Is he testing me?*

Cameron takes another sip of wine and looks at his phone. "No matter. You'll meet him shortly. He's joining us for dinner, but I thought it would be nice for the two of you to meet on the set today, before you begin work together during the next episodes. He must have changed his plans."

Blair can't believe she just heard Cameron say Reid is joining them for dinner. Perspiring and uneasy, she takes another sip from her martini. "What's the big deal about meeting him? I mean, he's only a guest star for an episode."

Cameron frowns and moves in closer to her. "Blair, have you lost your mind? He's a popular guy, one of *my* hottest stars, and you have three steamy episodes with him. The series needs a boost, and Reid's the one to do it. And you are the beneficiary of his guest star appearance, I might add."

"I'm the beneficiary? How so?"

Cameron shakes his head and looks at his watch. "It's almost 9:30. He's a half-hour late." He picks up his cell phone and calls Reid. Blair purses her lips and stares intently as Cameron waits for Reid to answer the phone. She hears that the call has rung over to voicemail. Cameron sighs and ends the call without leaving a message. "Well, while we're waiting on Reid, let me tell you something important. I had wanted Reid to meet you first, but since that apparently didn't happen, I guess I'll start before he gets here."

Before Cameron could start the discussion, Dominic the maître d' quietly appears behind Blair and catches Cameron's eye. He says nothing but gives Cameron a small envelope with a note inside. Cameron opens the envelope and pulls out a note:

Sorry, Cam. Just can't do it tonight. Felt ill when I got here. Was in the bathroom for twenty minutes. Rather than cause a scene, I'm going home. Talk tomorrow.
—Reid

Cameron frowns and reads the note again. Blair is curious as she can't see the note. She can tell that Cameron's disturbed by whatever it is he is reading. He slowly puts the note in his suit jacket pocket and bites his lower lip. Sitting back in his chair, he looks at Blair and holds his chin in his hand for a moment. "So, he's sick. He was here but had to leave. Damn."

Blair can't believe what Cameron just said. *Reid was here? Impossible!* She feels faint, and puts her napkin to her mouth, afraid she will vomit. Cameron rises from his chair to help her, but she faints and falls to the floor just before Cameron can catch her.

A Face in the Crowd

Blair's fainting spell causes quite a stir at Spago. Paramedics rush into the restaurant while Dom and two staff members hold the paparazzi back at the door. By the time the paramedics arrive at the table, Cameron has lifted Blair off the floor and the waiter is wiping her forehead with a cold cloth. The paramedics do their usual ritual of checking vital signs and asking Blair what happened.

Twenty minutes later they remove an oxygen mask and blood pressure monitor from Blair, and they pronounce her fit to go home. Cameron handles the paperwork, apologizes to the restaurant staff, and leaves a sizable wad of cash on the table. He calls Jimmy, who said he will wait in the car out front.

Cameron whispers to Blair, "You feel well enough to walk out through the front door, or do you want to use the back door?"

Blair smiles at Cameron and stands up from her chair. "I'm not a backdoor girl, Cameron. You know that."

Cameron nods his head, knowing that Blair is not brave, just sensible. Reporters are at the back door, and pictures of her leaving through the alley would be far worse than pictures of her leaving through the front door. Back door exits fuel speculation of scandal.

Diners in the main dining room clap as Blair walks out holding onto Cameron's arm. Cameron makes the obligatory apology to Dom for all the commotion and leaves another wad of cash with him. "Please take care of the staff and yourself with my apologies."

Jimmy is waiting with the car outside, attempting to fend off reporters and onlookers when Cameron and Blair make their way to the car. The pictures in the tabloids the following morning won't be flattering to Blair. She looks distraught.

On their way out the door of the restaurant, one persistent reporter shoves a microphone right in front of Cameron. "A fight? Was it a fight? Mr. Haines, did you and Ms. Kilian have a fight in there? Is that why the paramedics came?"

Cameron is silent but knows that this is a likely headline for tomorrow.

Just as Cameron is helping Blair into the backseat of Jimmy's car, she stops in her tracks and freezes. She's gazing across the top of the car at a tall man standing in the street. His arms folded and grinning at Blair with a big smile. He has blue eyes and blonde hair. He's wearing a tuxedo shirt with a bow tie, and a hooded jacket. When their glances meet, he pulls the hood up over his head, turns away and takes off running down the street.

Blair gasps and grabs the door frame. *Reid? But how could it be?*

"For God's sake, Blair, what's wrong?" Cameron grabs her chin to turn her head towards his. "What is it? Please, get in the car, Blair, you're just making a scene." Cameron pushes her head down into the back seat of the car as Blair is wide-eyed but silent. "Jimmy, get us out of here."

Cameron wipes his brow with his handkerchief, takes Blair's hand and leans over close to her. In just a whisper, he speaks. "Blair, what is going on? What were you looking at? What happened in the restaurant? I'm worried about you."

At first, Blair says nothing. Cameron persists. "You must tell me what's wrong, Blair. Tomorrow is an important day for you, and you are falling apart. You can't go on set tomorrow looking and feeling like you do tonight."

"You think I don't know that? I'm fine," Blair protests. " Just take me home. I'll be fine by tomorrow. Don't worry about your least valuable client letting you down on the set tomorrow."

Sitting back in his seat, Cameron takes a fresh handkerchief from his pocket and wipes Blair's face and neck. She's perspiring and her makeup is running. She smiles as he cleans her face, and she whispers, "Thank you."

Putting his handkerchief away, Cameron takes Blair's hand and turns sideways to face her. "You want me to go with you to the set tomorrow? Or at least for the initial script reading for the first episode with Reid?"

Blair shakes her head no. "You wanted me to know something. Why was Reid going to join us?"

Cameron is silent for a moment. "Well, at this point I'm not sure you're up to it."

"Not *up* to it? Me? Come on, Cam, I'm a tough bitch. Forget what happened tonight. You know me. What gives?"

Clearing his throat, Cameron leans in closer to Blair so Jimmy won't hear this part of their conversation. "No delicate way to put it, Blair. Reid isn't a guest star for three episodes. He will be a recurring character. A major one."

Blair shrugs. "Okay, so? He's a big star, and his coming onboard will help the show. And it's good for me since I'm his love interest, right?"

"Maybe."

"Maybe what?"

"He's being introduced into the show as your love interest, but the chemistry between you two will be critical."

Blair is silent, thinking back to their tryst on the set earlier that day. She tried to figure it out, and she thought, *What was Reid doing? Trying me out?*

Speaking softly, Cameron leans closer to Blair. "So, that's what I wanted to tell you, and I was hoping a nice meeting at dinner tonight would set the tone for your first script reading tomorrow. A warm introduction—if you know what I mean."

"Got it. We must 'click.' No big deal."

"Well, see, that's the hard part. If you don't click, he can replace you."

"Replace me? It's my show, and he's the guest star. What do you mean?"

"Ratings. It's all about the ratings, Blair. You know that. The show is a hit, but the ratings have slipped this season. Reid is being paid a lot of money to bring a new face and some star power to the show. He will be there for at least the full season. If you two don't click in three episodes, then you're out. They've already written the episode featuring your demise if things don't pan out. I wanted you to hear that from me before you hear the scuttle on the set tomorrow, or whenever word gets out."

"Well, how cozy for you, Cam. Reid is one of your biggest stars. As his agent, you get a nice slice of his fee, don't you? And he makes much more than me, so whether I stay or whether I go, you now make more money off that show than you did just putting me in it. How nice for you."

"I wasn't shopping him around, Blair. The producers wanted him. It just happens that I represent him. And you. They know that." He paused, then said, "And one more thing."

"There's more? Gee, with all that wonderful tatter of joyful news, what else do you have for me?"

"Reid makes the call."

"What call? You mean he decides if we're clicking or not? He decides if my character goes on or dies off in the show? I hope you aren't telling me that."

Shaking his head very matter-of-factly, Cameron says, "Yes, Blair, that is what I am telling you. They're giving him creative control over the show."

Blair smiles and looks out the window. "Well, damn it. That bastard."

Housekeeping

Jimmy pulls up in front of the Wilshire Palms, where the doorman comes to greet the car. Jimmy gets out to open the rear passenger door, but Cameron holds the door partly ajar. He looks up at Jimmy and asks, "Please give me and Ms. Kilian just a moment, okay?"

"Sure, boss."

Cameron turns to Blair, who is still giving Cameron the silent treatment after their conversation about Reid deciding her fate on the show. "You okay to go up alone? I'm happy to come in for a while if you like."

Blair feigns a smile and pulls back her hair. "Are you kidding? I don't think I can stand any more good news or acts of kindness from you tonight, Cam. I'll let you know about my chemistry with your golden boy on the set tomorrow. I'm sure you'll be tracking me every minute, anyway."

Cameron reaches over to kiss her goodnight, but Blair turns away and opens the door on her side of the car, instead of where Jimmy is standing on Cameron's side.

Jimmy runs to the other side of the car, helps Blair out the door, and escorts her to the entry of her building. She ignores the cheerful greeting from her building doorman, and strides silently past the smiling security guard at the front desk who welcomes her home. Once in the elevator, she leans against the back wall and exhales loudly. As the elevator door opens on her floor, she reaches in her purse for the key to the door. When she turns the key to unlock the deadbolt, it is obvious she did not lock the door when she left. She turns the knob, and her door opens. Shaking her head, she assumes she had forgotten to lock her door because she was in such a hurry to meet Cameron for dinner.

Once inside her apartment, she makes her way to the bar, but first glimpses herself in the mirror. Her thoughts reply to the image, *Could this terrible day have ended any more tragically for me?*

Something isn't right. The bar is immaculate. The cocktail shaker she used for her martini earlier in the evening is clean and put away. She goes to the balcony and opens the French doors. The balcony floor is spotless. No blood stains. No broken glass. Earlier that evening, Blair had left for the restaurant in a hurry, intending to clean it all up later.

Rushing to the bedroom, Blair looks in the cleaning bag where she placed her torn dress with the bloodstains. It's gone. Her other items from earlier in the week were there, but not the bloody dress. She runs to her phone to call the security desk downstairs. "It's Ms. Kilian. Has anyone been in my apartment while I was away?"

"Ah, no, Ms. Kilian. No one signed in for you tonight."

Blair is silent.

"You okay, Ms. Kilian? You want me to send someone up?"

"No, no. I'm simply confused."

Blair is due on the set early in the morning. Her car is coming to get her at 5:00 a.m., so she'll need to get up at 4:00 a.m. The night is almost over, and she knows she needs to get to bed. But she also knows someone has been in her apartment. She goes to the bar and pours some Nolet's gin over ice cubes.

She goes back to the balcony one more time and stares at the clean floor of the balcony. She then looks up to the darkened balcony on the tenth floor of the building next door. Still eerily silent. No commotion, no evidence of what she had witnessed earlier that evening. She closes the French doors to the balcony, and heads for her bedroom again, first passing by the dining room. Then she sees it. On her dining room table is a piece of paper with red writing:

Crime Stoppers. Report crimes you witness to the Beverly Hills P.D.

Blair freezes. She puts her drink down on the table and picks up the piece of paper. It's a small poster encouraging witnesses to report crimes, like the flyers you see taped to traffic light posts or telephone poles.

She sweats and feels clammy. *What in the world is happening to me?* she wonders. *Who has been here?* Running back to her balcony, Blair throws open the doors, goes to the railing and looks down at the back of the building next door. It is still very dark and quiet. No activity. She then looks up to the balcony on the tenth floor. There's a light on. She squints and counts the floors again to be sure it is the balcony from which Reid made his perfect swan dive. It is.

She goes back into her apartment, downs what's left of her Nolet's on the dining room table, and heads for the door of her apartment. On her way out to the elevator, she grabs her keys and slams the door behind her. When the elevator reaches the lobby, she runs out the front door and down the circular driveway in front of her building. Reaching the sidewalk, she turns toward the building next door and runs up the driveway to the entrance.

As she approaches the revolving door entrance to the Colonnade Condominiums, the doorman yells out to her and holds up his hand. "Whoa, there! What's the hurry, ma'am?"

Blair is frantic. "I need to see the manager. Right now."

"It's almost midnight, ma'am. Manager's not in. What's the problem?"

"I'm here to see Reid Garrett."

"No one in the building by that name. Well, eh, even if there was, I couldn't give out the names of any residents."

Watching the commotion from inside the lobby desk, the security guard comes out. "Is there a problem, Will?"

"Don't know. This woman is panicking, or practically."

The security guard looks at Blair and recognizes her. "Blair Kilian? It is you, right?"

Blair shakes her head yes and wipes the perspiration from her forehead.

"What's the problem? Do you need to see a resident? Everything okay?"

"I need to see Reid Garrett."

The security guard looks at Will, the doorman. "The actor? That's who she's looking for? Is he visiting one of our residents?"

Will shakes his head. "Not that I know of."

"Ms. Kilian, let me check the guest register. Perhaps he signed in before my shift began."

Blair shakes her head, "No, no, he's not visiting. He lives here. Tenth floor. East side, facing my building."

"You live in the Wilshire Palms?"

Blair, very agitated and confused, says, "Yes, yes, I do, and I can see Mr. Garrett's balcony from mine. I need to see him."

The security guard glances at Will, the doorman, then raises his eyebrows. He quickly takes Blair by the arm. "Let's check the visitor logs, Ms. Kilian. Come with me."

The security guard asks Blair to sit in his chair at the security desk. "My name is Ron. Ron Wu. I'm the night security guard here. So, tell me the unit you think Mr. Garrett lives in."

"Tenth floor. Corner unit facing east and south."

"That would be unit 1002. Balcony facing your building and wraps around the corner to face the back side of our building. The owner of that unit is not Mr. Reid Garrett. I'm sorry."

"That can't be right. Who lives there? Did they have a visitor tonight? Around six o'clock or 6:30?"

"Well, I can't tell you the name of the owner, but she's not even here so she couldn't have had any visitors. There's no one here on the visitor log signed in for Apartment 1002 for, well, more than a month."

Blair shakes her head, stands up to see the electronic log on the screen in front of Ron's desk. "Impossible. That's impossible."

Ron suddenly becomes very curious. "Ms. Kilian, why do

you say that's impossible? Did you see someone on that balcony earlier tonight?"

Blair's startled at the question and now realizes she may have given herself away. "No, I did not. But I was sure he lived here. And . . . and we work together, so I wanted to see him."

Ron becomes even more curious. "Work together, how so?"

"Never mind. It's not important. Just actor stuff. We will be on the same show next month."

"Ms. Kilian, are you here because you saw something on a balcony in our building tonight? Is that why you're here?"

"I never said that. I came here looking for someone I thought lived in this building. Obviously, I'm mistaken."

Two men dressed in suits approach the desk, so Ron steps in front of Blair and asks her to take a seat in the lobby while he helps the other visitors. One man has a notepad and Blair can hear someone speaking on a small radio in the hand of the other man.

Standing by a table in the lobby as Ron assists the two men, Blair sees glass doors out to the back of the building through the elevator bank. *The pool. Are those the doors to the pool?* Rushing down the center of the elevator bank, she reaches the glass doors leading out to a large terrace. She can see the pool lights below the terrace. Reaching the doors, she sees they're locked, and someone has posted a sign just outside on the terrace saying "Closed for Private Event." Yellow tape is draped on posts on the back terrace. She sees three policemen with flashlights looking at something in the bushes.

"Hey, Ms. Kilian, come back here." Ron, having seen her leave the lobby, yells out to her and is running towards her. "You can't be back here, or in the building. If you aren't here to see a resident, I need to ask you to leave."

Ron reaches for Blair's arm, but she pulls it away. "What are they looking for back there? What's going on?"

He points to the main lobby door. "Ms. Kilian, I need to ask you to leave. Now."

"Who was at the desk tonight around 6:30?"

"I was. I work 6 p.m. to 2 a.m."

"And no one went to apartment 1002?"

"No. We've been over that. You need to go."

"The pool. What was going on at the pool tonight?"

"Private party."

"Who? Whose party?"

"Ms. Kilian, I can't tell you that. We have a lot of celebrities and businesspeople in the building, and respecting their privacy is a big reason many of them live here. Your building is the same. You should know that. How would you like your fans jumping through security and asking questions about you?"

As Ron is nudging Blair towards the lobby door, she looks over her shoulder toward the doors to the pool. "What's going on? What are those men looking for?"

Ron shakes his head. "Nothing, just a little party mishap. A little too much to drink—if you know what I mean. No big deal and none of your business."

Blair is silent for a moment. If she reveals what, and who, she saw on the balcony of unit 1002 earlier that night, it could open a Pandora's box for her. If someone really dove off that balcony, she witnessed a suicide she didn't report. *Have the police discovered a body?*

The two men in suits leave the front desk and start toward the backdoors to the pool. One of them is speaking into a small handheld radio. As they pass by Ron and Blair, the one with the radio tells Ron to clear the lobby.

Ron obliges, "Yes sir, right away." He then grasps Blair by her shoulders and looks into her eyes. "Are you sure you're all right, Ms. Kilian? Should I call someone for you? I know Jerry and Ahmed, two of the security guards in your building. Do you know if either of them will be on duty tonight? Should I call them?"

"No. That's not necessary." She glances out to the pool deck and then looks back at Ron. "I must have the wrong address for Mr. Garrett."

"Very well, then. Would you like me to have Will, our door-man, escort you back to your building?"

Blair shakes her head and starts walking toward the door.

"No, thank you. I can find my way home."

As she exits the building, the doorman, Will, waves to her, "Good night, Ms. Kilian." She says nothing and rushes back to her building next door.

Entering the lobby of her building a few minutes later, Blair heads for the elevators. As she passes the security desk, the guard on duty calls out to her. "A note! Ms. Kilian, I have a note for you. It's so late I didn't want to call your apartment. I left it for Ahmed when he comes in at six, but since you're here, let me bring it over to you."

Blair is standing by an open elevator door as Erik, the night security guard, hands her an envelope with her name on it. Blair glances at the envelope, then frowns at Erik. "When did you get this? I walked through the lobby less than an hour ago and you saw me leave. You said nothing."

"Yes, Miss Kilian. You're right. A gentleman just delivered this note a few minutes ago. He asked for you and I told him you weren't in. He handed me this and asked that I give it to you when you returned."

"Who was he?"

"I don't know, ma'am. He didn't say. Nice-looking guy, though."

"What did he look like?"

"Blonde, tall. Gosh, I know he's an actor, but I can't quite remember the name. He was in that spy movie a few months ago." Erik rubs his chin, shaking his head. "Gee, what's his name?"

Blair feels flushed and woozy. She doesn't want to volunteer a name, especially if he looked like Reid Garrett. "Well, if you think of it, let me know."

"Yes, ma'am, will do. Good night."

Once the elevator door closes, Blair frantically opens the note. The brief message is in bold type and double-spaced:

Upon death, worthy souls anxiously cross over to the other side for a peaceful eternity.
Dark souls resist crossing over because they know a

tragic fate awaits them on the other side. That is why dark souls can still haunt the living . . . even when they are dead.

Late-night Diversion

After dropping off Blair at her apartment, Jimmy takes Cameron up to Sunset Boulevard, and then down San Vicente, past the London Hotel. Passing the schoolyard on the right, they see an enormous set of metal gates flanked by a tall hedge of Ficus trees. The car stops at the gates, and Cameron tells Jimmy to wait. He steps out of the car and walks to the intercom box beside the gates. A few seconds later, the large metal gates to the driveway swing open. Cameron walks in. Jimmy drives the car behind Cameron and follows him into the circular driveway in front of a quaint English Cottage.

The door to the cottage opens, and the subtle light from inside reveals a tall, slender figure. He's wearing a dark tailored suit, closely cropped beard, hands in his pockets, leaning against the doorway.

Stopping just short of the entrance to the cottage, Cameron smiles, "Good evening, Alton. Mr. Alton Price."

Alton nods his head but does not say a word. He waves his hand for Cameron to enter the cottage. As Cameron steps in, Alton goes to the car in the driveway and greets Jimmy. "You know where everything is, Jimmy. Make yourself at home."

Jimmy nods, "Thank you, Mr. Price."

Alton then enters the cottage where Cameron is waiting in the hallway. They shake hands. The cottage is immaculate and very modern on the inside. White walls, white floors, and stainless-steel baseboards. In the living room, Alton removed the original ceiling to expose a high vaulted roof with white-washed beams. This is the lair of Mr. Alton Price, the best fixer in Hollywood. He's handsome, well mannered, and an impeccable dresser. But those attributes are not important, because he is recognized as the best at fixing problems for actors, agents, studio tycoons, and business executives . . . and the occasional clergy or politician, but only when times are slow, because they can't pay like Hollywood types or business executives. Alton can also be very sinister when the situation demands it. Or when he's angry. Or just bored.

Alton waives Cameron into the living room, which overlooks a pool and lush gardens in the back. "Cam, you ruined my Thursday night. I assume this isn't a social call?"

At first, Cameron is silent. He knows Alton and has been in his cottage lair before. His prior visits have been as a client, or for a social event. Tonight is different. "I'm having second thoughts, Alton. Blair was a mess tonight."

Alton, standing by an open, glass sliding door, stares out at the pool while sipping his vodka martini. "What did you expect?"

"He's getting out of hand. You said you'd be sure that wouldn't happen."

"Yes, I did. And it's not of hand. Don't tell me how to do my business, Cam. Everything is unfolding as expected, or as we planned. I never told you it would be pretty."

Cameron is silent but walks to the glass sliding door where Alton is standing.

Alton turns to look at Cameron. "You're going soft in your old age, Cam." Alton hoists his martini. "Join me?"

"No, thanks. Seems that martinis are making people do bad things. Like jumping from buildings."

Finishing his martini in one gulp, Alton makes a coy smile. "I can do a beautiful swan dive too. Into my pool."

Cameron shakes his head and puts his hands in his pocket. "So we can't discuss this?"

"Nothing to discuss. Cam, go home. Stay focused."

"Just worried about Blair."

"Oh, come now, Cam. Worried about Blair? Let Blair worry about Blair. What's gotten into you? You're being too nice. Too sensitive. The most successful African American agent in Hollywood didn't get this far by being nice. I know your history, Cam. You're not known as being nice. You're getting soft now that you're over fifty. Be more like you were in your twenties. If this were about any of your other clients besides Blair, you wouldn't even be here tonight, would you?"

"Well, that was direct."

"Then keep to yourself, Cam."

"Okay, so what's the next step?"

"I'm taking care of that. We won't discuss it now. I don't need or want your input. You hired me because you can't take care of this problem yourself. So, go home."

Cameron pauses, then asks, "Is your houseguest still here?"

"Yes. And he's doing very well."

"May I see him?"

"No. We discussed this. You can't have any contact with him until . . ."

"But I'd . . ."

Alton cuts him off, prepares another martini for himself and presses a button on the bar. The front door opens, and Jimmy walks in.

Alton motions toward Jimmy. "Your car is waiting, Cam."

Cameron speaks, but Alton cuts him off again.

"Good night, Cam. You've interrupted my evening long enough. Sleep tight."

Alton shows Cameron to the car, Cameron lowers himself into the backseat, and then Jimmy drives the car toward the gates.

As the metal gates close behind Jimmy's car, Alton closes the front door. He turns around, and the door to Alton's office opens. A man steps out, and Alton smiles. "Well, seems your brother caused quite a stir tonight."

The man smiles. "When will this be over? I'm getting nervous."

Finishing his second martini, Alton hoists his glass and

looks at him. "It's the beginning of the end. Take your evening swim and turn in. Early day tomorrow."

Orphans in Bel Air

As the metal gates in the driveway of Alton's lair close behind him, Jimmy drives up the street and turns left at Sunset Boulevard. Not a word said between Jimmy and Cameron as they drive west on Sunset, through Beverly Hills and toward Bel Air. The quick dismissal by Alton was uncomfortable for them both. It embarrasses Cameron. Jimmy knows something bad will unfold. He has worked with both men for years, so he could sense the tension between Cameron and Alton.

Fifteen minutes later, Cameron is saying goodnight to Jimmy as the driver drops him off at his home. Before driving away, Jimmy attempts to say something comforting to him, but Cameron waives Jimmy off.

After Jimmy drives away, Cameron stands in the driveway, hands in his pockets, and gazes up at his formidable Bel Air mansion. It is a dark night, but his beautiful home is lit up like Versailles. It wasn't a simple journey for a black orphan born in South Central L.A. to make his way to the mansions of Bel Air. As little as forty years ago, restrictions prohibited African Americans and other minorities from buying homes in Bel Air and Beverly Hills. The only black and Hispanic residents of these neighborhoods were the servants who worked in homes like the one Cameron now had.

Buying a home in Bel Air was a lifelong dream for Cameron. How did a black boy born in an orphanage even know about Bel Air? He knew because of another African American boy who became an orphan at four years of age. That boy was Paul Revere Williams, and he became the first black architect accredited by the AIA in 1923. He designed over two thousand buildings during his career, including some of the most iconic homes in Beverly Hills, Bel Air and even Palm Springs. Many celebrities commissioned Paul Williams to design their homes, including Frank Sinatra, Lucille Ball and her husband, Desi Arnaz, and Cary Grant, to name a few. While Paul Williams homes adorned some of the best neighborhoods in California, he couldn't live in most of the neighborhoods where he designed homes.

Like so many other places in America, blacks and other minorities couldn't live in many of the finest neighborhoods. That irony made a huge impression on Cameron when his path crossed with that of Paul Williams at an architectural lecture in Los Angeles in the mid-seventies. Cameron knew that he too couldn't live in many of these neighborhoods for the same reason Paul Williams couldn't live in most neighborhoods where he designed homes for others. Cameron swore to himself he would one day live in Bel Air or Beverly Hills, in a home designed by Paul Williams. He now had that beautiful home in Bel Air—though not one designed by Paul Williams.

When Cameron was a young character actor, he discovered he was better at being a businessman than he would ever be at pursuing an acting career. He understood contracts, numbers, and how films and television shows get produced. When he became an agent, his friends told him that no celebrity would hire a black agent. Friends of Paul Williams told him the same thing: "Your own people can't afford to hire you, and white clients won't hire you either."

Paul Williams learned to draw renderings and illustrations upside down. This allowed potential clients to sit across from him, rather than next to him, which many would not do. Friends told Cameron that even black actors and celebrities would not hire him, because all the powerful agents in Hollywood were white. Even black actors wanted white agents.

Cameron persevered until he was one of the most successful

agents in Hollywood. And he was African American. Aside from being tall and handsome, Cameron was very articulate. When he was ready for junior high, he went to England to finish his schooling, thanks to a generous gift from a woman at church whom he never knew. The mystery woman paid for him to attend prep school and college in the UK. Aside from an excellent education, he came home with a charming British accent, and an articulate manner of speech.

Cameron had majored in Linguistics at Kings College, Cambridge, so he stood out from other agents, both in demeanor and eloquence. His presentation skills in promoting his clients became legendary. Before becoming a successful agent, Cameron often earned extra money by making grammatical edits in scripts and screenplays. He helped his acting clients to learn their lines, polish their speaking skills, and make the most of the dialogue in poorly written scripts. For a time, he was the best English coach in Hollywood.

Tonight, he now stands in the driveway of his home in Bel Air. Cameron smiles, takes his hands out of his pockets, and walks to the front door. And then he sees it. Yet again. Another note taped to the front door. Cameron stops for a moment. He goes up the steps to his front door and takes a deep breath. *How did he know I'd come home through the front door tonight? I drive my car into the garage and enter the house through the side door. He must have known I had a car service tonight. The dinner at Spago explains it.*

Removing the tape from the envelope, Cameron opens his front door and steps inside. He unseals the envelope to reveal a note, written on the same heavy paper stock as all the others:

A black man has a white daughter. She's your mistress, or at least we shall construct that narrative . . . more money, Mr. Haines. Just too many secrets for me to keep now. Make the next payment $1,000 more. And don't be late this time.

Throwing the note on the floor, Cameron folds his clasped hands around the back of his neck. *Another note, another headache.* His head throbs. Reaching for his cell phone, he texts Alton Price: "Another note. Stuck to my door. More money."

It's after midnight, but Alton texts back: "Are you surprised? Put the note with all the others. Go to bed. This will be over before too long."

The blackmail notes are financially and emotionally straining for Cameron. His secret could ruin his career and harm the two people he loves most in life. He's lived with the torment for thirty years, and now he pays a steep price to keep it quiet. *How much longer can I do this?* Cameron goes up the stairs into his closet, opens his safe and retrieves a shoebox from the back. He places the note inside the shoebox, already overflowing with notes. Cameron shoves the box to the back, closes the safe and falls onto his bed.

A Surprise Visitor

The alarm goes off as usual at 4:00 a.m. Blair is already awake. The studio car arrives to pick her up at 5:00 a.m. every day she is filming. She is usually fast asleep at 4:00 a.m., and the alarm wakens her from a dead sleep. Not this morning.

Blair has been awake most of the night. The scene of Reid Garrett diving off the tenth-floor balcony played repeatedly in her head. The one time she had briefly fallen asleep, she awoke thinking her vision of Reid's certain death was just a nightmare. A few seconds later, she realized it was not a nightmare, and she had awoken to reality. She sweat and felt sick to her stomach. Again.

And then there was the note. Before going to bed, she read it repeatedly, trying to understand what it meant. She had shoved it in a kitchen drawer, promising not to look at it when she awoke. And she didn't.

Once out of bed, Blair begins her normal morning routine for days on the set. Two glasses of lemon water followed by two cups of espresso. She completes the usual water and coffee ritual within minutes and then walks back to her bedroom. As she leaves the kitchen, she stops, looks to her living room and the French doors to the balcony. It's still pitch-black outside, but she stares at the doors, tempted to walk out on the balcony. She was awake most of the night expecting to hear sirens or something, anything, to tell her someone else witnessed Reid's swan dive from the balcony. She slowly walks to the French doors, which she had left ajar when she went to bed. If there were to be any sounds or commotion during the night, she wanted to hear it. She had also left her bedroom windows open, no doubt adding to her anxiety and sleepless night.

She pushes the balcony door open and listens. Nothing but the sound of traffic on Wilshire Boulevard in front of the building. She steps outside onto her balcony, looking directly down at the base of the building next door. Nothing to see or hear. She looks up to Reid's balcony on the tenth floor. Blair is dizzy and feels faint. She's startled to see a light on in the apartment. A bright light. Just like last night. The security guard told her that the apartment has been vacant for a couple months. The owner is out of town. She gazes at the light, then back down at the grounds below. Shaking her head, she goes inside.

Blair submerges her face in a bowl of ice water, then in another bowl filled with organic plant and other material her naturopathy doctor concocts for her at a very steep price. She repeats this ritual over and over, until her face is numb and smelling of witch hazel, herbs, and lemon. She pats her face dry with a sterilized cloth, and steps into her bathroom for her next ritual. The lemon water and espresso taken earlier work as a laxative for Blair. She takes a quick rinse in the shower. Just a rinse. The whole routine of make-up, bathing and grooming will take place at the studio.

A few minutes before 5:00 a.m., her phone rings, and the doorman informs her that her car is here. She's dressed in white yoga pants, a black rhinestone top, and black gloves. A white hat covers her still-damp hair, and she dons sunglasses, though it is still dark outside. It is rare that Blair would see any neighbors or anyone she knows that early in the morning, but she has had a few unfortunate incidents with the paparazzi on the way to the studio. She's learned to never be "unsightly," whether day or night. With one last glance in the mirror over her bar, she heads for the elevator to the lobby.

Once outside her building, Blair quickly steps into her waiting car. Her driver gives her a cheerful morning greeting and, as usual, Blair responds with a grunt and a wave of her hand.

On the way to the studio, Blair feels so ill, she almost asks the driver to stop. Her trepidation about what she will find on the set is feeding her anxiety to the point of making her sick. Reid Garrett is due on the set in two days. Is he dead or alive? He apparently holds her future—at least as regards the show—in his hands. But did he die jumping off the balcony? Or was it a ruse? Cameron expected him for dinner last night, but he didn't show. However, he did apparently leave a note with the maître d' at Spago. And then that face in the crowd. The tall blonde guy in a tuxedo shirt and bow tie. The one who put on his hoodie and ran off when Blair spotted him. He looked just like Reid, but how could it be? Her head was spinning with all the possibilities of what would unfold on the set.

Today is the wrap on the current episode. The reading for the episode that introduces Reid begins day after tomorrow. Will she arrive on set to discover Reid's dead body found last night, and everyone on the set aghast at the news? Will the police be there? What will she do if it was a ruse and Reid is there?

During her sleepless night, she kept expecting the phone to ring. Would Cameron, her agent, call her with the news? Or the director? Surely someone will have the news before she arrives on set this morning.

Passing through the studio gates, the car takes her directly to her dressing trailer. Her dresser is waiting outside and greets Blair as she exits the car. The dresser escorts Blair up the stairs to her trailer, takes her hat and sunglasses, helps her to the makeup chair, and brings her a cup of latte. The routine is the same for every morning on the set.

Before her dresser can begin the hair and makeup ritual, there is a knock on the door of her trailer. The director's assistant pops in, cheerful as a schoolboy. "Good morning, Ms. Kilian!"

Blair hates mornings, let alone morning visitors. "What brings you here at this dismal early hour?"

"Good news. Filming with Mr. Garrett is two days away, but he wants to meet you, so he'll join us on the set this morning. We've moved up your first script reading to this afternoon, right after filming."

Blair nearly chokes. "He's here? Reid Garrett will be on set?"

"Yes, ma'am! And so handsome! Eric just wanted to give you the heads-up." Eric is the director, whom Blair despises.

Blair asks the assistant, "You've *seen* him? You've seen Reid Garrett this morning?"

As the director's assistant is leaving Blair's trailer, he calls out, "Yes, Ms. Kilian. Everyone is so excited!"

Blair turns white and heads for her bathroom.

The Ghost Emerges

Blair's make-up artist is struggling to keep Blair in her chair long enough to finish preparing for the first shoot. "Ms. Kilian, please sit still! What's wrong with you this morning?"

"Margo, just finish! I mean it. Finish in two minutes. I've got to get out of here."

"Fine! You're happy with how you look, then go. Really. Just go."

Blair grabs the mirror from Margo, stands up and looks at herself in the hand mirror, and then at her reflection in the full-length mirror beside her. "Shit, my eyes look like ghouls."

"Exactly. So let me finish."

After about ten more minutes, Margo pronounces Blair ready for the set. A young girl waiting outside Blair's trailer drives her over to the set in a golf cart.

Arriving inside the soundstage, Blair quickly glances around to spot Reid. All she sees is the usual crew, the director, her costars, and cast. They gather the entire crew for the first shoot of the day. Blair takes her spot in her chair at the edge of the set for the first scene.

She sees something out of the corner of her eye. She turns halfway around in her chair to face the entrance to the soundstage, where a large door is being closed by the crew. Walking into the soundstage is a tall, blonde man wearing jeans, black knee-high Prada boots, and a white shirt with ruffles, like a pirate shirt. The shirt is partly open, revealing a handsome chest with light brown hair. He appears to be walking directly toward

Blair. The light from the entrance of the soundstage is at his back, obscuring his face. He stops a few feet away from Blair.

"Ms. Kilian, I presume?" He extends his hand and walks up closer to her.

Blair is silent and squinting to make out the details in his face. She slowly extends her hand before saying anything. The other cast and crew members are silent as they watch Blair greet the visitor. She offers a faint smile but says nothing as she stands up from her chair and moves closer to Reid. Studying his face, then his body, she is speechless. Something doesn't seem right, but she can't discern what it is. This *must* be Reid Garrett, and he looks just as she remembered him when they had their lunch time tryst yesterday. But there is something different about his manner, something unsettling. His face seems older, less animated and playful than the man she met yesterday.

Reid grins. "Cat got your tongue?"

Saying nothing, Blair turns to sit back down in her chair, grabs her script from the seat and motions to the director. "Let's get this going."

Reid knows Blair is ignoring him, so he folds his arms and smiles at the crew.

The director waves his hands toward Blair, "Well, if you say so! Are you directing today, Ms. Kilian?"

Visibly stunned, Blair is uncertain of what to say. She just sits there, looking back at the director.

After a brief silence, the director sets up the first scene and everyone takes their positions. Reid is still standing behind Blair. He moves close enough to her back that she can hear his breathing. Sitting in her chair, with Reid standing close behind, his breath is hitting her on top of her head. He softly touches the back of her neck with two fingers. Blair has goosebumps and pulls away by scooting forward in her chair.

She continues to ignore him as the actors on set prepare for the first shoot. Reid's presence behind her unnerves Blair. She perspires and looks for something to wipe her forehead. A large hand with a blue handkerchief appears in front of her mouth.

She grabs it, wipes her brow, and turns around in her chair. No one is there. Two members of the lighting crew to her side are laughing. It must have been Reid who handed her the handkerchief and then walked away.

The makeup artist on set rushes over to apply more makeup to Blair's forehead after seeing her wipe her forehead with the handkerchief. "Crap, we may have to call Margo in here to match that up. What do you think?" She hands a mirror to Blair, who looks closely at her forehead.

"I have no closeups today so this should be fine," Blair replies.

The filming is over in about four hours. Blair was uncomfortable when it was her turn on the set, and she bungled her lines twice. When she forgets a line for the third time, the director yells, "Cut. Ms. Kilian, do you need some time to compose yourself? These lines really aren't that complicated. What's wrong?"

Blair says nothing but shakes her head.

"Okay then, let's try this again," the director says to everyone. "This is the last scene of the episode, so let's make it good."

The last scene involves most of the cast, and Blair makes it through with no more mistakes. She returns to her chair, as do the other actors, waiting for the director to dismiss them or call for another take.

After looking at the monitor with some shots of the final scene, the director shouts, "Wrap. That's it. See you on Monday, ladies and gentlemen. Script reading for the actors starts in thirty minutes."

The crew cleans up the set to prepare for the next episode that begins filming after the weekend. Actors will return to the set for a first script reading of the next episode, which takes place around a table in the soundstage. Blair heads out of the soundstage and her driver takes her to her trailer. She casually looks around, but finds that Reid is not there, although he's expected for the script reading in half an hour. As she nears her own trailer, she sees that the crew has placed a new makeup trailer just across from hers. And it looks familiar. During the filming that day, the crew had moved Reid's trailer from the lot behind the soundstage to the area on the side, where the other key actors have theirs.

Entering her trailer, Blair smiles at Margo, who is waiting to remove Blair's makeup and help her change her clothes into something casual for the script reading. Margo folds her arms and smiles at Blair. "Well, did you meet him? Our new sexy savior for the show? Were you impressed?"

"Yes, I met him, and no, not impressed. Just another self-absorbed pretty boy."

Margo nods and starts removing the makeup from Blair's face. "Good, then. You don't have butterflies anymore and won't be throwing up before you go on set."

"I didn't throw up."

"Well, practically. You were so cranked up this morning. Glad it's all over. Oh, wardrobe dropped off your cleaning."

"What cleaning?" Blair is confused. "I sent nothing in."

"I didn't think you did, especially when I saw what it was." Margo goes to the closet and removes a cleaning bag with some garments on a hanger. Holding it up in front of Blair, Margo grins, "Since when do you wear a tuxedo jacket and a bow tie, with a hoodie over it?"

Blair stands up and lifts the plastic covering over the clothes on a hangar. "That fucking bastard."

13

His Latest Victim

Blair's driver is waiting outside her trailer to take her to the soundstage for the script reading. As she descends the stairs from her trailer, Blair walks by her driver in the golf cart without saying a word.

Confused, the driver follows Blair in the cart. "Ms. Kilian, don't you want a ride to the soundstage?"

"Can't you see I'm walking?"

"You don't want a ride? You'll be late. Script reading started ten minutes ago."

Blair waves her driver off, dons her sunglasses, and keeps walking to the soundstage. When she arrives at the side door, the director's assistant is waving his hand for her to hurry. Blair walks over to the large table where the actors, director and writers are all waiting for her to take her seat. Everyone else is seated and waiting, including Reid, who is holding court by telling some story energetically for the other actors and scriptwriters. As Blair takes her seat, Reid abruptly stops his story and smiles, "Well, look who's here."

The director clears his throat and looks at Blair. "Now that everyone is here, let's start with a read-through of the first scene."

For the next hour and a half, the actors read their lines and writers edit based on comments from the director or actors. The assistant director tracks the time, noting that the episode is running long. The writers cut some lines and consider a scene change to tighten things up. Since the episode introduces Reid as Blair's new love interest, a lot of focus is paid to the lack of chemistry between Reid and Blair when they read their lines. A playful chemistry had existed between the two of them during lunch yesterday, and the sex romp in Reid's trailer was passionate.

But yesterday Reid was witty, charming, and even playful. This Reid is hard-edged, serious, and brusque. Blair has a hard time reading her lines with any passion or interest. She has become very apprehensive about him, and she is furious about the tuxedo shirt, tie, and hoodie dry cleaning gag that was obviously Reid's doing.

The script reading is not the same as a rehearsal, which comes later. However, it is usually the first time the actors can interact with each other when they read their lines aloud for the first time. For this reading, it is obvious to everyone that there is no chemistry between Blair and Reid. The mood is almost hostile.

After the script reading ends, all eyes are on Reid and Blair. Eric, the director, slams his script on the table and stands up, yelling, "The script says you excite each other! You have the hots to be together! Instead, you both sound like you're reading a recipe instead of a steamy love scene!"

The soundstage goes silent.

Eric waves his hand at the writers and actors at the table and shouts, "Everyone out! We're done until Monday. Reid and Blair, you stay here until the others have left."

As the last of the cast departs the soundstage, the director pulls his chair over to the end of the table where Reid and Blair sit in silence.

"What gives? You two have a grudge I don't know about? I thought you had never met before. Am I wrong?"

Blair mumbles, "We've met."

Reid says nothing.

Eric looks at them both and pinches his lower lip with his right hand. "Well, here's the deal. You are both actors; highly paid actors, at that. You are being paid to act. That's what I expect you to do. I don't know what's going on, but you two should leave now and have dinner together. Do not come back to the set on

Monday morning with this attitude. I expect a hot chemistry between the two of you, a passionate reading of your lines, and that you fix whatever the hell happened in here today."

Reid stands up, preparing to speak.

Eric points a finger at Reid. "No. You had your chance to speak at the script reading. You were a robot. I'm through listening to both of you tonight." Eric puts on his jacket, gathers his papers and briefcase, and pushes his chair away from the table. "I don't want to hear another word from either of you until Monday morning. The first rehearsal had better be damn perfect. Fix this. Now!"

As Eric leaves the soundstage, Blair and Reid look at each other, waiting for the other to speak.

Reid moves closer to Blair and whispers, "So, we've met before. Liar!"

Blair smiles. "Oh, come now. You saying it wasn't memorable?"

"There's nothing memorable about you."

Blair looks into his eyes and reaches out to touch his face and neck.

"You feel, look different. Can't put my finger on it."

Reid frowns. "What, exactly, are you up to?"

"Not up to anything."

"Well, maybe you will change your mind at dinner."

Blair picks up her script from the table and walks away. "Dinner is a waste of time."

Reid shakes his head and smiles coyly. "Well, this isn't getting us anywhere is it?"

Blair walks toward the soundstage door. Reid follows her, and just as she is reaching for the door, Reid slams his hand on the door, right in front of her face. It startles Blair.

Reid leans in close. "I'll make this short. First, whether you stay as part of this show depends only on me. If you don't make me happy, you're out. You know that."

Blair turns her head away.

Reid leans in even closer to Blair. "So, here's the deal. You shape up by Monday morning. You become my passionate lover for the show, read your lines enthusiastically, and any time I want your company, you oblige. Anytime. Oh, and you bring me an envelope with five thousand dollars in it. First thing on Monday. Cash only. And you do that the first Monday of every month we're filming. The first Monday I get no cash, I exercise the clause in my contract to have you replaced."

Blair grabs the door handle, shoves Reid aside, and runs outside towards her trailer. Reid calls out for her to stop, but she doesn't, so he runs after her and grabs her by the arm as she tries to enter her trailer. He shoves the door open and pushes Blair inside. She falls to the floor. Reid closes the door behind him as he steps in and is now standing over Blair.

Beaming, Reid says, "And one more thing. Someone died last night. You witnessed it. I'll disclose that little tidbit to the police, anonymously. I've got evidence that you saw the suicide and didn't report it."

Blair stands, holding on to her makeup chair. "What? You look alive to me. You took your dive off the balcony and here you stand before me. You didn't die. I suspect you're the one that's been in my apartment, left that note at the front desk, and staged your little performance last night. Why? You don't even know me."

"Oh, I *do* know you. I know you very well, Blair Kilian. In fact, there are some very tantalizing things about you and your background that *I* know and *you* don't."

Blair lets out a faint laugh. "Well, that would amaze me. I hope it's tawdry and scandalous; it'll make me a more interesting actress."

"Babe, I doubt there's *anything* that could make you a more interesting actress."

Blair shrugs off the insult. "And another thing, what would Cameron think of you doing this to me? He's your agent too. Do you think he'd like one of his clients blackmailing the other?"

Reid laughs out loud, almost uncontrollably. "Cameron? You kidding? You're his charity case. You don't even know why he accepted you as a client. I do, and it's pathetic. I know the whole disgusting story. Don't expect him to help you. He knows exactly what's going on with you and me, and he won't . . . he *can't* stop it."

Reid undresses. He pulls Blair closer to him and unbuttons her blouse and skirt. Blair pulls back, but Reid is too strong for her to stop him.

She tries to slap him, but he grabs her hand and slaps her across her back. Blair screams, but there is no one to hear her.

Covering her mouth, Reid smiles. "Don't worry. I won't hurt that pretty face. I don't want you showing up Monday with a bruised face. Now let's have you oblige me, as you will do whenever I ask."

Reid rips off her blouse and pulls her pants down to her knees. She pushes back and reaches for the door, but he grabs her hair from behind and pulls her down to the floor.

It terrifies Blair as he pushes her down and pins her to the floor of her trailer. She tries to resist, but he is too strong. Blair resigns herself to the fact that she's being violently raped by Reid Garrett.

Guardian Angel, Revealed

Just after 3:00 p.m. on Friday afternoon, a small, black woman, wearing a dark blue dress and a white hat with a small veil, appears in Cameron's office. She looks to be in her late eighties or early nineties, and she tells Cameron's secretary that she wants to see Mr. Haines.

Cameron's secretary, Faye, hesitates for a moment but then asks the usual question. "Do you have an appointment?"

In a very soft and polite voice, the small, black woman replies, "Ma'am, you keep Mr. Haines' appointment book, and I am sure you'd know if I was someone who has an appointment with him."

Faye smiles, then clears her throat. "Mr. Haines doesn't see visitors without an appointment."

"Oh, I understand that," the woman replies. "But I need Mr. Haines to come with me right away to USC Medical Center. Someone important to him is dying."

Faye, a young woman of twenty-nine, also African American, raises her eyebrows and stands up from her desk. "May I tell him your name?"

"Yes. It's Irma. My name is Irma Mae Williams, but he won't know me."

Faye, uncertain what to do, says, "I see. Please have a seat for a minute. Mr. Haines is on the phone, but I will ask him to come out as soon as he finishes."

"Thank you, ma'am. It is urgent. It took me almost two hours to take the bus from South Central L.A. to Beverly Hills. I'm running late already."

Faye seats Irma in the lobby and then knocks on Cameron's door before entering. Closing the door behind her, she sees that Cameron is no longer on the phone. She tells him of the woman in the lobby wanting to take him to see someone who is dying.

Cameron leans forward in his desk, "Does she look crazy?"

Faye shakes her head no. "In fact, she's charming, well dressed, and says it took her almost two hours on the bus to get here from South Central L.A. Says you don't know her, but her name is Irma Mae Williams."

This intrigues Cameron since he was born in South Central L.A. and lived in an orphanage there, and then foster homes, until he left for prep school. "Show her in, Faye."

Cameron rises from his chair and puts on his jacket to greet his mysterious visitor. Faye enters Cameron's office, with Irma following behind. Cameron extends his hand to Irma, "Good morning, Ms. Williams. I'm Cameron Haines, but I guess you already know that."

"Oh, I do, Mr. Haines." She looks at Cameron intently, moving her eyes from the top of his head to his shoes. "You are just as handsome as I expected."

Cameron smiles, "Well, I'm glad I didn't disappoint you!"

Irma smiles and extends her tiny hand covered with a white glove. Cameron sees that it is a nice cotton glove, worn and pilled, but clean. He shakes her small hand gently.

Cameron waves his hand toward a large leather sofa, gesturing for Irma and Faye to both to take a seat.

"Thank you for your hospitality Mr. Haines, but we don't have time. At least, we have little time. Do you have a car?"

Cameron hesitates for a moment. "Yes, yes, I have a car."

"Please drive us to USC Medical Center right away."

"Ms. Williams, may I ask why you want me to go with you and who is the ill or dying person?"

"I promise you will know as soon as we get there. Please, may we just go? If I answer questions it could make us too late."

Cameron picks up his wallet and keys from a tray on the desk and turns to Faye. "Make a note that we are going to the USC Medical Center and I will call you from there within an hour and a half. If you don't hear from me, call the police."

Cameron's statement startles Irma. "Oh, that won't be necessary. I promise you won't be in any danger."

Cameron tilts his head towards Faye. "Do what I say. I will call once I know what is going on."

On the way to USC Medical Center, Cameron tries to talk with Irma. He asks questions about her background, whether she grew up in South Central, how many bus transfers she had to make to get to Beverly Hills. Irma said she did not mean to be rude, but she would answer all those questions after they got to the hospital. It takes just under an hour to arrive at USC Medical Center from Cameron's office in Beverly Hills. Irma asks him to use the valet parking so they can get to the intensive care unit right away. Cameron obliges, and about fifteen minutes later, Irma is escorting Cameron past the nursing desk in the intensive care unit, and into a small room with a frail black woman in bed.

Irma takes Cameron's hand and moves him to the head of the bed. She puts his hand close to the woman in bed who is motionless but still breathing. Irma taps the woman's hand with hers, and the dying woman's eyes open.

The woman in bed sees Cameron, and her eyes light up. She shifts herself up to see him better, smiles at Cameron and extends her hand closer to his. Cameron obliges and grasps her hand. She has a petite and well-manicured hand. When Cameron takes her hand into his, the hard calluses of her palm give testament to what must have been decades of hard, manual work. Cameron thought these to be the hands of a maid, housekeeper, or dishwasher. She beams at Cameron, holds his hand, but doesn't speak.

Cameron turns to Irma, who has just removed her hat and veil. Before Cameron can say anything, Irma says, "Mr. Haines, this is your mother. Her name is Jewell."

Cameron turns to look back at the woman lying in bed. His mother.

"I don't understand."

From behind him, Irma whispers to him, "She brought you to the orphanage shortly after you were born. The family she worked for told her she could not keep her job if she had a baby. So she left you with the nuns at the orphanage. She never forgot about you. She told me that if this day ever came, I was to tell you she is sorry. She saved as much money as she could to send you to England for your education. She knew it would be the only gift she could ever give you. The orphanage told her it had to be an anonymous gift, otherwise it would give the other orphans hope that their mother or father would someday return too, which never happens."

Cameron cries softly as a nurse enters the room because a buzzer sounded. She adjusts one of the intravenous tubes in his mother's arm, then shakes her head. His mother's grip loosens, her smile seems frozen and her eyes are closed. Cameron sees a flat line in the monitor at the head of the bed, and the nurse says, "I'm so sorry."

Cameron frowns and holds his mother's limp arm tighter. The nurse gives him a tissue. He asks her, "What happened?"

"Heart attack, preceded by a stroke yesterday, we think," she answers. "I'm sorry."

Cameron looks up, "How long has she been here?"

"Late last night. Her heart was very weak. She had rheumatic fever as a child, congestive heart failure for many years, several prior heart attacks. Then a stroke. And your relation to her?"

"Mother. This lady tells me she's my mother."

Irma nods her head, "Yes."

Cameron becomes upset. "That's it? That's all the time we have? She dies as soon as I got here?" Cameron stands up, wraps his arms around her small shoulders, and holds his dead mother in his arms. He kisses her on the forehead and strokes her arms. He is sobbing. He asks the nurse if he can sit with her for a while.

The nurse bites her lip and then nods approvingly. "Just for a little while. They will come to take her to the hospital morgue soon."

Irma taps Cameron on the shoulder. "She's made all the arrangements. Cremated. No service. She wants her ashes spread at sea. Unless you want them."

Cameron wipes his eyes and shakes his head. "For Christ's sake. I don't even know her full name. I don't believe this is happening."

Irma, speaking softly, says, "Grenier. Her name is Jewell Grenier."

"Why is my last name Haines?"

Irma explains, "Your mother and I worked for the Haines family for nearly our entire lives. The Haines family in Hancock Park. Haines Publishing. They ran a print company catering to black businesses."

"What? Why would I be a Haines?"

"Because you are. You are a Haines."

"The nuns told me they made up that name. No one was going to adopt a black orphan with no name, so they said they gave me that name."

"Even nuns can tell a fib." Irma shrugged.

"Then who is my father?"

"Prescott, the youngest Haines. He got your mother pregnant. They were in love. But a rich black family in Hancock Park would not let their son marry their maid. Not in the 1960s. Cameron, you know that rich black families, as few as there were in the sixties had, well, some snobbery to keep them apart from their past. It wasn't right, but that's the way it was. Rich white people didn't like their kids marrying the help, and, well, rich black people didn't like it either. They were . . . are devout Catholics, so abortion was out of the question. They made a deal with the Archbishop to have you taken in as an orphan, never to reveal your parents. Your mother convinced Mother Superior to put 'Haines' as your last name, on the premise it was a made-up name for a boy who would likely never get adopted. Your mother watched over you like a guardian angel, although forbidden from seeing you or contacting you."

Cameron thinks about it for a minute, and then asks, "So,

she was the lady from church the nuns told me paid for my education in England."

"Yes."

"Then I likely saw her at church, but didn't know who she was?" Irma nods her head. Another pause, then Cameron says, "And my father, Prescott. I think he died just recently. Did I read that in the papers?"

"Yes. He's dead. They sold the company."

Cameron, still sobbing, shakes his head and wipes his eyes with his handkerchief. "All this time she was alive, and so was my father. They never reached out to me. They left me with the orphan stigma forever. I don't know if I love my mother or hate her."

Irma, now crying herself, begs Cameron not to feel that way. "She loved you. She really did, Cameron. She did all she could do. She was ashamed for having a child out of wedlock. She never told the rest of her family what happened. Working in the Haines household as a live-in housekeeper, she often went months without seeing her family—your family. They never knew what happened. They thought her to be an old maid, literally, all of her life."

"And you, Irma? You were her friend?"

Irma nods her head, yes. "My best friend. We worked together in the Haines household for over fifty years. I was the cook. Well, mostly the cook until I got too old and then I washed dishes and helped your mother clean the house. They sold the big house years ago, and we got sent off to a senior living facility on Pico. We shared a room that the Haines family paid for. Still pays for. For me now. Just me."

Overcome in grief, Cameron holds his head in his hands. "She abandoned me. She could have come forward all these years, so I could have known her. I can't forgive her. This is so unfair."

Irma takes Cameron by the hand and tilts his chin towards her. "She was ashamed, Cameron. Especially when you became famous and successful, she didn't want to spoil your image. A black maid who bore you out of wedlock with her employer's son. How would that look in the tabloids? That's all she thought about.

She didn't want to shame you. And she was frightened for you."

"Frightened? Why?"

"Because someone came around a few weeks ago, the last time she was in the hospital. He rattled your mother. Said he wanted more information on her background and, well, your name came up. Your mother lied and said she didn't know who you were. But it left her uneasy. She said it was better for you to be an orphan with unknown parents, rather than the parents you really had."

Cameron looks at Irma. "Did you see this man or talk to him?"

"He was here last night, but when I came in and saw him, he left. Said nothing. Your mother was unconscious, so I thought I should just come get you first thing this morning. I didn't give it another thought."

Cameron shivers. He knows exactly who that person had to be.

15

That Missing Party Guest

"What? That can't be. He was lying right next to the fall mat. How does a dead man just walk away? Tony, you're being lied to."

"Reid, shut up. The cops couldn't find anything. They looked for a guest that passed out at the party, but they found nothing. They saw some broken bushes and marks left by the fall mat, but there wasn't a body. Are you sure your phony caterer friends saw what they told you they saw?"

Reid is silent.

"Reid?" Tony asks pensively.

"Shit. Should I call his wife?" Reid asks.

"How stupid is that? Call his wife and ask if Derek has shown up today? Won't she ask you why you're calling? And, by the way, his wife has already contacted the police. Derek didn't come home last night, so she called the cops. She filed a missing person's report."

Reid becomes agitated and confused. "Derek's body wasn't in the bushes by the pool deck of the Colonnade, but he also didn't come home last night. What the fuck happened?"

Tony clears his throat, then whispers. "Reid, that's what I'm asking you. Someone is onto you. I'm guessing it's Alton Price. He was there, I'm sure of it. Someone tipped him off or knew something would happen. And now you've got a missing accomplice who's dead. That's how he operates. He's likely hiding the body to use against you at an opportune time. Or use the dead body for another purpose in one of his schemes."

"Tony, you're talking in riddles. What do you mean, 'accomplice'?"

"For God's sake, Reid, you conspired with Derek to fake a death, your own death. Fake a fall. Didn't he know what he was doing? Come on."

"Well," Reid said slowly, "he saw my martini foreplay with Blair across our balconies. He was laughing. He found it funny."

"And, Reid, I've been meaning to ask you something else. When you told me to take my drone to the top of the Wilshire Palms and watch all of this unfold with your little stunt next door in the Colonnade, and Ms. Kilian on her balcony below, how did you get her to appear on her balcony at that moment?"

"Hey, wait, you filmed it all, didn't you? Tony, please don't tell me you botched that."

"I got it, or as much as I could get on my drone camera. I've got her face on film as she watches Derek's body vanish behind the hedges after his swan dive. The timing was perfect. I know how we got you into the rented apartment and your phony caterers down below, but how did you get Ms. Kilian to be on her balcony and watch a stranger commit suicide at that exact moment?"

Reid is silent.

"Reid," Tony persists, "I need to know. Was there someone else involved in your stunt we might need to worry about?"

"Yes, someone else involved, and no, you don't have to worry."

"Who, Reid? Who helped you get Blair Kilian on her balcony last evening?"

"Does it matter?"

"Yes. If I'm to help you stay out of the way of the cops, I need to know everyone else involved. Otherwise, I can't help you should they get serious about finding the caterers and the guy who rented the pool deck for a film shoot." Tony continued: "There's also the Alton Price problem. So how did you get Blair Kilian on her balcony last night to witness your performance?"

"Cameron Haines."

"What? Cameron Haines, your agent?"

"He's Blair's agent, too."

"I know that. So Cameron arranged for Blair to be on her balcony at the exact time necessary to witness your faked suicide?"

"Yep."

"How did he do that?"

"Don't know. I knew Blair and I would work together on that mini-series, and I told him I had a little welcoming joke to play on Blair. I just asked him to have her on her balcony by 6:30 last night. He didn't want to do it, so we argued. But then I reminded him why he pays me a big fat check every month. He was angry but said he would take care of it. And he did."

"Does he know what happened?"

"About Derek? About the stunt getting fucked up?"

"Yes, that's what I'm asking you. Does he know?"

"I don't think so. He thinks I pulled it off and . . . and . . . well, let's just say he thinks I pulled it off. Without a hitch."

Tony is silent and then speaks slowly. "Shit, why did you have to involve him at all? What does he know about your blackmail scheme? Does he know about all the others that pay us, besides him?"

"Okay, Tony, I'm done with playing twenty questions. You work for me. Have you forgotten that?"

"Since when? We're partners. Don't overstep with me."

"Rules are changing, Tony. Too many partners being cut in on the income and I'm the one doing all the work."

"Really?" Tony steamed. "All the work? Who sets up our victims with incriminating events? Who keeps the cops at bay when there's a fuck up—like this one? Who's doling out acting parts to a mediocre, pretty-boy actor who doesn't deserve them? You think you can do all that by yourself? Are you forgetting who you're dealing with? You are the most expendable partner. Don't forget that. And one more fuck-up like this and I can't protect you."

"Sorry. I'm tired. What else do you want to know?"

"I want to be sure I understand about Derek. He's only your stunt double in pulling off the swan dive. Right? That's it? He knows nothing more?"

"That's it. But what does that matter now?" Reid asks. "He's dead."

"So you were seducing Ms. Kilian from your balcony, attracting her interest. You rush inside to put on your tuxedo jacket for the swan dive. But you never came back out. Instead, it was Derek in the tuxedo, not you, but it all happened so quickly, I'm sure our dimwitted starlet never noticed. She thought it was you diving off the balcony. Derek knew what you two were doing. Right?"

"Well, he knew he was doubling for me, making it look like me doing that swan dive. I told him it was for a film shoot—just a short film I'm making. He just thought he was diving off the balcony dressed as me. That's it. He didn't know the rest."

"The rest being that you set her up to witness a suicide or a murder, then blackmailed her for not reporting it? And recruiting her to our dues-paying club because of her other little parental secret?"

"Yep, and to torment her—make her think she's crazy. Makes it easier to extort money from a bimbo like her. It's what I do, Tony. You know that. Stop pretending this is all a surprise to you. I'm getting annoyed."

Tony asks, "He knew you were flirting with Blair Kilian before his jump, then he posed as you to make it look like you jumped off the balcony?"

"Yes, he knew. But he's dead, so what's the point?"

"What's the point? The cops may figure it out! They're asking a lot of questions. And our partner there is asking a lot of questions about how this got so messed up. He thinks you're adding too much drama to recruiting new members. He thinks you're taking too much risk just to have a little sadistic fun."

"Okay, Tony, so I will ask one more time: What is the point?"

"That IS the point, Reid! We need to plan for what Derek's wife says when his body turns up. And that's not the scary part, Reid."

"What? What's the scary part?"

"Where is Derek's body? *That's* the scary part! You've been blackmailing and extorting Hollywood stars and agents for years. Maybe you're now outsmarted. Did you think of that?"

"Doubt it."

"Reid, perhaps it's time to stop. Why do you keep doing it, anyway?"

"I enjoy it. And it's made me rich. I like it better than acting. You see how many checks we receive every month! You get your share, and it's a lot of money. I love doing it! I hate all those primped up actors and agents. They think they're so perfect. So impervious. It's my job to exploit their faults and imperfections . . . and to make them pay for them. It makes their fame a little less enjoyable. Their own vanity becomes dark. So dark, in fact, that sometimes they kill themselves."

"Like Evelyn Sackalow?" Tony asks. "It made you feel good when she killed herself?"

"Only sad part of her suicide is that is the checks stopped. Bummer."

"My god, Reid! I'm thinking you like torturing our victims more than taking their money from them."

"So, fuck off, Tony. It's what I do, and I pay you very well to help me."

"Well, on that point, Reid, where's the money from our King of Hollywood? The last two payments were short."

"I revised our deal with him."

"And why did you do that? Looks like we're getting less money from him."

"*We* are getting less money, but *I* am getting some better paying acting gigs. And connections to some new members I want to add to our victim's club. Higher paying members, that is. Back off, Tony. This is my gig."

"Well, star boy, I'm bowing out from here on. If you want to continue this nasty business, don't include me in any of your new stunts. Extortion and blackmail are one thing; murder is another."

Reid shook his head. "I can't stop. I won't. Tony, you've been my partner in all of this for years. Who will take care of the photographs and wiretaps for me if you're gone?"

Tony is silent for a moment. "Plenty of other crooked private investigators and corrupt cops will be happy to take my place for you. But whoever replaces me can't fix what happened last night."

"What about our other key partner at city hall?" Reid asks.

"He comes with me. If I leave, he goes too. And most of our club members go with me too."

"That's not fair! That's not what we all agreed."

"Fair or not, if you insist on this reckless torture of our paying victims and keep messing up our recruits, then you're out."

"Then I need to take care of anyone standing in my way."

Tony is silent for a moment. He then whispers into the phone, "And who would that include?"

Reid says nothing and then hangs up.

Lies and Secrets

Reid throws his cell phone across the room, where it smashes against the headboard of his bed. He's furious that his phony suicide performance has gone awry. Though Blair is none the wiser, he's now got an accidental death on his hands, and a potential problem with the police. Losing his partners will make it harder to keep up his share of the business.

He pulls back the cover and sheets on his bed, undresses, throwing each piece of clothing across the room as it comes off. The last piece to come off is his underwear, which is blood-stained in front. Reid becomes faint as he drags down his underwear. No obvious injury, just some blood. He's relieved that it's Blair's blood and not his. Holding his head in his hands, he pulls his hair until each fist grasps a clump of his thick blonde hair. He pulls until it hurts, and some hair comes out in his hands. *Did I hurt her worse than I thought? I don't remember seeing any blood when I left.*

He swallows two Xanax, with a chaser of bourbon before showering. Sitting on the floor of the shower, he sees the blood on his torso wash down the drain. The events of the day begin as a flashback in his mind. Meeting Blair on the set, her lie that they've met before, raping her, and then learning that the police didn't find Derek's body after the fall.

Tony has quit. He was a partner in Reid's crimes of blackmail and extortion for years. Reid knows suicide is always an alternative, but he's tried that twice before. Tony rescued him both times, but he's not around now. *Maybe that's a good thing,* he thinks.

The Xanax and bourbon have kicked in. He can't stand up, but he can barely reach the handle to turn off the shower. Reid is too unsteady to walk, so he crawls across his bathroom floor to his bed, leaving a trail of soapy water on the tile and carpet. He pulls his wet body up onto his bed and is fast asleep. His recurring nightmare soon begins.

"You adopted brat!"

Reid says nothing in response to his seventeen-year-old classmate at boarding school.

"I said you're an adopted, spoiled brat. Fight me!"

Finally, Reid replies, "You're a liar, Sullivan! Just a fat, ugly liar."

"You're adopted. And you're spoiled. You and your fucking car. Show off! Your parents have to spoil you because you're just an orphan."

Reid turns around and slams Sullivan in the face with his chemistry book. As Sullivan hits the ground, Reid lands on top of him and unleashes his fury on Sullivan's face.

Reid remembers nothing after that until he is sitting in the principal's office. His parents arrive after meeting with the police and the principal. They've also met with Sullivan's parents before their son Bobby was taken to the hospital.

Reid's father extends his hand. "Let's go, son."

"Is it true?"

Reid's mother tries to take his other hand, but he shakes it away.

"Tell me!" he cries. "What Sullivan said. Is it true?"

His parents look at each other and his mother begins to weep.

Reid is furious. His face is red, "So it *is* true! I'm not your son. Why didn't you tell me?"

Shaking her head, his mother tries to take his hand

again, but Reid pushes it away. She insists, "We never knew the right time to tell you, son."

"Well, this is the worst time, isn't it? At school in front of my classmates? How did *he* know? How did Sullivan know?"

His parents, exasperated, shake their heads, looking down at the floor.

"*Tell* me! How did Sullivan know you adopted me?"

His parents take each other's hand, and his father says, "His mother told him."

"What? Bobby's mother, Mrs. Sullivan? How did she know?"

Taking a seat across from Reid, his father tells the story. "Son, we love you more than anything else on earth. We couldn't have children, so we adopted you from the Catholic orphanage in Denver. Saint Catherine's, near where we used to go to church, Reid. They told us an automobile accident killed both your parents. You were only eight months old."

Reid is crying, shaking his head. "But how? How did Mrs. Sullivan know? How? And why did she tell Bobby?"

Reid's father takes a deep breath, "She used to work at the orphanage. She was a nun. She left the convent and orphanage a couple months after we adopted you. She was pregnant with Bobby when we met her, and then she married Mr. Sullivan, who is Bobby's father. That's why the two of you are just ten months apart in age."

"So, if I'm an orphan, he's a bastard. Bobby the Bastard!"

"No, Reid, we don't talk like that," his father replied. "They got married. No one is a bastard or an orphan. You are our son. Bobby is their son."

"Why did you never tell me I'm adopted, and the Sullivan's know all about it? And *why* did she tell Bobby before you told me?"

Neither of his parents said anything.

"My name? What was my name when you adopted me, Mom?"

"Why is that important? We're your parents, Reid."

"What was my name? Who were my parents?"

"Luke. Luke Swanson was your name. We changed it to Reid and gave you our last name, which is what you do when you adopt a child. It was different back then. Adoption was more secretive. The orphanage never gave us the names of your parents. And we never asked."

"Then who told you my birth name was Luke Swanson?"

"Mrs. Sullivan. She told us. You know we've been friends ever since you and Bobby were born. They moved across town about ten years ago and, well, when they sent Bobby to the same prep school we chose for you, we just reconnected."

"But why, why did she tell Bobby before you told me?"

Silence again from both parents.

"Why? Tell me why she did such a cruel thing?"

"She's angry," his father eventually replies. "She's on a mission to purge what she thinks are her misdeeds at the orphanage. We fought with her about it. It's too much to go through for a seventeen-year-old. Just know we love you and we're sorry we didn't tell you years ago."

"The fight with Mrs. Sullivan—what did you fight about? Was it about me?"

Reid's parents look at each other, and his father clears his throat before speaking. "Mrs. Sullivan lied to us. When she was a nun, she handled your adoption and told us you were a single child with deceased parents, killed in a car accident."

"And so?"

"Reid, your parents were alive. They just gave you up."

"Why?"

"Don't know. We just learned this about a month ago as part of her purging process. She's called other adoptive parents, if she can find them, and is doing the same thing to them. She wants to clear up any lies she told them, even if the truth is painful. She also told Bobby that he was born before she and Mr. Sullivan married. And that she was a nun and left the convent after she got pregnant. I don't know why that is so important to her, but she felt it was part of the process."

"So, Bobby is angry?"

"Obviously."

Everyone is silent. Reid's mother takes out a handkerchief to wipe his face. She leans forward, "And son, there's one more thing."

Reid's father speaks up, "No. *No*, that's unnecessary."

Reid pushes his mother's hand away from his face, "What? What's 'unnecessary'? *Please* don't lie to me anymore."

After a brief silence, his mother speaks. "You apparently have a twin brother."

"What? Where is he, and why were we separated?"

"We don't know where he is, and neither does Mrs. Sullivan. The clergy in charge of the orphanage felt that twins were too difficult for one set of adoptive parents. So they split you up. We never knew that until she told us, just last month. Your father and I were heartsick . . . for you, for us, and for your twin brother. What a heartless thing to do. We would have loved to have you both. I'm sorry, son. Sorry to give you all this at once. I hope you can forgive us and Mrs. Sullivan."

Reid's face is red. He breathes heavily, "No. No, I can't. I'll forgive none of you. Ever. Especially her."

Two weeks later, Mrs. Sullivan is dead. Murdered. The killer stabbed her numerous times and then dressed her in a nun's habit. A note was left on her forehead: "A sin against a child is the worst kind of sin. There can be no redemption."

The nightmare jolts Reid awake, and he sits up in bed in a cold sweat, shivering. The bed sheets are wet. He has this same nightmare over and over. He wishes it were only a nightmare. But it's not.

Last Month's Revelation

Four weeks ago . . .

A knock on the door. Cameron Haines looks up from his desk, "Yes? Is that you, Faye?"

The door opens, and his secretary Faye steps in, closing the door behind her. She is in shock, leaning against the door.

"You okay? Why the knock?"

Faye clears her throat, "Mr. Haines. I just wanted to prepare you."

Cameron stands up from his desk. "Prepare me? For what? What's wrong? You look like you're ill. Do you need to go home?"

"It's startling, and, and before he comes in, I just wanted to prepare you. He says he's Reid Garrett's brother. Twin brother. He wants to see you."

"What? Reid has never mentioned a brother. Sounds like a scam. Faye, you know how many people claim relations to celebrities. Someone looking for a handout. Why are you even letting him in?"

"You'll see. May I show him in?"

Cameron walks around the desk, and waives his hand for Faye to show the guest in. "And please compose yourself."

"Oh, and he's pretty beat up."

Faye opens the door, and he walks in. "Mr. Haines, this gentleman says his name is Landon Griffith . . . and that he's Reid Garrett's twin brother. Mr. Griffith, this is Cameron Haines."

Landon extends his hand, but Cameron refuses. Landon's

swollen face has stitches over some nasty cuts and bruises, but Cameron can see that he's identical to Reid. Without saying a word, or shaking the extended hand, Cameron examines Landon, looking at the top of his head and back to his face. Cameron finally says, "I'm sorry; please excuse my bad manners. It's just that I'm stunned at the resemblance."

Landon drops his hand to his side. "I understand, Mr. Haines. Thank you for seeing me. I don't know who else to talk to."

Cameron extends his hand, they shake, and he shows Landon to the couch. "Is it just a coincidence or are you Reid's twin brother? And why, might I ask, are you so beat up? Do you need to see a doctor?"

"I've seen a doctor, thank you."

"What happened?"

"Reid and I had a fight. I guess he wasn't as excited to learn he has a twin brother as I thought he'd be."

"What? You've already met Reid, and you had a fight?"

"Yes, sir."

"When and how did you meet him?"

"At his house. I shocked him, and it made him angry. Well, not angry . . . *furious*. Yes, that's the word. Furious."

"How did you know where he lived?"

"Mr. Campanelli told me."

"Tony Campanelli? Good grief! So how did you find him?"

Landon explains, "I thought he was Reid's agent. My mother looked him up. She got it wrong, but I went to see him. He was about as startled as you. He called Reid, and he said for us to meet at his house."

"When was this?"

"Over a week ago."

"Where have you been since then?"

"The hospital, then hiding. Deciding what to do. That's why I'm here."

Cameron stands up, "Tell me what happened at Reid's house."

Landon begins, "Reid opened the door, invited me in. After inspecting me, he asked me to follow him to another room, which turned out to be his home gym. Once we were there, he made me take off my clothes so he could see exactly how *identical* I was. Guess he wasn't happy with what he saw. Said there was only one Reid Garrett, and the spotlight wasn't big enough for anyone else . . . especially a twin. He asked if I was there for money, and I said no. I just wanted to meet my brother. That enraged him, and he started punching me and throwing weights at me. I was sure he would kill me. I shoved him, and he fell backwards over a bench, hitting his head on the floor. He was still conscious, but groggy, so I grabbed my clothes, ran out of the house and drove away."

"My god, I'm sorry. That's terrible. Where did you go then?"

"To the hospital. The emergency room at Cedars-Sinai. They stitched me up, checked me out for broken bones, and released me. They said I had to file a police report, but I haven't."

"Did they ask you what happened?"

"Yes, I just told them two guys beat me up on the street trying to rob me. That's why they said I needed to file a police report."

"Where have you been since then?"

"A little hotel up on Sunset Boulevard. I found out you are Reid's agent, so that's why I'm here. I thought you could help me with my brother."

"What is it you want?"

"I want nothing, Mr. Haines. I just wanted you to know what happened, and if you think Reid might react better if you told him I'm his brother. You could tell him I'm not some stranger trying to shake him down for money."

"Landon, how *do* I know you're Reid's brother? I mean, yes, you're a dead ringer for him. Even your mannerisms and speech are just like his. Or, I should say, your mannerisms are like Reid's *used* to be. Before . . . "

"Before what?"

"Never mind," Cameron said, shaking his head. "What proof do you have that you are his twin and not just a look-alike?"

"I wasn't sure until a month ago. When Reid first became famous, I noticed our resemblance. My friends and family would tease me about it. I just thought it was a coincidence, but I followed his career. I learned about his family, where he was from. I couldn't find any actual connection, except that we looked *so* much alike. But then I found out his birthday is the same as mine. Just another coincidence?"

Landon continued: "My family adopted me and told me a car accident killed my parents. My family knew nothing about my parents or where they were from. The orphanage where I briefly lived is closed. I contacted the Catholic Archdiocese of Denver and they told me that adoption records are secret and, in this case, likely discarded when the orphanage was closed. They refused to help me. It seemed like a dead end, but my mother told me I should follow my heart and go meet Reid. His public biography doesn't indicate that his parents adopted him. The Garretts are a wealthy family, and his upbringing was far more comfortable than mine. My parents love me, but they have never had much money. My mother died a few weeks ago, just after she told me to follow my destiny and find the truth about Reid."

"You came here to Los Angeles with nothing more than that?" Cameron asked.

"Well, one more thing happened. About a month before my mom died, a woman called to say she was a nun at the orphanage when they adopted me. The lady was no longer a nun, but she wanted to let my parents know she had lied to them during my adoption and wanted to meet us to clear things up."

"Did she?"

"She was scheduled to meet my Mom for coffee, but she never showed up. We thought it was just a scam. Someone looking for money. Then my mom died."

"That's it? That's where it ended?"

"Yes. I came here to meet Reid. I wasn't expecting *that* kind of reception. I thought he'd be happy to know he has a brother. Instead, he wanted to kill me."

"Has Reid tried to reach you?"

"No. He didn't even ask for my name or where I was from. Nothing. As soon as he got a good look at me, he just wanted me dead."

Cameron walks around his office for a few moments, rubbing his chin.

"Can you help me, Mr. Haines? I know Reid would feel better if you could vouch for me. I want nothing from him or you. If he's my brother, I just want to get to know him. My parents are both dead, and I'm an only child. If Reid is my twin brother, then he'll be the only family I have. That would be a magnificent gift. I don't care about his fame, but I'd love to know my brother."

"Landon, I have no kind way to tell you; Reid is not a pleasant person. In fact, Reid's ruthless and self-centered. I'm certain if I vouched for you and we could prove you *are* his brother, he'd want to kill you even more. It pains me to say that, but I assure you, it's true."

Landon's face is stoic. He shakes his head, "That can't be true. Tell me why you won't help me. The truth."

Cameron sits next to Landon and puts his hand on his shoulder. "Landon, I've known Reid a long time. He's one of my highest-paid clients and one of the most famous. He's a one-man show. When he told you there's no room in the spotlight for anyone else, that's how he thinks. Having a twin would diminish his fame and take the spotlight away. The media would smother you with attention—and even sympathy. Reid would hate that and kill you before it could happen."

"That's not the answer I wanted to hear."

"I know it isn't."

"So, I'm just supposed to go back home? That's it?"

"Before doing that, I'd like you to spend some time with someone who is better at solving these kinds of problems than me. Can you stay in L.A. for a while longer?"

"If it would help me meet my brother, then yes, I'll do whatever you suggest."

Cameron pulls his cell phone from his pocket and dials a number. "Alton, are you in your office right now? Okay, then I'm sending a gentleman over to meet you. Listen to his story and call me tonight."

Hours later, his cell phone rings and Cameron answers. Before he can say anything the voice on the other end says, "I'd like to keep him for a while."

"Good. Then you can help him with Reid?"

"Not exactly. But I can help *you* with Reid."

"Alton, what are you saying?"

Alton hangs up.

18

A Deadly Gift

Four weeks later, Friday afternoon—the day after the botched fake suicide . . .

Alton tells his houseguest to go to the guest room and stay there until he comes for him. He goes outside, across the yard to the pool house, and opens the door. A young man is sleeping on a daybed inside, tied up and gagged.

Another man enters the pool house and smiles at Alton. "He's in good shape, but, man, will he have a headache when he wakes up!"

Alton takes the man's pulse and rolls him over on his side. "He looks good, Rob. Thanks for staying with him the last twenty-four hours. You've kept him unconscious the entire time?"

"Yes, sir. I diapered him and cleaned him up twice. A little water, but no food. I didn't want him to be awake to see me or where he's been."

"Perfect; just as I asked. Let's get the diaper off and get him into the back seat of your car. When did you give him the last pill?"

"About three hours ago. He should be asleep for at least an hour . . . give or take."

Alton and Rob place Derek, the stunt diver, in the back seat of Rob's car. Alton pats Derek on the forehead, "Sorry, young man. You won't remember a thing, but you'll get a nice reward for you and your wife, in due time."

Rob closes the back door of the car and shows a piece of paper to Alton. "This the right address?"

Looking at the piece of paper, Alton replies, "Yes. That's Tony Campanelli's home. He carries a gun so be careful."

Rob nods his head. "So, I place him at the front gate and leave?"

"Exactly. Be sure no one sees you and prop him up safely. He should wake up soon, so get moving. I don't want him to see you."

"How will Mr. Campanelli know Derek is outside his house?"

"Leave that to me. Reid Garrett will know about it just as soon as you drop Derek off. I'll be sure of that. It should take about fifteen minutes for him to get to Tony's house."

"What if Mr. Campanelli comes out first? Before I leave?"

"He won't. It's Friday night; he's had dinner with his weekly call girl, and she'll leave around 10:30 or 11:00 p.m. Like clockwork. He's *occupied* until then."

"Do I text you when I've made the drop?" Rob asked.

"No. I've placed a tracker on your car. It's under your hood by the battery. Once you've gotten home, retrieve it, smash it with your foot, and toss it out."

"Got it. So this Derek guy really hit the fall mat, but you made it look like he missed?"

"Absolutely," Alton confirmed. "We were waiting a few feet away in a ficus hedge. Tracked him all the way down. He hit the mat perfectly. We grabbed him as soon as he hit the mat and shot him with the tranquilizer. Even for a perfect stuntman, you need a few seconds to compose yourself after you hit the mat following a high dive. It can really knock the wind out of you. Adam and I grabbed him right away, administered the sedative, took him off the mat and moved it about ten feet. Reid's fake caterers came over shortly thereafter and saw the body lying in the bushes, several feet from the mat. We put Derek on his back with fake blood rolling out of his nostrils."

Rob considered all of this, then asked, "So, when you brought him to your place and had me clean him up, that wasn't real blood I cleaned out of his nose and face?"

"No. Didn't it seem a little pasty to you?"

"Yep, it was like red cornstarch."

"Exactly. Reid was careless. Once he told Cameron where to have Blair and at what time, we figured out who reserved the pool for the party and the apartment he would use to make his stunt."

"How did you know all that?"

"That's enough of the story for now, Rob. Get moving. He'll wake up in about an hour and you've got a twenty-minute drive up Laurel Canyon."

"On it, boss."

Alton tracks Rob's car up Laurel Canyon, until he sees the beeping signal come to a stop. After less than two minutes, the tracker shows Rob's car turn around and drive back down Laurel Canyon. Alton's phone buzzes with a text. *He drops off ok. All good. Watching for next arrival.*

Alton nods, but does not respond. Oksana's English is clumsy, but as a former Russian KGB agent, she's reliable and tough. Had something gone awry with Rob's drop off, she could handle a scuffle, and she's great with a gun. Alton never relies on just one person for an important task. No matter how qualified they are or how trustworthy, no one ever knows *the whole* story or completes a task unsupervised. Oksana was waiting across the street from Campanelli's house to witness the drop off. Now she waits for Reid to arrive.

Sitting in his office, surrounded by video screens and electronic equipment, Alton sends an anonymous text to Reid Garrett. *Get off your butt and pick up Derek at Tony's house. Hurry before the police get there first.*

Alton smiles. The encrypted text will erase itself once read. Reid will be furious, and it will surprise Tony. Alton wishes he were standing in the bushes with Oksana to watch it all. But she's good with the night camera, so Alton will see it all later.

Oksana waits patiently until she sees the front door of Tony's house open. Tony runs down the driveway in his bathrobe. A naked woman stands in the doorway with her hand over her mouth. Tony kneels in front of Derek, shakes his shoulders, and slaps his face. Reid must have just called him.

Tony yells something out to the naked lady in the doorway, but Oksana can't hear it. Headlights illuminate Tony's face and Derek's body as a car rapidly approaches, then screeches to a halt. Reid Garrett jumps out, pushing Tony to the ground and grabbing Derek, who is waking up. Tony and Reid are shouting at one another as Reid picks up Derek's limp body and places him in the passenger seat of his car.

Tony stands up and grabs Reid from the back as he is placing Derek in his car. Turning around, Reid punches Tony, who falls back on the pavement, just outside his driveway. Reid jumps into his car, turns it around and backs into Tony's body. Twice. Startled, Oksana hears Tony scream and then two loud thuds. Reid gets out of the car and looks at Tony, who is dead or unconscious. After spitting on him, followed by a swift kick to the head, Reid drives away, headlights off.

Oksana has recorded everything on an infrared night vision camera. Once Reid's car is out of sight, Oksana runs across the street and reaches out to Tony, whose motionless body is lying in a pool of blood on the pavement. Before she looks for a pulse, she puts on gloves and looks around to be sure no one else is on the dimly lit street. Her examination is quick.

Back in her car, Oksana drives away and texts Alton: "Reid takes Derek's body in car. He runs over Mr. C. Not dead. I bring video to you now."

Alton takes a deep breath, "Good god, he tried to kill him. Shit."

19

The Fall Guy

Fleeing from the gruesome scene at Tony Campanelli's home, Reid is driving recklessly down Laurel Canyon toward Sunset Boulevard. Derek, groggy from his sedative, yells for Reid to stop the car before he gets sick, but Reid ignores him. Derek lowers the passenger window and vomits, covering the side of Reid's red Ferrari in a colorful goo.

"Shit, Derek! You idiot!"

Derek wipes his mouth with his sleeve and then answers Reid in a raspy voice. "I asked you to stop."

"I don't stop for liars and traitors."

"What? What are you talking about?"

"You were in on it, weren't you? Who tipped you off to mess up our stunt? Alton Price? Was Tony in on it too?"

"Reid, what are you talking about? I've got some serious questions for you. What happened, what day is it, where have I been, and how'd I get this bitch of a headache?"

"Fifteen thousand dollars wasn't enough for a one-minute performance? How much did Price pay you to mess it up? Why did you fuck me over?"

"Reid, stop. Please. Tell me what happened after I landed. It was a perfect landing. Perfect. Before I could even roll over on the mat, someone grabbed me and injected my arm. That's the last I remember until I woke up with you beating me up in the driveway a few minutes ago."

"Liar!"

"Reid, I'm not lying. What happened? I'm sore all over. Nauseous. And here, look at my arm. Do you see this big red splotch? That's still sore from whatever they injected me with. What happened after the fall?"

Reid looks over at Derek and shakes his head, but he says nothing.

"You taking me home?" Derek asks. "What day is it?"

"Friday."

"So where was I Thursday night, after the fall? And all day today? Where was I?"

"That's what I want to ask you. Where the fuck were you after you hit the fall mat, and who drove you to Tony Campanelli's house?"

"I don't know. And I don't know anyone with that name. Tony . . . whatever. I feel like shit and want to go home. God, Marianna will be so pissed. And worried. Have you spoken with her?"

"No, I haven't spoken with your wife. She knows nothing about what happened. She reported you as a missing person when you didn't come home Thursday night."

"Shit, oh shit. Reid, you can't tell her I made a jump. Please."

"Depends."

"Depends? On what?"

"On how helpful you are to me."

"For fuck's sake Reid, I made a ten-story jump for you! Risked my life for fifteen thousand dollars because I need the money and owed you a favor. What else do you want from me?"

"First off, silence. No one must know why I hired you. No one, ever."

"That was part of our deal, Reid. I already agreed to that."

"And I want to know where you were and who hired you to fuck up the dive."

"I didn't fuck up the dive. Think about it. If I fucked it up, I'd be dead. You don't survive after you hit the ground falling ten stories. I hit the mat, just as planned. What happened right after that is a mystery to me. I don't know, Reid. And frankly, I'm a little scared."

"Scared of what?"

"Not what . . . who. I'm scared of you because of the way you're talking, and I'm scared of whoever drugged me and kidnapped me for the past twenty-four hours. Who is it, Reid? What went wrong? Why did they mess up our little performance? Is there something you're not telling me?"

Reid says nothing for blocks.

Derek interrupts Reid's thoughts. "What are we going to tell Marianna? About where I've been?"

Reid is still silent and turns down Santa Monica Boulevard towards the Melrose district where Derek lives with his wife, Marianna, and their new baby, Rachel.

"Reid? Talk to me."

"I can't believe you didn't get a look at anyone near the fall mat before you got tranquilized. How can you ask me to believe that?"

"You know me, Reid. You know I'm a great stuntman and a high-fall expert. That takes concentration and calculation all the way down. I'm focused on the center of that mat the entire fall until the moment I roll my head under for impact. You know that. I'm focused on one thing, no matter what's near the mat. And I can tell you for sure that no one was anywhere near that mat when I made my dive. No one. I wouldn't have made the leap if anyone were even near that mat when I dove off the balcony. Once I hit the mat, it takes my breath away and I need a moment to focus. Someone grabbed me the moment I hit the mat."

Reid says nothing until he turns the corner onto Derek's street.

"Reid, what do I tell Marianna? Will you come in and vouch for me? What's our story?"

"You joined me for an interview as my stand-in for some light action work. For my next film. I hosted dinner afterwards, and you drank too much. You spent the night at my place and slept off your hangover until I came home from the studio tonight and I drove you home."

Derek shakes his head, "Shit, she will be furious if she thinks

I got so drunk I had to sleep it off."

Reid grunts, "Oh, come on, Derek, she knows you have a drinking problem."

"Had. Had a drinking problem. I've been clean."

"How many more lies tonight, Derek? You're still a boozer. And a *loser*."

"Okay, I'll take my punishment from her. What about the money? You owe me fifteen thousand dollars."

"I'll think about it."

"What? I risk my life and you decide not to pay me for it?"

"Once I'm sure you aren't lying, I'll pay you the rest. Here's a down payment." Reid hands Derek a wad of cash.

Derek counts it out. "A thousand dollars? That's it? You fucker."

"Oh, one more outburst like that and Derek is a poor boy. Now get out of my vomit-covered car and apologize to your wife for being a has-been stuntman who drinks too much. Or should I say, a fall guy who drinks too much? Oh, that's funny, isn't it! A fall guy!"

As Reid pulls up in front of Derek's house, he pushes the passenger door open, and gives Derek a strong shove out the door. "I don't want Marianna to see me. Stick to the story. If she doesn't believe you, have her call me."

Before Derek can even get up off the sidewalk in front of his house, Reid screeches off.

Body Double

It's a hazy Saturday morning in Los Angeles, and Alton Price is hosting a breakfast for a guest. His houseboy set a formal table on the patio by the pool, and he prepared an Italian-style breakfast preceded by Bloody Marys.

The buzzer at the front gate rings. Alton, just getting out of the shower yells out, "Marcello, will you get that, please?"

"Yes, sir."

Alton hears Marcello have a brief conversation over the intercom with whoever has just rung the buzzer at the gate. Marcello then calls out to Alton, "Mr. Price, it is Mr. Haines. He says he needs to see you."

Alton mutters, "I'll bet he does."

"Should I let him in, sir?"

Alton yells out, "Tell him I'd rather he went home, but if he insists on coming in, please show him to my office."

"Yes, sir."

Getting out of his car, Cameron sees Marcello waiting to greet him at the front door of Alton's cottage.

"Good morning, Mr. Haines."

"Good morning, Marcello. Sorry to show up unexpectedly, again."

With a nod and a faint smile, Marcello shows Cameron to Alton's office, which is off the main hallway. Alton's bedroom adjoins the office, connected by a secret door. Alton emerges from his bedroom in a bathrobe, holding a cup of coffee, and sighs. "Well, Cam, two nights ago you show up and ruin my evening, and now you show up on a Saturday morning and interrupt my breakfast. Have your forgotten that custom of making an appointment?"

Cameron is visibly upset. "I know I'm being an ass, but when are you going to stop this, Alton? How much longer will it go on?"

"Oh, come now, Cameron. Are you fussing about Reid trying to extort Blair? You knew that would happen. You know exactly what he's up to. We discussed all of that weeks ago."

Cameron holds his head in his hands. "I . . . I think he raped her."

Alton puts his coffee cup down on the desk and walks over to Cameron. "What makes you think he raped her?"

"I called Blair to check in with her this morning. I was curious how things went on the set yesterday. I already got Eric's version—he's the director."

"I know him, Cam."

"Well, he said the reading went terribly and that Reid and Blair were to work out their differences by Monday."

"I spoke to Blair about an hour ago," Cameron continued, "and, well, she was freezing cold with me. Told me she wanted a new agent. She rambled about my apparently knowing everything and abandoning her, just like her father did. Said she was expecting Reid to be a jerk since he held her future in his hands, but that I hadn't told her rape and extortion were part of the deal. Then she hung up."

Alton is silent for a moment, pacing about the office while deep in thought. "Well then, Cam, we will have to move our timing up. I'm sorry about the rape. It's unforgivable—if it's true. And the father abandonment comment, I know that must have really hurt."

Cameron, tears in his eyes, shakes his head.

"You know we'll make him pay for all he's done. And if we're adding rape to the list of his other despicable deeds, then so be it. The punishment will be that much more severe."

Alton gives Cameron a handkerchief to wipe his tears and

blow his nose. As Cameron stands up, Alton gives him a hug. "I'll take care of things, Cam. You know I will."

Cameron shakes his head and turns to walk out of the office.

As Cameron proceeds down the hallway toward the front door, Alton yells out to him. "Oh, one more thing. I've got a question for you before you leave."

Cameron turns around to face Alton.

Walking down the hallway towards Cameron, Alton asks, "How well do you know Tony Campanelli?"

Cameron sighs, "As if this morning isn't already terrible, you make it worse?"

"Answer my question."

"We've met."

"Someone tried to kill him last night."

Startled, Cameron replies, "Do I need to guess who?"

"You don't."

"Was Campanelli in on the faked suicide?"

"He's in on *all* of Reid's schemes. Or at least he was." Alton pushes a button on his desk and then looks up at Cameron. "You're staying for breakfast. It's time we discussed how this will end."

Marcello appears at the office doorway, "Yes, sir?"

"Please add a place setting to the table; Mr. Haines will join us for breakfast."

"Yes, Mr. Price."

As Marcello leaves the office, Cameron speaks up. "I thought we were meeting for lunch Monday to discuss what happens next."

"Let's meet now. You're here, my special guest is here, so let's make this Saturday morning worthwhile. I'll meet you out by the pool in ten minutes. Ask Marcello to make you a drink."

Cameron is enjoying his Bloody Mary at a table by the pool when he hears the living room sliding door open and a tall blonde man steps out. Cameron jumps up so quickly he almost knocks over the table. "Reid! What are you doing here?"

Before the blonde man can speak, Alton emerges from behind him, grinning. The tall blonde man is now smiling too.

Cameron squints, "You're dressed just like him. And your hair, it's now fixed the same way as his."

Alton is all smiles. "Well, we fooled you for a minute! Yes, Cam, this is Landon. You haven't seen him since you sent him over to me from your office about a month ago."

"He was so bruised and swollen; I have to admit I didn't see *exactly* how identical they are until now."

Landon speaks up. "You know you don't have to refer to me in the third person. I'm standing right here."

"Forgive me. It's just that your appearance startled me when I first met you in my office, and I'm equally startled now." Walking closer, Cameron extends his hand. "You've got his mannerisms now, and dress like him too."

"Alton has been a great tutor."

"Yes. I see that."

As the three of them walk over to the breakfast table, Alton waives to Marcello to start breakfast. "Landon performed beautifully, seducing Blair at the studio. She did not know it wasn't Reid, and he fooled the onlookers too."

Cameron shakes his head, "I understand. But now what? Blair had never met Reid in person, so he could fool her. But many people know him personally. *Very* personally—if you know what I mean."

"Take a big gulp of that Bloody Mary, Cam. I'm about to divulge something for you to think about."

Finishing his Bloody Mary in one gulp, Cameron places his glass on the table, folds his hands in his lap and smiles. "All yours, Mr. Price."

Alton picks up a newspaper and tosses it over to Cameron. The headline startles Cameron: "Actor Reid Garrett Injured in Accident That Kills His Brother."

Alton retrieves the phony paper from Cameron. "That would be quite an attention-grabber headline, don't you think?"

"Have you lost your mind, Alton?"

"Not quite. I've been discussing Landon's future with him. His future as Reid Garrett."

Cameron frowns. "What?"

"His future as Reid Garrett instead of Landon Griffith."

"And exactly how would that happen? Are you suggesting what I think you are? That's insane."

"It's the best ending, Cam."

"You told me you'd take care of all of this once and for all. Frankly, when you said that, I wasn't sure if that meant you would restrain Reid or just make him go away. I didn't think you meant a body swap, or whatever it is you're suggesting."

"Oh, come now, Cam. You thought I'd kill him. Why are you using those nicer words? 'Restrain'? 'Go away'? You wanted him dead. But you'd lose a lot of money if your number one client suddenly died. There goes his income and *your* hefty percentage."

Cameron shakes his head but says nothing.

"This was not part of my original plan. I was to just remove Reid from your life. That's it. But when Mr. Griffith here showed up as a perfect duplicate of our problem star boy, I had a better idea. Let's just create a more *perfect* Reid Garrett."

Cameron is shaking his head as Marcello appears with another Bloody Mary. "Alton, that may work in the movies, but how would you possibly make it work in real life?"

"Cam, think about it. I eliminate Reid, and you lose one of your biggest moneymakers as a client. Second, no disappearance is perfect. There's always the risk that they uncover my dirty deed, or people get suspicious. You're involved in this up to your eyeballs, even though I'm the one having all the fun."

"Such gallows humor, Alton?"

"I'm serious. You know I love ending the lives of nasty souls. And I still plan on ending the life of Mr. Reid Garrett. The question is whether it's better for Landon to have a new life as Reid, and if that's a safer option for you, too."

Turning toward Landon, Cameron asks, "Would you really give up your identity to live the rest of your life as someone else? I can't believe that."

Landon stands up and walks a few feet from the table. "At first, I didn't like it. I'm not ashamed of Landon Griffith, or unhappy with my life. But I'll never have the fame or money Reid has."

Cameron objects, "But it's not *you!* Don't you get that, Landon? It's not really *your* life. It's comfortable and exciting, but it's *not* Landon. It's Reid. And, might I add, there are many people in this town that hate Reid Garrett."

"Oh, and I love that, Mr. Haines! I want to turn that around. It will be fun to remake Reid, in a way. It's a bit of revenge too, isn't it?"

Cameron and Alton look at each other. They both think there must be a bit of deviousness in Landon, too.

Alton leans in close to Cameron, and whispers in his ear, "Cameron, Landon is Reid's twin. Identical twin. There's a bit of a sinister streak in Landon, I can tell you that. Not as bad as Reid, but he's been with me for four weeks. I've seen it. Not sure we can trust him. Not yet, and maybe never."

Landon overhears part of the conversation and puts up his hand, "Please, don't tell me I'm devious like my brother. I'm not that guy."

Marcello arrives at the table with Italian frittatas, sausages, and fresh fruit. He also offers coffee and more Bloody Marys.

Before taking his first bite, Cameron puts down his fork and looks up at Alton. "But what if we're found out? A lot of moving parts are at work here, a lot that can go wrong." Looking over at Landon, "And can you even act? Can you read a script? Can you be an actor like your brother?"

Alton interrupts, "Oh for God's sake, Cam. Reid's a lousy actor. Face it. He's good looking, sexy, and he can memorize a script, but he's not known as one of Hollywood's best actors."

Landon assures them, "I *can* do it. I *want* to do it."

Before either of them can respond, Cameron's cell phone rings. The caller ID says "REID GARRETT." Cameron looks up at Alton before answering the phone. "Speak of the devil."

Alton nods, "Take it."

"Good morning, Reid." Alton and Landon can hear Reid screaming at Cameron. "Reid, settle down. Get a hold of yourself.

Reid? Reid?" Cameron looks up from his phone. "He hung up. He's furious that Tony didn't die. He wants to know how much Blair knows about his scheme and if I know you're the one that fucked it up. Says he will expose my secret and Blair's too. He will kill both of our careers."

Alton points at Cameron, "It's also not good for *us* if Tony Campanelli lives."

Cameron asks why.

Alton answers, "I'll explain later. Here's what we need to do. You get a hold of Blair and tell her Reid is coming over for a script reading tonight. She's not to be fearful because you'll be there too."

"What? Are you crazy? We can't put Reid in the same room with me and Blair right now!"

"It won't be Reid. It'll be Landon. We've got to let her in on the plan. Otherwise, it won't work."

"Shit." Cameron pushes his plate away and asks Landon to give him a moment with Alton. Landon nods and walks back inside the cottage. "Alton, the more people that know, the greater the chance this comes out someday."

"I'm very aware of that. I'll ensure that doesn't happen."

"And what about Landon? He'll have something over you and me for the rest of our lives."

"No one ever has anything over me, Cam. No one. If we discover that we can't trust Landon, then things change. We'll talk about that another time. For now, you just be sure Blair is ready for her script reading tonight."

An Errand Turns Messy

As Cameron is leaving the driveway of Alton's cottage, Alton waves him off and closes the front door. "Landon, you know what you need to do."

"Read my lines? Again?"

"Yes, over and over. I've got an errand to run, but when I'm back in a couple hours, we'll do a complete reading of the next episode. I'll read Blair's lines; you handle Reid's."

"What about the other parts?"

Alton smiles. "Marcello will read all the other lines for us. In Italian!"

As Landon goes into the den to study his lines, Alton uses a keypad and eyeball recognition scanner to open the door across the hall from his office. The door opens to a windowless room. Alton takes his seat in a large leather chair surrounded by a half-circle desk and more than a dozen television monitors of various sizes. This is Alton's lair, where he conducts his electronic surveillance of targets and clients and monitors his most secret activities from the shadows. It is also where he can access criminal and other personal background records from around the world; some legally, but most through clandestine sources. Alton honed his surveillance skills during his eleven years in the CIA, four of which he served as a foreign operative. He's overqualified to be Hollywood's best "fixer," but he grew tired of living anonymously and alone while on secret CIA assignments overseas.

He plugs a device the size of a pack of cigarettes into his computer and adjusts the settings on a large video monitor. With a few keystrokes, he hacks into the security cameras in the home of Tony Campanelli. Tony is still in the hospital recovering from his injuries last night, but Alton wants to be sure there is no one else at home this Saturday afternoon. Alton and his small team will execute what he calls a "residential retrieval" operation. Law enforcement authorities would call it an illegal entry, search and seizure.

A buzzer goes off and the monitor clicks on for the outside gate to Alton's driveway. He looks up, pushes a button on his desk, and the gates open. A black van enters his driveway as Alton picks up his jacket and a small briefcase. When Alton approaches the van in the driveway, the side door opens, and he steps inside. The door closes immediately behind him and the van leaves the driveway, heading up the street toward Sunset Boulevard.

Rob Elliott, a member of Alton's team, is driving as Alton takes his seat in the van, just behind him. Rob turns around briefly, "Afternoon, boss."

Alton winks at Rob. "Oksana is already there. Told her to wait across the street."

"Got it."

About fifteen minutes later they pull up in front of Tony's home off Laurel Canyon in the Hollywood Hills. Alton texts a question mark to Oksana, who soon emerges from a Ficus hedge across the street. The side door of the van opens and Oksana steps in. Her name in Russian is "Оксана," but in English she spells it "Oksana." Alton first met her on foreign assignment. She is a former KGB agent who got traded for a US spy during the waning years of the Soviet Union. Both were traitors against their government. The Russian KGB captured her while she was working as a double agent for the CIA. She "switched teams," as they say. The American spy was working for the CIA but became a double agent for the KGB during Vladimir Putin's days running the KGB. They both got discovered as double agents and incarcerated by their own governments.

Ultimately, the two traitors got swapped in a single deal. She's bitter, angry, and just the type Alton needs when he fears he may encounter desperate people. The KGB trained Oksana as a killer and kidnapper. She did more of the former than the latter. If she kills someone and gets caught, the CIA will probably get her released. She still knows a lot of secrets, so Alton often says, "Oksana has a lifetime pass." Decades ago she was a tall woman, thin and beautiful. The years have not been kind to her. Too many gunshot wounds, stabbings, and brutal fights have taken their toll. Today she is still over six feet tall but overweight; her face shows the pain she has inflicted on others, and the pain others have inflicted on her.

Oksana gives Alton a kiss on the cheek, "How is my little bubala?"

Alton hates being called that, but he smiles and gives her a wink. "Questions from either of you before we go in?"

Oksana and Rob both shake their head, no.

"Cool, then let's ditch the van where we planned, and head in."

Rob parks the van off the street on a patch of dirt at the corner, obscured by a large Ficus hedge and an avocado tree. In most sections of the Hollywood Hills, the streets are narrow, curvy, and older sections have no sidewalks. This street has dirt along the side of the road and lots of vegetation.

Alton, Oksana, and Rob hop over the fence behind a hedge. Alton turned off the security alarm and cameras from inside the van just moments ago.

"We'll have only about forty-five minutes if the alarm company notices the outage and sends the security patrol to check it out. We have to hustle."

Alton uses a slim device the size of a credit card to open the front door, and each of them runs to their preassigned location in Tony's home. Alton goes to the office and sees a large file cabinet. He quickly picks the lock and retrieves a stash of client records, recognizing many of the names as the celebrities Reid is blackmailing. The wall safe is more of a challenge, but Alton gets it open and retrieves some documents and jewelry. He already knew what to look for, but as he opens the safe, he spots a silent alarm switch he was unaware of. A wire and sensor inside the door look unusual to him.

Oksana searches Tony's bedroom for anything he may have stashed there instead of in his office. She is also looking for any incriminating personal items that Alton might use to keep Tony silent. Bedroom toys and "party favors" are a favorite to retrieve.

Rob checks the garage for things Tony may have kept in one of his cars. It's always a long shot, but people like Tony and Alton often keep monitoring or other devices in their cars. They often contain some interesting information.

The back of the watch on Alton's wrist vibrates. He goes to the window of Tony's office and sees a man using a clicker to open the front gate to Tony's property. "Shit." He texts Oksana and Rob, "We have a visitor. Meet at the van ASAP." As the car approaches the front of the house, Alton recognizes the car. A red Ferrari. Alton says aloud, "Damn, this messes things up."

22

Turnabout

The driveway gate opens slowly, and Reid is impatient. With the gates only half open, he slams his car through the gates of Tony Campanelli's home, tires squealing as he races up the long driveway to the front door.

The Ferrari lands with a thud on the first row of steps to the entry. Reid throws open the driver's door, runs up the front steps and uses a key to unlock the front door. Once inside, he enters the alarm code on a keypad in the hallway. In his haste, he doesn't notice the alarm is already off, and he heads down a long hallway to Tony's office. Pulling a ring of keys from his pocket, he quickly identifies a tag on a key that says "Tony files." He opens the top drawer and sees that all the client files are missing. Using a second key, he opens the lower drawer but only sees household and other files of no interest to him. Turning away from the file cabinet, Reid walks over to Tony's desk. After examining the papers on top of the desk, he pulls out all the drawers and rifles through the contents. He finds nothing he is looking for.

Teeth clenched, Reid shouts, "Shit! Where are they? That fucker." He surveys the room and surmises he is too late. *Someone has already been here,* he realizes.

Eyeing the safe on the wall, Reid pulls a piece of paper from his pocket with the combination. Before he can turn the dial to the first number, he sees the safe is already open, and it is empty. At that moment, the alarm goes off, triggering a loud siren and lights flashing in the hallway. *Damn it, I know I disarmed it.*

Sitting in the black van outside, Alton has just turned on the house alarm remotely as Reid was opening the safe. The alarm goes off, and the camera in the office has come back on and gets a clear shot of Reid running down the hallway to the keypad to silence the alarm. Alton's equipment in the van is capturing the camera images of Reid as he runs from the office down the hall and struggles to enter the code for the alarm. Alton shuts off the alarm just before Reid enters the last number of the alarm code.

Reid looks up at the security camera in the hallway by the alarm keypad. *Someone is fucking with me.* He flips his middle finger up at the hallway camera and smiles. On his way out the door, he lifts a flower vase from a side table and throws it at the camera. He misses.

Alton, Rob and Oksana are watching Reid's tantrum on the camera inside the van parked outside.

Rob turns to Alton and asks, "Why is he so angry? What is he looking for?"

Alton points to the floor of the darkened van, and the stack of client files he retrieved from the cabinet in Tony's office. "Those. He came here looking for those."

"Why?"

"Because those are files Reid and Tony keep on the people they're blackmailing. They're full of salacious details these celebrities, politicians and businesspeople want kept secret. Without what's in those files, Reid can't keep up his extortion and blackmail schemes. At least, not most of them."

Rob grins and winks at Alton. "Congratulations, boss. What a treasure trove you now have."

"Exactly."

"So, you'll use those files to stop Reid? Turn him in?"

"No! Quite the opposite."

"What?" Rob is confused.

"We don't want Reid getting into any trouble," Alton explains. "His reputation needs to remain squeaky clean, at least in public. Our *new* Reid Garrett won't have a future if people find out about any of this. Those files are for us to keep safely locked away so no one can prove what Reid was doing."

"Seems unfair. Why should he get away with it?"

"What makes you think he's getting away with it?"

Oksana laughs and pats Rob on the back. "His punishment vill be eternal. Da best kind."

Rob says nothing. He understands what Oksana means. That's the only part of working for Alton that Rob dislikes . . . the killing. It's rare, but it's how some jobs end.

They hear the rumble of Reid's Ferrari coming down Tony's driveway and rolling over the gates he smashed earlier. Reid drives out of Tony's driveway and takes the turn toward Laurel Canyon at breakneck speed.

Rob returns to the driver's seat at the front of the van. "Follow him, boss?"

"No. Let's get out of here. Is our license plate still covered?"

"Yes, boss."

"Good, leave it covered until you get to Laurel Canyon, then flip the switch. I'm sure we disabled the gate cameras, but just in case we missed anything, leave them covered for now. The house alarm is going off, so the security patrol should arrive soon. Drop Oksana off at the London Hotel, and then go back to my place and put everything away as usual. Stay with Landon until I get back. I've got a quick stop to make on the way home."

Alton slowly opens the side door of the van and steps outside, taking his briefcase.

"Where are you going, boss? How are you getting there?"

"I'm taking Oksana's car she's hidden across the street. Go on, get moving, get out of here. I'll be in touch." Just before stepping out of the van, Alton's cell phone rings. The caller ID says "CAMERON." "Cam? What's up?"

"Blair is on her way to Reid's house. She called me back about the message I left for her on the script reading with Reid tonight at her apartment. She says she'll do the reading at Reid's house. Alone. I'm not welcome."

"What?"

"She said since I can't take care of Reid for her, she'll do it herself."

Incredulous, Alton asks, "You mean she couldn't just wait and see Reid tonight at her apartment for the script reading?"

Cameron replies, "She said Reid will have his *last* script reading with her tonight. His very last script reading. Alton, I'm worried. She's no match for him."

Alton steps back inside the van and closes the door. "Damn. What's she up to?"

"Don't know, but I'm worried. What should I do?"

"Stay put, Cam. I'll get back to you. If you hear from her again, call me right away." Alton hangs up before Cam can respond.

Rob asks, "What's up, boss?"

"Change of plans. Blair is meeting Reid at his house. I'll go there now, and you follow me. But don't keep up with me. Take your time, park the van somewhere near Reid's house where they won't see you. Get the drone ready and do nothing until you hear from me."

"Got it."

Alton looks to Oksana, "You have your gun, I assume?"

She nods her head yes.

"Silencer?"

"Alvays."

"Come with me."

Alton leaves the van with Oksana close behind. Oksana drives a Mustang Shelby GT500, courtesy of Alton. He wanted to buy her an Aston Martin, but with her height and girth, she couldn't fit into it—at least, not comfortably. The black-on-black Shelby GT500 was the second choice, but it comes in handy for car chases and pursuits. Alton waives Oksana into the passenger seat, and he takes the wheel of the Mustang. As he pulls away from the curb, Cameron calls him again. Alton answers, "Cam, what now?"

"Should I meet you at Reid's?"

"Absolutely not. Stay put. I'll be at Reid's in about twenty minutes. Does Blair still drive a Mercedes convertible? Black?"

"Yes, that's right. One more thing."

"What? Make it quick."

"She might have a gun, Alton."

"What do you mean she *might* have a gun?"

"Mine. She's got mine."

Alton is silent for a moment. "Cam, what were you thinking?"

"I know, I know. After Reid raped her, I brought it over to her and told her to hang on to it. It freaked her out and she wouldn't even touch it. Maybe she doesn't have it with her. Just wanted you to know."

"Shit, Cameron. Anything else you need to tell me?"

The Chemistry Between Us

Reid greets Blair at his front door wearing only a swimsuit. "Ah, my favorite actress and trailer fuck! Come in."

Dressed as if she is going to a cocktail party, Blair smiles faintly at Reid. "I'm ready for my reading. Shooting starts day after tomorrow. You have your script?"

Reid shows her in, snatching a kiss on the cheek as she walks by. "I'm too excited to read my script right now. I need something relaxing."

"Let's have a drink, then," Blair suggests.

"That's not what I had in mind. Let's go to the bedroom first."

Blair asks again, "A drink, please? Then whatever you want. I need my job and I don't want you to let me go from the show."

Reid replies, "Are you daft? I told you what you need to do to stay on the show. And I *showed* you what you need to do. In your trailer. Staying on the show has nothing to do with how you read your script. It's the on-demand sex and the money you pay me. That's what decides."

Blair remains calm and smiles. "Gin martini? You join me?"

"As long as it's a prelude to the bedroom."

"It is." Blair smiles and eyes the bar at the end of the living room. "I'll make us our cocktails. And I brought a little candy with me."

Reid smiles as Blair throws a small vial of white powder and a thin straw on the coffee table. "I love snow! Let's save half for the bedroom."

Blair looks in the mirror over the bar and sees Reid opening the vial of cocaine and making lines on the coffee table behind her. She makes two large gin martinis, one laced with the drug tramadol, a powerful painkiller. She had mixed the cocaine with methamphetamine, a combination that can cause a stroke. Her martini is mostly water, with just a hint of gin.

"I'm starting without you, baby." Reid snorts two lines of the cocaine, not noticing it's laced with meth. He leans back on the sofa, tilts his head up and snorts the deadly combo deeper into his nasal cavities. "Oh, Kilian, that's nice. You surprise me."

Blair arrives with the martinis and sets Reid's down in front of him. She unbuttons her blouse before hoisting her drink and taking the first sip.

Reid smiles and leans forward to pick up his martini from the table. "Coke and gin, what a combination." He takes a sip, then shakes his head as he swallows. "Shit, woman, that's nasty."

"It's the coke. It affects your taste buds. You know that. Just drink up and let's get to the bedroom."

Reid stands up without his drink and starts toward the bedroom.

"Finish your drink, Mr. Garrett. If you are as rough with me in your bedroom as you were in my trailer, we both need this drink before we start." Blair removes her blouse and throws it on the sofa. She's not wearing a bra.

Reid hesitates for a moment, then grabs his drink from the coffee table. He throws his head back and finishes the drink in one swallow, his face grimacing as he slams the glass down on the coffee table. "You're not only a terrible actress, but you make a lousy martini!"

Blair finishes her martini and takes Reid's hand. As they walk down the hallway to Reid's bedroom, he fondles her breasts, then stumbles. Blair catches him before he falls. "You okay, my sexy leading man? Don't tell me you're a lightweight."

Shaking his head, Reid places one hand on the wall to steady himself. "What was in that drink? I'm feeling sick...lightheaded."

Blair smiles, "Oh come now, Mr. Garrett, you're no stranger

to coke and booze."

Reid is pale and perspiring. "You half-breed bitch, what did you give me? I . . . I can't stand up."

"Half-breed?"

Nearly choking, Reid blurts out, "Half-breed bastard child!"

Startled, Blair pulls Reid's face toward hers but says nothing.

Reid looks like he is about to faint, so Blair places her arms under Reid's armpits to keep him from falling. "Let's get you into bed." As they enter the bedroom, Reid lapses into unconsciousness, so Blair must drag him the last few feet to the bed. His head hits the bed, but he slips off. Blair struggles to lift his torso and feet, but she eventually has his entire body on the bed. His breathing is shallow. She puts a pillow under his neck, laying his head back, nostrils facing up. Reaching inside her dress, Blair pulls out two nose droppers, each filled with more cocaine laced with methamphetamine. She empties a full dropper in each nostril. Standing up from the bed, she hears something in the hallway. Turning around, she runs to the hallway but sees nothing.

Returning to the living room, Blair puts on her blouse, takes the glass Reid drank from and puts it in a plastic bag she brought in her purse. She wipes clean the glass she drank from, cleaning it with rubbing alcohol to remove any prints. She then takes the glass to the bedroom where she lifts Reid's hand and places his fingers around the stem, remembering he's left-handed. His breathing is even more shallow. Back to the living room, she fills the glass halfway with gin and places it on the table. She carefully wipes up the lines of coke she laced with methamphetamine and places it in a bag in her purse. After wiping the table with rubbing alcohol, she takes a vial from her purse filled with cocaine but not laced with methamphetamine. She makes a few neat lines, then rubs two off, so it looks like someone finished two lines. Reaching for the vial and straw on the table, she drops both in the plastic bag with the glass Reid drank from. Looking around the room, Blair remembers to clean the bar where she made the drinks and to wash the martini shaker.

Walking to the front door, she hesitates before turning the

doorknob. She doesn't want Reid dead; only too incapacitated to read his lines. Just enough of a disability to get him off the show and replaced with another actor. A stroke would be the best she hoped for, but not death. Turning away from the door, Blair runs down the hallway to check on Reid one last time. He hasn't moved. Leaning toward his face, she can hear his breathing, but it's labored. He's also wheezing, and one nostril is bleeding. Deciding to stick with her original plan, she heads for the door and runs to her car.

Unbeknownst to Blair or Reid, Alton has been watching all the living room activity from behind the swinging door to the kitchen. He had arrived on the back patio shortly after Reid took his first snort of cocaine. Blair almost spotted him earlier as he watched her from the hallway while she filled Reid's nostrils with more cocaine. He made a noise scuffing his shoe against the baseboard, so he hid in the bathroom off the hallway when Blair came down the hall, thinking she heard a noise. As Blair began her clean up activity in the living room, Alton moved across the hallway to the back entrance of the kitchen. Oksana was still on the rear patio to give Alton backup if Blair had gotten careless with a gun.

When Blair starts her car, Alton goes to the front window to see her pulling away. He then runs down the hallway to check on Reid, whose pulse is weak and his breathing erratic. Alton texts Oksana: "All clear, come to the master bedroom." He then calls Rob, who is waiting down the street in the van.

Rob's cell phone rings. "Yes, boss?"

"Get the van to the front door right away. Reid is in awful shape."

"Is he shot?"

"No, heavily drugged. Meet you in front as soon as you can get here."

Oksana pops her head in the master bedroom door, her gun still in her hand. "Vat she do to him?"

"Cocaine and something she put in his drink. He's barely breathing."

Oksana takes Reid's pulse and puts her hand on his forehead. "Overdose on something. Heart racing, breathing bad."

Alton nods in agreement. "Help me carry him to the front door. Rob should be outside."

They carry Reid outside as Rob arrives, opening the side door of the van. Oksana and Rob lay Reid on the floor of the van, and Alton goes back to remove his handprints from the doorknob. Closing the front door behind him, he tells Oksana to get her car and go home until she hears from him.

Inside the van, Alton tells Rob to drive back to the cottage while he calls Doctor Odem.

"Doc, it's Alton. I've got a celebrity with a potential cocaine overdose and something else mixed in with gin. His breath is rancid, which makes me think he took crystal meth or something similar. His mouth smells like a meth addict. Foul. Can you meet me at my cottage right away? Thanks, Doc."

Rob is driving a little too fast, so Alton tells him to slow down and not draw attention. Rob looks over at Alton. "Is he going to die?"

"Hopefully not. But meth, alcohol and cocaine can be a terrible combination. Depends on how much she gave him."

"Can the Doctor help him?"

"Dr. Odem is the best. He's discreetly handled overdoses for celebrities and businesspeople for decades. Rob, you know the drill. You never saw Dr. Odem, no matter what happens. And if Reid dies, you know what we have to do to protect Dr. Odem."

"Yes, boss. I do."

A light begins to flash on a device Alton has on the dashboard of the van. It means that the bugging device Alton planted in Blair's car has come on because it is recording something in her car.

Rob points to the device. "You plant something in her car?"

"Yep, just before I went to the back patio. Her top was down in the Mercedes, so I put it under her front seat. Hand me the headsets. Hurry."

Alton is listening in on a conversation Blair is having on her cell phone as she drives home.

"Damn it. I don't believe she's doing this. She's reporting an overdose of Reid Garrett to 911. Holy crap, that upends our plans."

24

The An Early Debut

Rob turns on the recording and they hear Blair's voice. She's in a panic or pretending that she is. "I need to report an overdose. Please hurry." She gives Reid's name, address, and a frantic statement that he tried to accost her during a script reading and she had to flee when it became obvious, he was on drugs or something. She tells the 911 dispatcher she feared for her life and just ran away.

It startles Rob. "Why did she do that? She's crazy. Why tell them she was there?"

Alton shakes his head and slams his fist into the door of the van. "Damn it. She's smarter than I thought. I underestimated her."

"What? She just spilled the beans on what she did!"

"No, she didn't," Alton explains. "She doesn't want Reid to die, so her guilt made her call 911. But it's a Catch-22. If Reid lives, he will probably remember some of what happened and try to pin it on Blair. By reporting it as an overdose and his trying to assault her, she can explain why she was there and that his story is drug-induced. Good insurance for her, whether he lives or dies. But, shit, she may have just ruined our plan for a new Reid Garrett if this trashes his reputation."

Rob drives the van into the driveway of Alton's cottage. Alton and Rob jump out and carry Reid to a bed in the guest room. They don't want Landon to see him, so they avoid the pool house where Landon is staying. Alton tells Rob to put the van away and then bring Landon to his surveillance room.

After he secures Reid in the guest room, Alton runs down the hallway to his surveillance room. He uses his eye scanner and security code to open the door to his secret lair across the hall from his office. This highly secure room, with lead walls and an array of computer and TV monitors, contains the most sophisticated surveillance equipment available. Alton gained some of it illegally when he left his last post with the CIA. He uses his police scanner to pick up any phone communications between the police, the fire department and the paramedics dispatched to Reid's house. He can also pick up cell phone conversations if he chooses to. After scrolling through several 911 dispatch calls, he finds the EMT team that arrived at Reid's house a few minutes ago.

After one paramedic calls in the routine confirmation items, he hears her report the call as a false alarm. "Patient refused treatment, appears fine. Caller and alleged assailant reported to police for investigation."

Alton shakes his head. *How could that be? There shouldn't be anyone there.*

Rob pushes the buzzer outside the secure room and Alton unlocks the door. "Boss, he's gone. I've looked for him everywhere and he's not here. His clothes gone too."

"What? Landon isn't here?"

"No, sir."

Alton looks back at the chatter on the EMT scanner, and then over at Rob. "I think our twin star boy tricked us. The paramedic at Reid's house just called in a false alarm."

"Boss, there's nobody there."

"Oh yes, there is. They're saying the patient is refusing treatment. He's a tall, blonde male in his thirties. Says his name is Reid Garrett. But if we've got Reid Garrett here, then that has to be Landon at his house."

"What? Shit, Landon is over there posing as Reid? How could that happen?"

"Exactly. I think the two of them, the brothers, have had us. Or Landon knew what was happening and stepped into his new life early. Go to the guest room and get Reid's wallet. It was in his front left pocket when we brought him here. Put it in my car, and bring the car around front, ASAP!"

"Yes, sir,"

"And Rob, stay here close to Reid until the doctor arrives. Don't let anyone in except Doctor Odem."

"Got it. I'll have your car out front in two minutes."

Alton grabs his briefcase and what he refers to as his "medical kit" and heads out the front door of the cottage. Rob has just brought Alton's car out from the garage and parked it right by the front steps.

Rob says, "Good luck, boss. I'll let you know what Dr. Odem says when he gets here."

25

The Trouble with Doubles

"I'm fine, sir. Really."

The paramedic is shining a light in Reid's eyes and nose and taking his blood pressure. But it's not Reid; it's Landon posing as Reid.

The paramedic asks, "Any headache?"

"No, ma'am." Landon smiles and winks at the paramedic who is an attractive Latina.

The paramedic swabs Landon's nose for any evidence of drugs and asks to see his tongue. "Well, it's been nice meeting a celebrity, but I don't like false alarms." The pretty paramedic packs up her gear and waves away her associate. "I'll take these to the lab, but I can tell by looking at you you're fine. Your breathalyzer reading was acceptable, and I don't see any evidence of drugs. But we will still need to have your mouth and nose swabs checked by the lab. Let me finish my report so we can get on to people who really need us."

Landon whispers, "Sorry about the 911 call."

"So am I. Do you know why your girlfriend reported you as being overdosed?"

"I don't have a girlfriend."

"Then who is the lady who called 911?"

"I don't know."

"You don't know a Ms. Blair Kilian?"

"She's an actress. We're filming a show together. She was to meet me here to rehearse a script."

"Okay, so did you have a rehearsal?"

"No. I've just arrived home to meet with her and there's no one here."

"Was somebody else here at your house?"

"Not that I know of."

"Well, save your story for the police. They should be here any minute. We've called it in as a non-emergency and now we will report it as a false alarm, so they'll likely have some questions for you. Are you sure no one else is here inside your house?"

"Absolutely."

"Then why were you just standing here on the porch when we arrived?"

"I just got here. I was expecting Ms. Kilian, but you showed up just as I arrived."

"Well, tell it to the police. Our work's finished."

Just as the paramedics are leaving, two LAPD officers arrive. The paramedic hands them a piece of paper and they have a brief conversation. Landon can't hear what they are saying, but the paramedic points to him as a police officer nods his head and walks over to Landon.

"Mr. Garrett?"

"Yes, sir."

"Making a phony 911 call is a serious issue. The fine is a thousand dollars and up to a year in jail. Can you tell me what happened?"

"As I explained to the paramedic, the actress Blair Kilian, and I were to meet here to rehearse a script. I just arrived moments before the paramedics arrived. Maybe she was mad because I was late?"

"So you were just standing here on your porch when the paramedics arrived?"

"Yes, sir."

"Where is your car, Mr. Garrett?"

"I assume it is in the garage."

"What kind of car do you have?"

"Ferrari."

"What kind of Ferrari?"

"Red."

"I didn't ask for the color, I asked for the model. Maybe I should see it."

Landon doesn't know what kind of Ferrari Reid drives, but before Landon can think of an answer, he sees a black Bentley come down the driveway. The police officer turns around and motions to his partner. "Go see who that is."

As the officer approaches the car, Alton jumps out and walks toward Landon and the officer questioning him. He walks right past the other officer without saying a word.

As soon as he recognizes Alton Price, Landon mumbles, "Shit, what's he doing here?"

The LAPD officer interviewing Landon sees Alton pass right by his patrol partner and arrive on the doorstep.

"Excuse me sir, who are you?"

"Price. Alton Price. Is there a problem, officer?"

"Depends. Why are you here?"

"I'm here for a meeting with Mr. Garrett and his agent."

"Why are you all meeting here?"

"Script reading."

"And who else was to be here?"

"I don't think that's important. Why are you here with Mr. Garrett? Is there something wrong, officer?"

Landon speaks up, "Mr. Price, everything is fine. You can leave. There's no script reading."

Alton raises an eyebrow. "Have you cancelled the script reading?"

Before Landon can answer, the LAPD officer asks Landon if can see his driver's license for identification.

"What? You don't recognize Reid Garrett?"

"Sir, I know who you are, but I need to verify that it is you. ID, please."

Before Landon can think of what to say, Alton pipes up. "Reid, you keep your wallet on the credenza by the front door. I'll get it for you." Before anyone can say anything, Alton opens the door and steps inside. Moments later, he appears on the doorstep and hands Reid's wallet to the LAPD officer.

The officer examines the driver's license and looks at a couple credit cards. He hands the wallet to Reid. "Very well, but before we go may we have a look inside?"

Alton responds before Reid, "No, officer, you may not look in the house."

The officer turns to Alton, "I asked that question of Mr. Garrett, not you. Mr. Garrett, may we step inside?"

"No, there's no reason to."

"Look, Mr. Garrett, we've got a report of an overdose, an attempted assault, and a false report to 911."

Putting his hands up in the air, Landon steps closer to the officer. "Officer, there's no overdose. I'm fine."

The police officer looks at Landon. "Paramedic said you're clean, just some alcohol. Mind if we look around just to be sure no one else is here?"

"Yes, I mind. Nothing happened here, so unless you have a search warrant, I'd like you to leave. I'm not the one that called 911. You should take that up with Ms. Kilian. Why didn't you talk to her first?"

The two police officers look at each other. "Well, Mr. Garrett, we don't have a warrant so if that is how you feel, we'll leave. If the paramedic found any evidence of illicit drugs on you, we'd have cause to search the premises, but we don't, so we'll go. When we get a statement from Ms. Kilian, I may have additional questions for you."

As the officers walk toward their patrol car, Alton grabs Landon's shoulder and squeezes it tightly. "You almost botched that up. If I hadn't arrived, you'd be on your way downtown to police headquarters."

Landon nods his head. He's relieved the police are leaving because he is sweating and lightheaded.

As the LAPD officers leave the driveway, Cameron Haines arrives. He gets out of the car, looks at the departing police car, then walks over to Landon and Alton who are still standing on the porch of Reid's house. Cameron is not sure if he's looking at Landon or Reid. "What the hell is up here?" he asks.

Alton motions them both to go inside, where all three are now standing by the couch. They see the lines of cocaine on the table and a half-finished martini glass. Alton instructs them not to touch anything on the table.

Without saying a word, Alton grabs Landon by his neck and throws him on the sofa. "Looks like you're more of a twin than I thought. The dark streak runs in Reid's veins *and yours!*"

26

The Better Offer

Landon's head hits the back of the sofa with a thud. He protests, "Whoa, let me explain, Mr. Price!"

"Try me," replies Alton. "But if you're lying, I won't have to worry about which version of Reid Garrett gets handed over to the police."

"Why are you so mad? Wasn't this the plan all along? I'd become Reid, Reid would disappear, and my old identity would go away, right?"

"You jumped the gun. This wasn't the time to make the switch. The timing was up to me, not you. I'm suspicious. How did you end up here today?"

Eyeing the unfinished martini on the coffee table, Landon reaches for it as he settles in more comfortably on the sofa. "Change of plans, Mr. Price. Change of plans."

As Landon reaches the martini to his lips, Alton says, "I asked you not to touch anything on the coffee table."

Saying nothing, Landon downs the rest of the martini concoction. "Not the best martini I've ever had, that's for sure. I think it is just straight gin. And it's warm."

Alton picks up the empty martini glass, sniffs the rim and swipes his finger across the bottom of the glass. Putting his finger on his tongue, Alton puts the glass down. "Landon, you're as stupid as your brother. This is just gin, but it could have been something else."

"I don't care. See, here's the deal, Mr. Price. The *new* deal. I've got a better offer, so I don't need your help."

Alton frowns at Landon, then sits down next to him on the sofa. He motions for Cameron to sit down on the other side of Landon. "Hollywood is full of better offers, Landon. Some are real, some are traps, and some are lies. The hard part is figuring out the difference. So, let's hear your better offer."

"I can be rich without having my brother killed or hidden away. That's the deal. Cleaner alternative than yours, Mr. Price."

"I'm presuming this offer came from Reid?"

Landon smirks. "Maybe."

"And how did Reid hear about our little plan?"

"He didn't, as far as I know. He got suspicious after he met Blair Kilian on the set and then had sex with her. She insisted they had met the day before. And she said something when he was having sex with her."

"You mean when he was raping her. In her trailer."

"She said something about being a different man the day before, in his trailer. That man was me, as you know."

"The day before Reid raped her. Say it, Landon. Your brother raped her."

"Okay, he raped her. I won't sugarcoat it. Anyway, when you botched up his little fake suicide stunt, he put it all together and thought I was working with you or somehow involved. He called me this morning after you and Rob left. Told me I'd get rich being his assistant, and he'd share his business proceeds with me. We could even get a lot of publicity about my actual identity, and our orphan story. He thought it had lots of possibilities and he wants to work together."

"Proceeds? He offered you a part of his actor's income?"

"Not exactly."

"Then what, Landon? What did he offer you a part of?"

"The income from celebrities."

Alton laughs and replies, "It's called blackmail and extortion. He offered to cut you in on his crimes of blackmail and extortion."

"Okay, yes, that's it. His side business."

"Awfully pleasant name for crimes, isn't it? So why the hell are you here?"

Landon says nothing and stares away from the table.

Alton grabs Landon by his shirt collar. "Look at me! Why are you here? What were you and Reid going to do with Blair?"

"To fuck with her, and to startle her with my existence, and then to . . . to increase what she had to pay Reid to keep her job and hide what she is. And who she is."

"And what or who is she, Landon?"

"You don't know? Reid said you knew." Landon looks over to Cameron. "*You* know, don't you, Mr. Haines?"

Cameron says nothing but looks over to Alton.

Alton pulls Landon closer. "And what is it we surely know?"

Landon squirms on the sofa, looking over his shoulder at Cameron, then back at Alton. "Blair is half black. She's the illegitimate daughter of Cameron Haines."

Cameron looks down toward the floor. "God damn Reid. Damn him."

Landon shakes his head and smiles. "So it *is* the truth!"

Alton puts his hand up before Cameron can say anything. "Landon, how do you know either of those statements are true?"

"Reid told me. Said he has lots of dirt like that on tons of celebrities and movie people. People in the industry."

"Proof? Did he offer you proof? Because without proof, it's just slander, and they can sue you and your brother. And, even if it is true, extortion and blackmail are illegal. Ultimately, you are both headed for jail."

"He said he has all the proof on everything he blackmails celebrities for."

"And when he's caught, you are an accomplice. Your brother is setting you up as the stooge for the day he gets caught. Or he wants you out of the way and is baiting you before he can kill you."

"Say what you will, Mr. Price, but Reid offered me a better option than you did. Murdering my brother so I can take his place is worse than what Reid is doing. I came out here to be with my brother. He's my only family. He's not perfect, but he's offering me an exciting and wealthy life."

"Did he apologize for trying to kill you when you first met?"

"Yes, he did. I think he was sincere."

Alton stands up from the sofa. "So why weren't you here at the house with Reid when Blair arrived? Why did you show up later?"

"He wanted an hour with her. Told me to come by no sooner than 11:00 a.m. When I got here, the paramedics virtually followed me into the driveway."

"You never went inside?"

"No."

"Do you know where Reid is?"

"No. Should we look around? I'm worried."

"Landon, give me your cell phone."

"Why?"

"I said give it to me, before I rip it out of our pocket!"

Landon reaches into his pants pocket and retrieves his cell phone. Alton grabs it out of his hand.

Flipping through his recent call list, Alton sees three calls from Reid to Landon earlier in the morning. "Why three calls? What was the purpose of each of them?"

"Well, the first call was to make me the offer. I told him I would think about it. I had some questions, so I called him back. Then I accepted, and the third call he told me what to do. And that's why I'm here. Where is Reid? Have you looked for him here in the house? And why did Blair call 911?"

"I'm most disappointed, Landon. Your brother is very devious, and he is just using you. You're too naïve to figure that out and he's sucking you in to his criminal activity. Being identical twins, I might have guessed that you'd have some, or all, of Reid's self-absorption and poor judgment."

Landon lets out a sigh. "It's my choice. I don't need a lecture from you."

Alton reaches inside his pocket and pulls out a small vial with a needle at the end. He reaches over towards Landon, grabs his neck, and injects the vial before Landon has time to react.

"What was that? What did you do to me? Tell me!" Landon

struggles with Alton and Cameron helps restrain him on the couch. After about three minutes, Landon becomes groggy and his eyes close.

Alton and Cameron say nothing as Landon keels over and falls off the sofa onto the floor.

Collateral Damage

Alton and Cameron leave Reid's house in Alton's Bentley and make their way to Blair's condominium on Wilshire Boulevard.

Alton places a call to Oksana. "Oksana get to Reid's house as soon as possible. You'll find a guy passed out on the living room floor. He's Reid's twin brother. I'll explain later. Don't let it startle you. Keep him there and stay with him. If he comes to before I'm back, give him a Propofol injection. All I had in my kit was a small dose of midazolam, so he might wake up in an hour or two. Whatever happens, don't let him regain consciousness or see you."

Oksana assures Alton she will take care of everything.

Cameron is fidgeting. "Alton, I'm not sure this is the right thing to do. Everything between me and Blair will change, and maybe not for the better."

"Cam, listen up. We have no choice. Blair must know the truth, no matter what we decide about Reid and Landon. They both know your secret, so it's time to end the charade. I warned you about this when Blair first came to America. I told you that your secret would be out, eventually."

"You did. And here we are."

"Exactly. Let me do the talking at first."

As they arrive at the Wilshire Palms, they see a police car parked in front of the building. The valet takes Alton's car and he and Cameron proceed to the security desk. The guard on duty recognizes Cameron as a frequent visitor. "Good afternoon, Mr. Haines! Good to see you!"

"Nice to see you, Ahmed," Cameron replies. "Is Ms. Kilian home?"

"She is, but I'm afraid those guys just got here ahead of you." Ahmed points to the police car in front of the building entrance. "No reason you can't go up though."

"We can wait," Cameron says.

Alton looks at Cameron. "No, we can't wait. Let's go up now. We don't want her telling the cops the wrong story. You know what I mean."

Cameron nods, and Ahmed says, "Go on up. I'll sign you in, Mr. Haines. And your guest?"

"Alton Price," Cameron replies.

"Got it. I'll let Ms. Kilian know you're coming up."

As the elevator door closes, Alton tells Cameron to stay calm. "Let me do the talking first. I want to be sure Blair doesn't say too much about Reid's condition when she left."

"Got it."

When the elevator door opens, they see Blair standing in the doorway to her apartment. "Well, I guess this is my day for visitors, isn't it?"

Cameron tries to give Blair a kiss on the cheek, but she turns away. "Ahmed told you we were on our way up?"

"He did." Alton extends his hand to Blair, and she smiles. "I can only guess I'm in *real* trouble when I have two cops in my living room *and* Alton Price at my doorstep."

Alton kisses her hand and grins. "It's your lucky day. You've been a busy girl. I'm quite impressed. Didn't know you had it in you."

In the background, a police officer clears his throat. "Ms. Kilian, may we regain your attention?"

"You have my full attention."

As Blair, Alton, and Cameron enter the living room, the two police officers stand up, one of them holding a clipboard. "I'm Officer Stan Witkowski, and this is Officer Daniela Salazar."

Blair introduces Cameron and Alton to the officers.

Alton speaks up before the police officers can resume their questions to Blair. "Officers, I think I can save you some time. We just came from Mr. Garrett's house, and I'm afraid this whole thing was very unfair to Ms. Kilian. He became angry with her for refusing his advances and well, he behaved as if he was drunk or on drugs to intimidate her. It was a terrible prank that upset Ms. Kilian."

Officer Salazar cuts Alton off. "We just started asking Ms. Kilian a few questions and you've jumped ahead to Mr. Garrett. We have the report from the officers on scene. We know what it says about Mr. Garrett's condition, but we'd like to hear from Ms. Kilian, please."

Alton's statements have confused Blair. "You were just there and saw Reid?"

Alton nods, "He's fine, Blair. He owes you an apology, and it's his fault you made that 911 call. This is all very unnecessary."

Blair can't believe what Alton just said.

Officer Salazar lets out a sigh. "Prank or not, it's illegal to put in false calls to 911."

Alton shakes his head. "Blair didn't know it was false when she made the call. Reid fooled her, and that's not right, but it is what happened. I believe his attorney will contact you to make amends."

"Well, we'll go speak with Mr. Garrett, and if he makes a confession, then Ms. Kilian here is off the hook. If not, we'll be back."

"Fair enough. Thank you, officers."

Closing her clipboard, Officer Salazar stands up and heads for the door. Officer Witkowski follows behind, neither one of them saying anything as they leave.

As soon as the door closes, Blair stands up. "What the hell is going on? That story you told the cops about Reid is a lie. He was unconscious when I left."

"We're protecting you, Blair. You tried to kill Reid. If the cops found him in the condition you left him, you'd be on your way to jail."

"Well, I didn't do an outstanding job of killing him if you just saw him in perfect condition. Besides, he did that to himself. Too much booze and cocaine over a lot of years. That's not my fault."

"I lied. Reid is not ok. To be sure he doesn't die, the doctor asked me to find out exactly what you gave him. The doctor smells meth on his breath and sees cocaine in his nostrils. Did you mix the meth in with the gin?"

"I told you. He did that to himself."

"Blair, you're lying. I saw you pour cocaine down his nose in the bedroom and clean up his martini glass before you left his house. I got some nice shots on my cell phone. You set it up to look like he did it to himself, but you enabled it."

Blair stands up, placing her hands on her hips. "You were snooping on me? At Reid's house?"

Alton nods. "I'm here to help you, Blair. But you have to help me first."

"Really? You're going to help me just like my agent here helped me get raped by the guy who's extorting money from me to keep my job? I hate you, Cameron!"

"Later, Blair. You and Cameron can cover all that later. Right now, I just need to know what you gave Reid before I saw you clean up his martini glass."

"Crystal meth and gin."

"How much meth?"

"About 50 milligrams. I ground up five 10 milligram tabs of crystal meth in his martini."

"Shit, Blair. Plus, the gin and the cocaine? Did you really want to kill him?"

"No, just mess him up. Like he was doing to me. He weighs almost two hundred pounds. That's not enough to kill him, and he's taken lots of drugs before. You know his reputation in town. You bailed him out and took him to the Betty Ford clinic for drug rehab at least two times that I know of. I'm sure there's more. He's no angel."

"What makes you such an expert, Blair?" Alton asks.

"You have your sources, I have mine. He might have a stroke

or some memory loss if I'm lucky. But one thing's for sure. He won't be in any condition to read his lines on Monday."

Cameron stares on in silence, never having seen this side of Blair.

Alton texts Dr. Odem the information Blair has just given him, then looks up at Blair. Doctor Odem acknowledges Alton's text instantly. Looking up at Blair, Alton says, "Well, it looks like he won't be reading any more lines, perhaps forever."

28

Our British Roots

Alton tells Cameron and Blair to listen to him closely. "You two stay here. Don't talk with the police or anyone else until you hear from me. Don't leave the apartment."

Blair stands up and grabs Alton by the sleeve. "Why? What's going on? I will not be reduced to a prisoner in my home."

"Just for a few hours, Blair. You don't have a choice. And while you two are both together, Cameron will tell you how Reid knows your background, and well, where you came from."

Cameron objects, "No. Not now."

"Yes, Cam. *Now*. Tell Blair about her background, how Reid knows about her. Nothing else. I'll be back in a few hours. I expect to find you both here so we can wrap up this mess."

Neither of them says anything as Alton grabs his jacket and heads for the elevator. As soon as Alton is in the hallway waiting for the elevator, he texts Cameron, directing him to say nothing about Landon. Cameron looks up from his phone and moves closer to Blair, both seated on the sofa.

Blair frowns. "Cameron, no matter what little story you tell me, I can't forgive you for not stopping Reid. And I don't want you as my agent. So, tell your story, then I want you to leave."

Clearing his throat, Cameron whispers, "I don't blame you. What I need to tell you is something you should know. It's not something that redeems me for my actions. You can still hate me and get another agent."

"I didn't really mean that I hate you. As I said, I can't forgive you for what you let Reid do to me."

"Understood, but you need to know that Alton and I had a plan to deal with Reid and he got ahead of us. We were both trying to protect you and deal with Reid. The rape, I just don't know what to say. We knew he tormented and extorted celebrities, but we didn't think he was violent. Now we know better. But that's not what I'm here to tell you, so let's leave that for another time."

"Do I need a drink for this story, or will it be short and sweet?"

"Why don't you fix us both one of your famous martinis. But not the kind you made for Reid."

Blair makes a coy smile and goes to her bar to fix two martinis. Cameron gets up and goes toward the French doors to her balcony. "May I?" he asks.

"May you what?"

"May I go out on your balcony?"

"Why not? Just watch for falling stars."

Cameron smiles. Blair has an odd sense of humor, which gets mixed in with her anger. Cameron finds it charming, since he was the same when he was younger. Witty sense of humor, but serious about success. Perhaps too serious. Out on the balcony, Cameron looks up to the building next door, counting the floors until he sees the tenth-floor balcony where Reid's stunt double made his jump. He's surprised by how high it seems and can imagine seeing a man swan-diving from that balcony would terrify any observer. And the thought of Blair poisoning Reid and covering it up is hard for him to accept. She is tougher, or meaner, than he thought.

Blair joins Cameron on the balcony, placing two martinis on the table at the corner of her balcony. "Well, here we go. Want to relive the whole nasty event? This is where it all started."

Picking up his glass, Cameron says, "I thought it started at the studio commissary."

"Ah, you're right. Here's to the charming Reid I met at the commissary, and to hell with him after that. May he rest in peace, or at least in pieces."

They both sip from their martinis and take a seat at the

corner table on the balcony.

Placing her martini on the table, Blair looks over at Cameron. "Okay, let's get on with it."

"Blair, my mother dropped me off at an orphanage in South Central Los Angeles when I was an infant. The nuns raised me in the orphanage. No one wanted to adopt me, but I prayed all the time that someone would. In the summer before I was to start junior high school, Mother Superior told me to pack my things, and that I was going to boarding school in England. I was frightened and confused. I cried, wondering who I'd wronged to send me away. Mother Superior cried too, saying she would miss me, but this was a special gift. A woman at church provided a generous scholarship for me to finish my education in England. A week later, I found myself at a boys' boarding school that helped kids prepare for college. In my case, I was trying for Kings College, Cambridge. My first year was terrifying. I was one of just three black kids, the other two from Africa. The British boys didn't know what to make of me. They picked on me and bullied me. Later, some of my classmates and most of my teachers supported me. To my astonishment, they admitted me to Kings College and my life changed."

"I've seen your degree in your office, Cam. I knew all about your education and time in England. The orphan thing is news to me, but why does that matter?"

"I'm getting to that. After graduation, I went into acting and did well in West End theaters in London, and others around the United Kingdom."

"Cam, I know all of that. You were a young and successful actor but being a black actor in Britain in the 1980s wasn't great. That's why you came to America. This is all in your bio. I knew it before I met you. Get to the part I don't know."

"The part you don't know is that while working on my last play in London, I had a part that played opposite your mother, Judith Kilian."

"Cam, I know that part. My mother sent me to America to meet you, hoping you'd be my agent. Which you are. Or were. I know you two go way back to your early twenties."

"Blair, what I am trying to tell you is that your father didn't die. That is what you've always been told. But he's not dead."

"What? Cameron, I've been to my father's grave. Many times. My mum and I would go there often. All the holidays, and his birthday."

"There's no one in that grave."

"Liar! Why are you saying these things?"

"Blair, I'm your father. I got your mother pregnant. We were in love, but there's no way England would accept an interracial couple in the 1980s. It would have ruined both of our careers, especially your mother's career, which was already so far along. But we didn't want an abortion. Your mother wanted to raise you as her own, but no one was to know you had a black father. It would have been terrible for you, and for her."

"Oh my God, why didn't I ever figure that out? Mum didn't speak of you often, but once I found a bunch of her old theatre notices. One was a playbill with the entire cast on the front. Mum looked at it and cried. I asked her what was wrong, and she said it was just a terrible play. But I saw how she looked at your picture. I just thought it brought back memories of when she was younger."

"I stayed away so as not to raise any suspicions. It has been heartbreaking. Still is."

"Well, to some extent, I am not surprised. My olive skin, large features, and curly hair, which I spend a fortune straightening. Mum always told me my father was a Sicilian, very dark with black curly hair. That's how she justified my looking so different. She said I was exotic because I'm half-Sicilian."

"Your mother is a superb actress."

"More like a great liar."

"We love you, Blair. I hated to give you up, but it was best for you and your mother. I agreed to go to America to pursue my career and your mother would concoct a story about your father dying."

"Then who is the man in the grave, and what about the stories my mum told me about him? That's all a lie?"

"I will let your mother tell all of that to you. She's a superb actress, remember that. She made up a wonderful character that never existed."

"What about my birth certificate?"

"It says Kilian, and that is your mother's last name. Have you not noticed that there is no father listed on your birth certificate? It is all legitimate. You know she told you she wanted to keep her last name when she married your father and that he had died by the time you were born, so she left his name off. Didn't that make you the least bit curious?"

"My father that never existed."

"Yes."

"So it's just that easy? Playing a make-believe part as if she's in a play?"

"She's been protecting you, Blair."

"Does she know what you're telling me?"

"She does. Not happy about it, but I told her why."

"Why are you telling me? Why now, after all these years?"

"Because Reid knows the story. That's why he's blackmailing you. And me."

Blair is shaking her head, "I don't believe what you're telling me. Why would one of Hollywood's most popular talent agents let his star client blackmail him? What the hell is wrong with you?"

"To protect you."

"Really, or is it to protect *you?*"

"I screwed up, Blair. When your mother sent you to me to act as your agent, you must have wondered why I took you on. You're my daughter. I want you to succeed. Your mother kept me posted on every step of your life. I have two boxes full of pictures, report cards, recitals, plays, and acting auditions for all thirty-three years of your life. I should have been honest with you when you first arrived. It was really you that worried me.

Cameron continues, "Can you imagine the headline? 'Top Hollywood Agent Takes On Mixed-race Illegitimate Daughter as a New Client.' You know this town, Blair. If that *were* the headline, what they'd say about you behind your back would be worse. And let's be honest: it would have tainted your career for good. No one would appreciate you for who you are, knowing you're my daughter. They'd laugh you off. You are a good enough actress that you built your own following by yourself—not because you're my daughter."

"You could have told me and let me make a choice to hide it. Or not. For God's sake Cameron, this is really messing me up. Who all knows this besides Reid?"

"Tony Campanelli and Alton Price. I think that's it."

"How did they know?" Blair asks.

"It was easy. Tony and Reid built quite a lucrative business out of blackmail and extortion schemes for Hollywood actors, executives, directors. It was easy to track my history in the UK, the romance I had with your mother, and then the birth certificate with your mother's name. Father listed as deceased, but no record of him, and he's not on your birth certificate. Reid and Tony even tracked down my mother, and Reid went so see her just before she died. Reid was looking for just one more piece of dirt to use against us."

Blair stands up from her chair, looks up at the balcony where Reid's stuntman made his fall, and turns to Cameron. "So, now what?"

Cameron takes a sip from his martini. "Now, we get even."

Fallen Star

Alton arrives at his cottage to find Dr. Odem frantically attempting to save Reid's life. He's using saline and some medications to get the meth and cocaine out of his system.

Eventually, Dr. Odem turns to address Alton. "Alton, I'm not sure what to tell you. First off, this guy is obviously a frequent drug user. This latest drug and alcohol combination may not be fatal on their own, but his organs appear damaged. Without being in the hospital or lab, I can't tell how badly, but my sense is he's severely compromised."

"Will he make it?"

"You'll know in about an hour. Not much else I can do. But Alton, if he makes it, he will be in terrible shape."

Alton whispers to himself, "Karma is amazing, isn't it?"

"What did you say, Alton?"

"Never mind. What about his acting career?"

Dr. Odem takes a deep breath and a long exhale. "It looks like he had a stroke, but I won't be able to tell until he comes to, and I can't be here when that happens. You know that."

"Got it."

"He needs to be on life support. You need to get him to a hospital, or wherever you plan to take him for recovery. I can't do any more here."

Alton nods his head but says nothing. He never discloses his plans to Dr. Odem. He wants him to have plausible deniability should the authorities ever question him. "I'll take care of it,

Doc. You can be on your way. What do I owe you?"

"The usual."

"Ten thousand, cash?"

Dr. Odem nods his head. "I'll leave the IV drip in, but you must take it out to transport him."

Alton goes to his office and returns with a large manila envelope. "Plus a little extra for all the trouble."

"Thanks, Alton. Sorry this one won't have a happy ending."

"Not your worry. I'll check the gate cameras to be sure no one is watching outside before you leave. I'll text you when I'm sure it's clear, then just drive out as soon as the gates open."

Dr. Odem waits in his car in the driveway for Alton to text him, which he does for about five minutes. When the text shows up, Dr. Odem leaves the driveway, and the gates close behind him.

Leaving his office, Alton spots Rob in the hallway, standing outside the guest room. "Let's get him in the van and to his house as soon as we can get there."

The color drains from Rob's face. "Is he not going to make it, or is he in such good shape we're taking him home?"

"Leave that to me. Let's get him back to his house right away."

"Yes, sir. I'll bring the van 'round front."

Alton gets a text message on his cell phone from Oksana. "Where body?"

Alton replies, "On sofa. You in the house yet?"

Oksana texts back, "Arrive already, no one in house."

It shocks Alton. *Shit, how did he wake up so quickly? Did I mess up the dosage?* He calls Oksana, tells her to keep looking around the property and to stay there until he arrives.

After they load Reid's body into the van, Rob drives and Alton sits in the back with Reid. He notices how ashen Reid's face is, and how his breathing is getting even slower and shallower. Rob turns around to ask how the patient is doing. Alton looks up at Rob, "Stop asking that. It's not your worry, Rob."

"But sir, shouldn't we take him to the hospital?"

"No. Reid likely won't make it, but if we take him to the hospital, it could implicate Blair and Cameron, whether he lives or dies. It could even implicate other innocent people like Derek, the stuntman. It's a snowball we can't control if we take that course of action. And Reid has no one to blame but himself for the condition he's in. You know the torment and misery he has caused so many people."

"It always comes back to karma for you, doesn't it? That is how you justify when someone dies. Or you kill them."

"Rob, look at the course of events. Reid taunted and tormented people just for his entertainment and financial gain. He's getting his payback. I'm not deciding if he lives or dies. He's decided that for himself. He's a bad person."

"But sometimes you help bad people."

"I help *good* people who sometimes do *bad* things. We all have good and bad inside of use. As we get older, one side takes over, but even good people can do bad things on occasion. Reid is not in that category—you know that. He's a bad person who does bad things."

"Then you just let him die?"

"I'm not a doctor. You know what we get paid to do. I've been through this with you before, and whenever someone is about to die, you ask the same questions. Maybe you need to think more carefully about your line of work."

"You might be right."

Alton smiles at Rob, and Rob smiles back. They both know that Alton is right; it's simply hard for Rob to accept it.

As they approach Reid's house, Alton asks Rob to pull over just before the driveway to his home. "I texted Oksana we were on our way. I want to make sure she is in there alone."

"Wouldn't she have told you if someone was there?"

"Not if the cops showed up unannounced. Wait here."

Alton leaves the van and hops over the hedge near the side of the house. He sees Oksana's car in the driveway, and some lights on in the house. He texts Oksana to be sure she is alone. *"You alone? Y or N?"*

She replies, *"Y."*

★

Oksana lets Alton in through the front door. She puts her hands up and shakes her head. "No one here."

"When did you get here?"

"Hour ago, maybe less."

"And no sign of him anywhere?" Alton asks.

"No. I look outside; check the house, garage. No one here."

"How about clothes or anything that looks like it belonged to Landon?"

"I show you." Oksana takes Alton to the back bedroom, which must be a guest room. There are a few clothes on the bed that Alton recognizes as belonging to Landon. He remembers them from when Landon stayed in his guest room. But Landon's duffel bag and toiletries bag are missing. He must have had time to take them with him before he fled.

Alton shakes his head. "Shit, that's all the midazolam I had in my bag. It wasn't enough to sedate him for long. Damn. Oksana, please gather up these clothes on the bed, the sheets, and the towels in the bathroom. Get anything else that looks like it belonged to Landon and put them in a big trash bag. You should find them in the kitchen. Please bring everything to the living room. I'll help Rob carry Reid back to his bedroom. He's in terrible shape, Oksana. It may startle you."

Rob pulls the van up to the front door, and he and Alton carry Reid back to his bedroom, where Blair had left him. The bed is still messy with some blood stains from a nosebleed and cocaine dusted on the pillow where Blair poured it down his nostrils. They are both wearing gloves so their prints will be nowhere in the house.

Once Reid is on the bed, Alton and Rob join Oksana in the living room. Alton tells Oksana and Rob to get ready to leave and to be sure their prints will be nowhere in the house. Before leaving, Alton picks up the martini glass Landon drank from and he tosses it in his bag. He leaves the lines of coke on the coffee table undisturbed. After one last scan of the living room, all three of them meet in the driveway.

Alton's cell phone rings. It's Cameron. He says, "Tony

Campanelli is on his way over there."

"What? I thought he was in the hospital," Alton replies.

"He got out this morning and had a driver bring him over here to see Blair, thinking Reid was here."

"Why?" Alton asks.

"He says that Reid told him he had a script reading with Blair Kilian this afternoon and that the reading was at Blair's apartment."

"Interesting. Reid knew Blair was coming to his place, so he must have diverted Campanelli to Blair's apartment to buy him some time. Did he hurt either of you?"

"No."

Alton thinks for a moment, then asks, "Did Blair tell him she was at Reid's earlier?"

"No. She played it cool and said she knew nothing about a script reading."

"Why is Campanelli going to Reid's?"

"He's on his way over there to look for Reid—and his files. He thinks Reid stole his client files. Says Reid also tried to kill him in his driveway. That he ran over him and that's why he's in a wheelchair. He also suspects it involves you, but I said nothing. I think the driver is also serving as his bodyguard."

"You tell him anything of what's happened?" Alton asks.

Cameron replies, "No. We just listened to him rant, and when he couldn't reach Reid on the phone, he told his driver to take him to Reid's house."

"Okay, I'll deal with it," Alton says.

"Alton, Tony is in a wheelchair, but his driver or bodyguard is a big burly guy who looks to be wearing a gun under his coat; I think it's a shoulder holster. And you know Tony Campanelli always carries a gun."

Alton says, "Shit! Stay put, Cam. I'll be in touch."

Bloody Reunion

Alton planned to have Rob and Oksana depart while he set the last stage for Reid's overdose death at his house. With Landon now missing and backing out of the deal to replace Reid, Alton lets events take a different course. Reid's condition is hopeless, so the aim at this point is to be sure the cops can't trace Reid's death back to Blair. Alton never lets his workers see his handiwork for a death scene, so he always dismisses them. He allows no witnesses. But with Tony on his way over, he sees another opportunity to solve two problems at once.

"Rob, you head back to the cottage," Alton directs. "Stay put until I call you. I've got a few details to check here, and then Oksana will take me back."

Rob nods his head, "Sure boss."

"And Rob, please take those two bags of Landon's belongings and the sheets and towels Oksana collected. Take them with you to the cottage. I think it's a delightful night for you to sit by the fire in my living room."

"What? It's not that cold."

"Take the items in those bags, and if Landon left anything at the cottage, put all of them in the fireplace with the items in the bags. Get the sheets and towels Dr. Odem used with Reid and put those in the fireplace too. Scrub the usual places for fingerprints. Stay warm until the fire goes out."

"Got it, boss. I know what to do."

Alton smiles as Rob drives away, satisfied that Rob got the

message. Alton's fireplace in the cottage is huge. That's because it has six gas burners. Alton bought it from a funeral home that went out of business. The fireplace is six feet tall and eight feet deep. Alton enlarged it when he bought the cottage and remodeled it. It makes a beautiful fire for burning evidence, records and, in this case, clothing and sheets. He equipped it with an emissions scrubber to avoid polluting the neighborhood and to evade detection of the authorities. Rob knows how to dispose of the ashes.

Turning to Oksana, Alton smiles. "Got time to give me a hand with a burly bodyguard?"

Oksana puts her hands on her hips, "He is good-looking?"

"It's a surprise."

"I need my gun?" she asks.

"Yes, but don't use it unless you have to. This is a KGB-style takedown. Your specialty. When your target approaches the front door, you take him down before he sees me or anyone else. Make him unconscious and hide him out front until I come out. Please try not to kill him."

Oksana nods her head and scans the front of Reid's house for a place to hide. She and Alton slip behind a half-wall by the garage where Reid keeps four large trash cans.

Within minutes, Tony's Rolls-Royce enters the driveway to Reid's house and pulls up to the front entry. A large bald man with a mustache gets out of the driver's side and goes to the trunk to retrieve Tony's wheelchair.

Alton sees surprise in Oksana's face, and whispers to her, "What is it? Something wrong?"

"I . . . I know dat man."

"What? The driver? Who is he and how do you know him?"

"Bodyguard at Russian consulate in San Francisco. I date him."

"You dated him? Good grief, can this task get any more complicated? Will he recognize you?"

"Vee have good time—if you know vat I mean."

"Good god, Oksana, I get it. Can you make him unconscious

without him recognizing you?"

"Russian women much smarter than Russian men. You know dat."

"Okay, well, don't fuck it up. If he recognizes you before you make him unconscious, we must kill him. Got that?"

"Don't worry. I vant to date him again so no kill."

Alton shakes his head in disbelief that Oksana has slept with the burly bodyguard. Oksana doesn't date; she only has sex.

The Russian bodyguard helps Tony Campanelli into his wheelchair and then rolls him up to the front door. Without knocking or ringing the doorbell, the bodyguard kicks in the front door. Before Alton can even stand up, Oksana runs to the front door and body slams the Russian into the doorjamb. It startles Tony Campanelli, but before he can say anything Alton has shoved him out of his wheelchair and onto the front porch, holding his face down so he can't see Oksana and his bodyguard struggle. Alton knows that it really doesn't matter what Tony sees, because he's never leaving here. It's the Russian bodyguard they need to make sure doesn't see or remember any faces. He plans to leave him alive.

Oksana injects a sedative into the Russian's neck as he tries to stand up. Before he is even fully unconscious, Oksana is dragging his body over to the trash cans by the driveway. His head has a huge gash that is bleeding. Oksana wraps a towel around his head, so he won't leave a trail of blood to the trash cans. She and her burly former date are quickly out of sight.

Alton picks up Tony, who is in pain and screaming. Placing his hand over Tony's mouth, Alton whispers, "You are carrying your gun, Mr. Campanelli?"

He nods his head and grunts. Alton reaches inside Tony's coat and grabs his Glock G17 pistol. "Time to say goodbye, Tony."

Tony continues screaming profanities as Alton carries him across the threshold and throws him onto the sofa in Reid's living room. Alton pulls a piece of cloth from a plastic bag and puts it over Tony's nose and mouth. He struggles for a moment, but then passes out on the sofa.

Alton dons rubber gloves and heads to the master bedroom to retrieve Reid. He is still unconscious and barely breathing. Lifting him off the bed, Alton carries Reid to the living room, where he places him opposite Tony on the sofa. He has both men sitting sideways on the sofa, facing each other with their torsos resting against the back of the sofa. Alton puts Tony's Glock in Reid's left hand, and pulls the trigger twice, at close range. Tony is silent as his bloody head slumps over into Reid's lap. He places Reid's left hand with the gun at his side on the sofa.

Alton surveys his handiwork to be sure the angle of the bullets makes sense from where Reid and Tony are each seated. He places a lighted marijuana cigarette dipped in meth in Reid's right hand, with his arm over the top of the back of the sofa, leaning the cigarette on a part of the sofa where Alton covers it with gin. He splashes gin on Tony's bloody corpse and puts a martini glass in his hand.

Standing by the entry door, which is lying on the ground, Alton surveys the room one more time. The death scene pleases him. Two nasty souls on the sofa, both dead. The lighted marijuana cigarette has nicely ignited the fabric on the top of sofa, and the flames quickly spread. He knows the smoke detector will soon go off even though the front door is open, so he turns away and looks for Oksana out front.

After a few seconds, Oksana stands up from behind the wall near the trash cans. Alton runs over to her, "Let's carry your Russian lover to the front door. Then we will turn him over and drag him face down to the front door of the Rolls." Within minutes, the Russian bodyguard is unconscious and lying by the driver's door.

Alton opens the door to Tony's Rolls-Royce and places the head and torso in the front well of the driver's side, with his legs hanging out of the open door. He removes the bloody towel from the bodyguard's head and makes blood marks in the driveway from the front door to the car. The marks are faint, but the police will find them. He wants it to appear the bodyguard crawled from the front door back to the car, trying to get away from someone.

The smoke alarm is going off in the house, and Alton sees smoke coming from the opening for the front door. "Time to scram, Oksana." They both jump in Oksana's car and Alton tells her to stop just outside the driveway on the street. Alton jumps out, still wearing his gloves, and pulls the electric gates closed. It will slow up the fire department for another minute when they arrive, ensuring the living room engulfs in flames.

As they drive off, Oksana turns to Alton. "I can guess vat you did inside, no?"

"No. You can't guess, so you don't know. Too bad about the fire. I didn't know Reid smoked."

Oksana smiles and kisses Alton on the cheek. "You owe me dinner."

"And we need an alibi, so let's head over to Taix. Quickly."

Taix French Restaurant on Sunset Boulevard in Echo Park is a favorite of Alton's. It's east on Sunset, and Alton's cottage is off Sunset in West Hollywood, so a bit of a drive from his lair, but he loves it there. Plus, the staff knows him so well they will vouch for him if he needs an alibi.

The valet knows Alton by name, so Alton doesn't want the valet to see him arrive this late. He tells Oksana to park around the corner and wait ten minutes before she comes in the front door of the restaurant. He doesn't want the valet knowing what time he arrived. Alton sneaks around the back of the restaurant, through the kitchen, waving to two of the staff that know him. It's busy and no one in the kitchen is looking at their watch. Passing the waiters' station between the kitchen and the bar, Alton spies a dirty martini glass on a bus tray full of dishes. He grabs it and slips quietly into the bar. The bar is busy, so he slides against the back wall and then shoves his way up to the bar, holding his empty glass. "Hey, Marco, can I get one more of my usual? My lady friend is almost an hour late."

"Mr. Price, how did I miss you? You cheating on me? Someone else makes your drinks now?"

Feigning a guilty look to play along with the bartender, he replies, "You were busy, so I helped myself. So sorry."

"I hate when you do that. Makes me feel bad, but it is crazy tonight."

"No worry, just my usual when you have a chance. And I'll be right back. I've been waiting for my date for almost an hour. If she's not up front by now, I'll need a new date to go with that drink!"

Marco smiles as Alton makes his way to the maître d' at the front desk, who recognizes Alton as he emerges from the bar. "Ah, Mr. Price, your lovely lady, from Russia with love, is waiting over there. She just arrived and asked for you."

Alton smiles. "Well, about time. I've been waiting in the bar for almost an hour for her." He waves to Oksana, who starts making her way over to the maître d'.

"Mr. Price, I can never pronounce her name, but I know she is one of your frequent lady friends."

"Not to worry, André. No one can pronounce her name. She loves it when you call her 'From Russia with Love.'" Alton knows that Oksana really hates being called that and can't understand why André can't remember her name after all the times she has eaten there. "You have a table for me and my companion?"

"I'll make one for you. Wait here."

"I'll grab my second drink from Marco and be right back." Alton takes Oksana by the hand and they both go to the bar to retrieve Alton's drink. Marco has placed it on the bar next to a candle. "Thank you, Marco. May I ask you to make a drink for my companion here before André seats us?"

Marco knows that Oksana drinks six shots of straight vodka in a cocktail glass with just two ice cubes. He also knows she likes a cheap Russian vodka they keep for some Russian families that come in as regulars.

André finds them both in the bar. "Your table is ready. Sorry you had to wait here so long, but I have one of your favorite tables all set."

As Alton and Oksana make their way through the dining room to the table, lots of heads turn. Alton is strikingly handsome, and Oksana is strikingly large and tall. People often wonder if she is really a woman or a drag queen, and what in the world a great-looking guy like Alton is doing with her.

Alton's cell phone rings as soon as they sit at the table. The caller ID says "Cameron." It's the third time he has called since he and Oksana left Reid's burning house. Alton dismisses the call.

Oksana sees Cameron's name when Alton places his cell phone on the table. "You vant me to leave while you speak with Mr. Haines?"

"I'm not speaking with him until he sees the news about Reid, whenever that will be. I want to be sure he and Blair hear about Reid in whatever way the news reports it."

"Vy?"

"Because I don't want them knowing anything about what happened except what they hear in the news. You know why."

Alton and Oksana raise their glasses for a toast. Before Alton can say anything, Oksana whispers, "Two fewer vicked souls in the vorld tonight."

Alton smiles and winks at her, finishing his martini.

31

House Call

Cameron throws his cell phone down on the coffee table in Blair's living room. "Alton always answers. I never have to call him multiple times. Something's up. He's in trouble or avoiding me."

Blair stands up to refill her martini. "I'm scared, Cam. Tony Campanelli accused Reid of stealing his client files from his house and implicated you and Alton. Is it true?"

"They said his security camera has Reid on video going through his house while Tony was in the hospital. Files are missing and Reid flipped off the camera in the hallway. Tony thinks Reid flipped the bird at him, and that Reid has his files. I don't know why he thinks I'm involved." Then he adds, "You know I'm not."

"Doesn't matter. He came here first before he went to Reid's."

"That's only because he thought Alton was here, which he was, so someone in your building must have tipped him off. How well do you know your security guards?"

"For god's sake, Cam, since when are you so damn naïve? It's L.A.! Every doorman and security guard in town gets bribed by the paparazzi, lawyers, or private investigators. My building is no different."

"They're onto Alton, that's for sure, but I doubt he worked with Reid to get the files. Doesn't add up."

"That big bodyguard looked nasty, and he had a gun," Blair remarked. "And you said Tony Campanelli always carries a gun, too. You think something went wrong at Reid's? Should we go over there?"

"Call the valet for my car," Cameron says. "Let's drive over to Reid's, and if Alton's not there, we'll pay a visit to his cottage."

About thirty minutes later, Cameron and Blair drive up the street to Reid's house. Three blocks away, they see firetrucks, police cars, and a crowd of people in the street. Cameron pulls his car over to the curb. "Damn, are they in front of Reid's house?"

Blair opens her door and steps up onto the curb. "I can't tell. It's too dark and a firetruck blocks the street. This doesn't look good, Cameron. Let's get out of here."

Before Cameron can reply, his cell phone rings. He hopes it's Alton. The caller ID shows the name of a gossip journalist from *The Hollywood Reporter,* so Cameron doesn't answer. "Why would he be calling?" A few moments later, Cameron sees the caller has left a voicemail, so Cameron opens the message. The reporter wants a comment from Cameron regarding the condition of Reid Garrett following the fire at his home. He leaves his number for a call back. "So that fire *was* at Reid's house. A reporter wants to know what information I have since I'm Reid's agent."

Cameron turns his car around and tells Blair to turn the radio to 1070 AM, the twenty-four-hour news radio in Los Angeles. A reporter reads the traffic report as Cameron makes his way to Alton's cottage in West Hollywood.

As they drive down Sunset Boulevard at half past the hour, the news comes on the radio. The newscaster says a fire broke out at the Hollywood Hills home of actor Reid Garrett. The Los Angeles Fire Department extinguished the blaze, but Mr. Garrett's condition is unknown. Cameron's cell phone rings again, this time from the local NBC news affiliate. He doesn't answer. "Blair, I've got to get to get back there to see what happened. Maybe you shouldn't be there with me."

"Oh god, no. Please drop me off and I'll get a ride home. Cam, I did not start a fire. I just left Reid on the bed. That's all. What the hell happened?"

"I don't know. Now I'm really worried that Alton isn't calling me back. Where is he?"

Cameron pulls up to the Mondrian Hotel on Sunset Boulevard.

As Blair gathers her purse and prepares to step out, the news report has an update. Two burned bodies have been found inside Reid Garrett's home. Identities are still unknown. "Oh my god, Cam! Could the bodies be Reid and Alton?"

"I don't know. You just get yourself home and speak to no one. If the cops come back, call me right away, and I'll call my attorney to come over."

Blair nods and steps out of the car as Cameron dials Alton's cell phone again.

★

Back at Taix restaurant, Alton and Oksana are finishing their meal when Alton sees that Cameron has finally left a message, so he listens to it. "Voila, there it is. Two burned bodies at Reid's house. He's worried one of them is me."

Oksana puts her hand on Alton's. "Reid, dead?"

"Seems so. Two burned bodies. Now I can call Cameron and start working on what the police know. And be sure your Russian bodyguard is okay but not talking too much. Let's get going."

Alton pays the bill, says his goodbye to the maître d', and escorts Oksana to the car. "You head home. I'll get a lift back to the cottage. I need to use my surveillance equipment. I don't think you will hear from anyone, but if you do, call me."

Oksana gives Alton a kiss and a hug and drives away.

Before summoning his ride, Alton calls Cameron, who answers right away. "Oh, thank God you're okay, Alton. It is you, isn't it?"

"It's me, Cam. What's happened?"

"You haven't heard? Shit, Alton, it's all over the news. Fire at Reid's house. Two bodies burned. One must be Reid. Is the other Landon? He was there when you and I left to see Blair."

"Did you hear any more from Campanelli?"

"That's what I would ask you. He didn't find you at Reid's?"

Alton is silent.

"Did you hear me?"

Alton ignores the question a second time. "Cam, unless you need me there, I'd like to get to my cottage and find out what the police know about the cause of the fire and the two victims."

"You don't already know?"

"Cam, what did I just say."

"Got it. And no, I don't need you here. But what do I do about Reid? Reporters are calling and he's my client."

"Tell them the truth. That you don't know anything about what happened at Reid's."

Cameron is silent for a moment. "What about the police, and what about Blair? We were both at Reid's house earlier today. I was there with you."

"Cam, if the police contact you or Blair about Reid, just tell them the truth. Tell them Tony Campanelli and a bodyguard visited you both earlier today looking for Reid. They told you they were going to Reid's house, and that is the last you heard. That's all you need to do, Cam. Don't lie about it. I understand Reid's face is on Campanelli's security cameras during a break-in. Documents implicating Campanelli as his accomplice could turn up."

"How will they turn up?"

"Cam just do as I say. Be honest about what you know, and don't speculate. Things have a way of turning up in situations like this."

"Wow, okay. So, this Reid nightmare is almost over?"

"Not quite, Cam. I'll call you tomorrow."

Cameron sees that Alton has hung up.

32

Two Souls for the Devil

Alton arrives back at his cottage and runs down the hallway to the surveillance room. Using his eye scanner, the door opens and closes quickly behind him. He knows that Rob is somewhere in the cottage, but he's not ready to see him.

The files Alton, Rob, and Oksana retrieved from Tony Campanelli's home earlier today are sitting in three boxes in the corner of his surveillance room. Two of the boxes contain the blackmail files Reid and Tony used for years to extort money from celebrities and business executives. The other box contains some of Tony's client files—including Reid's, which is the largest. He retrieves the file titled "Reid Garrett Living Trust and Will" and runs all the documents through a scanner. Alton plans to return the original file to Tony's desk and keep a copy for himself in an encrypted electronic vault.

While the scanner copies the living trust and will, Alton retrieves a file titled "Sackalow," and places it in his briefcase. Evelyn Sackalow was a successful costume designer who had two families; one husband and two children in Los Angeles, and a girlfriend and an adopted daughter in New York. Neither family knew of the other; but Reid did.

Evelyn and Reid worked together on a couple films and they struck up a friendship. Her adopted daughter in New York was a huge fan of Reid's, so she asked her mother if she could come to the set one day and meet him. Evelyn told Reid that the girl was her teenage niece from New York. Reid agreed to meet her, and a few weeks later a fourteen-year-old girl showed up on set with Evelyn, who reminded Reid that the girl was her niece. It was a brief visit, two pictures with Reid and an autograph. When they said their goodbyes, the little girl grinned and turned away to take Evelyn's hand. As they walked off the set, Reid overheard the little girl say, "Thank you, Mommy, that was so cool!" Evelyn turned around to see Reid as they were walking away, smiled, and put her finger over her mouth with a faint, "Shush."

Reid loved discovering little secrets. While a loyal friend would likely say nothing about this disclosure, it was a gift to people like Reid who made blackmail and extortion a fun and lucrative hobby. Within minutes, Reid called Tony Campanelli and told him what he had just overheard. Two days later, Tony and one of his associates in New York uncovered everything about the two families, including names, addresses, birthdates and living arrangements. A week later, Evelyn found an envelope on her dressing table at the studio telling her to pay Reid six thousand dollars a month to protect her family secrets from each other and the press. Evelyn made the monthly payment for over six years. Reid increased the payments every year until Evelyn could no longer handle the financial pressure of supporting two families, making Reid's ever-increasing payments, and the anxiety of her secret being exposed whenever her money ran out.

Three weeks ago, Evelyn's car plunged off a cliff from the Pacific Coast Highway, north of where she lived in Malibu. She died at the scene. At first, the police called it an accident, but the toxicology report determined that Evelyn had a high concentration of alcohol and sedatives in her system, raising the prospect of suicide. When *both* the husband in L.A. *and* the girlfriend from New York showed up at the morgue to identify the body, Evelyn's secret was exposed, and both of her families were devastated by the deception. Reid and Tony split almost a half-million dollars in extortion payments from Evelyn over those six years.

Now, Alton will use Evelyn's file to expose the scheme Tony and Reid had going for years. All the other celebrities and business executives in the other files are still alive, so Alton opted to keep those files hidden away. No point in hurting those people, but Evelyn was already dead and her secret exposed. Alton will be sure Evelyn dishes out some revenge from the grave. He also plans to make one brief note to accompany Evelyn's file when he places it on Tony's desk, just to make the Reid and Campanelli connection even more obvious. It will also be a clue for police that Campanelli and Reid had a reason for an enormous disagreement when Campanelli was at Reid's house. It will help justify the gruesome death scene on the sofa. They are both dead, but Alton will ensure their legacies are ruined and that their scheme removes any suspicion of Blair being involved in Reid's death.

The will and trust should make the relationship between the two men even more obvious. Campanelli is a beneficiary in the estate of Reid Garrett, along with a charitable trust created upon Reid's death. Tony Campanelli manages the trust. With Reid and Campanelli both dead, the final disposition of their estates may get complicated.

After making an electronic copy of Evelyn's file, Alton places the original in his briefcase, along with the original copy of the Reid Garrett Living Trust and Will. When he goes to close the second box of the client files, he sees a very thick file at the back of the row of files. Intrigued, he pulls it out. The title on the file is written in large black script, *Hollywood REX*. Alton does not understand what that means, but he thumbs through the file for several minutes. Placing the file down on his lap, he whispers to himself, "I'll be damned. Holy crap. What was this self-absorbed star boy thinking? Good god."

Perspiring, Alton removes the file from the box and places it in his wall safe. Looking at his watch, he sees it is time to go, so he takes a deep breath and opens the door from his surveillance room to the hallway of his cottage.

Sitting down the hallway, Rob spots Alton emerging from his surveillance room with a briefcase and car keys. "Hey boss, I'm so glad to see you. I thought you might be dead."

"Dead? Why?"

"You know. The fire at Reid's. The other unidentified body. I thought it might be you. The pictures on the news are terrible."

"It's all okay, Rob. I've got a brief errand to run, and then I'll be back shortly."

"Who is the other dead body?" Rob asks.

"Other dead body?"

"You know what I mean, sir. Who else was with Reid at the house?"

"The police will have to tell us that."

Rob smiles, knowing that Alton will not answer questions. "Okay, boss, I'll be here."

"Did you enjoy the fireplace as I asked you?"

"Fires out. Fireplace is all clean."

"Good boy. See you in a couple hours. Take it easy. I won't need you for the rest of the night."

"Guess I'll say a prayer for those two souls in heaven."

Alton stops at the door and turns to face Rob. "You can pray for their souls, Rob, but I'm pretty sure they're *not* in heaven."

Alton arrives at Tony Campanelli's home and parks the van on a patch of dirt behind a Ficus hedge and an avocado tree, near the driveway gates. He uses his equipment in the van to turn off the house alarm, just as he did earlier today when retrieving the extortion files. Dressed in a black jumpsuit, Alton hops the fence, uses his card to open the front door, and is in Tony's office in less than five minutes. He places the file with Reid's Living Trust and Will on top of a stack of other files in the corner of his desk and lays Evelyn Sackalow's client file right in the middle of the desk. Alton pulls a crumpled piece of paper from a plastic bag and throws it in the trash can beside Tony's desk. He had typed a note on Reid Garrett's letterhead, and it says, "Tony, I've got the $6,400 I owe you from the last Sackalow payments. Pick it up at my house Saturday afternoon. Bring her file with you; you won't get the money until you do. —Reid"

Wearing gloves, he crumples the note in a ball to make it look like Tony crushed it in his palm and threw it in the trash after reading it. Alton thinks the note is cheesy and might look suspicious to detectives, but he'll take his chances. The detectives will get Reid and Tony's bank records and see lots of large deposits over many years. Since Reid was careful never to accept a check for his blackmail payments, it will be hard to expose the other celebrity victims without seeing their files, all of which are now in Alton's possession—except for Evelyn Sackalow's file, which now sits prominently in the center of Tony Campanelli's desk. He also wants the police to see that Tony is the executor of Reid's estate and has power of attorney for healthcare decisions.

When LAPD detectives look in Evelyn's file, they'll find a record of cash payments and the split between Reid and Tony, plus a mysterious third party with the initial "R." The file also contains the damning personal information about her two families exposed upon her death. The Sackalow file and the crumpled note about the money should explain why Tony was at Reid's house earlier today, and why they might have had a heated argument. It's not as tight as Alton would prefer, but he surmises it is enough to justify the ugly death scene at Reid's.

The potential loose end is what could happen if Landon turns up. When the detectives pull the cell phone records for Reid, they will see he called Landon's cell phone earlier today. They won't know who Landon is unless he turns up or until they can find him. If he turns up, Alton wants the police to make the connection that Landon was helping Reid in his extortion scheme. When DNA tests ultimately reveal that Landon and Reid are brothers, that should help incriminate Landon if, or when, he shows up.

Alton knows he must find Landon before any of that can happen. Landon knows too much about the original plans Alton had for him to assume Reid's identity. Alton needs to be sure Landon does not tell his story to the police. This means that Landon needs to be permanently missing. One way or the other.

Alton takes one last look at Campanelli's office, satisfied with what the LAPD detectives will find when they arrive. He leaves the house, turns on the alarm system from the van, and drives away.

33

Too Many Russians

Back at Reid's house, the firemen extinguish the blaze and hot spots, while two paramedics revive the Russian bodyguard found unconscious on the floor of the Rolls-Royce when they arrived.

An unmarked police car pulls into the driveway, and an older man in a rumpled business suit, tie, overcoat, and gray fedora hat gets out of the car. He's in his late sixties, gray hair under the fedora, closely cropped. His pale and wrinkled face shows the strain of investigating hundreds of murders over his forty-five-year career at the LAPD. As he surveys the activity at the mansion, the veteran LAPD homicide detective grins and nods his head. Another celebrity murder, another Hollywood mansion, another gruesome crime.

He looks at the scene unfolding below him. A sprawling Hollywood Hills mansion, a five-car garage, and the Los Angeles skyline in the background. An entry door charred with smoke and the roof damaged from a fire still smoldering. Paramedics, firefighters, news crews mill around up at the street and a dead celebrity lies inside. He wonders why the rich and famous often have more gruesome murders than ordinary folks. In the San Fernando Valley, or even South Los Angeles, most murders are a simple gunshot or two. A domestic dispute gone bad. Occasionally he sees a gang murder, and those can be gruesome. But it's the way the rich and famous kill each other that has fascinated Detective Edward Reams for most of his life. These spoiled people have everything to live for, yet they kill with such vengeance.

Murders of the rich and famous always happen in neighborhoods where cops can't ever afford to live. Forty-five years of murders, especially by the rich and famous, have made Detective Reams more than bitter; he often finds he has no sympathy whatsoever for the victims. It's not like the shooting of a six-year-old girl in a gang mishap. Murders of celebrities and rich people are not tragic like that; he often thinks the rich victims deserve what they got. Or at least, to some extent.

When the investigator has no sympathy for the victim, it takes the passion out of investigations. The Police Chief gave that observation to Detective Reams when he was slow to uncover a critical clue in the double-homicide of a rich oil executive and his mistress. The chief encouraged Reams to think about retirement. "Your heart's not in it, Ed. You've gone cold."

Reams ignored the advice. "I'm still a good cop and a skilled detective," he responded.

Reams adjusts his overcoat and hat and walks over to the paramedics. "Good evening. I'm Detective Ed Reams, Homicide, LAPD. This man doesn't look dead to me. Is he not a victim?"

An attractive, young, African American woman stands up and introduces herself as Paramedic Jane Hobbs, and then she introduces her colleague, Eric Stamner. She thinks Detective Reams looks like Spencer Tracy. "No sir, this one's not dead. Just beat up a bit. The deceased are inside."

"How many?" Reams asks.

"Two dead in the living room. Looks like a shooting, but both victims are severely burned. We haven't touched them. That job is for the coroner. Nothing we can do."

"My assistant and a police photographer were to meet me here. Their car is out on the street. Have you seen them?"

"Yes, sir. They spoke with our Russian patient here and then went inside the house."

Reams nods and then walks through several inches of water and firehoses in the driveway toward the entrance of the house. The front door lay burned on the floor just inside the entry. He assumes the firefighters kicked it in. Across the room, two burned bodies slump over on what's left of a large, semi-circular sofa. The stench of burned flesh is not new to Reams, but he never gets used to it.

"Ed, we're over here." Reams turns around to see his assistant, Evan Perry, and an LAPD photographer coming down the hallway to the living room from the bedroom.

"Fill me in, Evan. Who is the congenial couple here on the sofa?"

"Two victims, one of whom we assume is Reid Garrett. Looks like he consumed some cocaine and alcohol in the bedroom and possibly the living room before his guest arrived. There's cocaine on the pillow, some blood, and an empty cocktail glass on the nightstand. We think that's Mr. Garrett with the gun in his hand, although both bodies are severely burned. There's enough blood on the pillow for the lab to let us know if it's Garrett or not, but we think it is. The coroner will have to confirm the identities of both bodies."

Reams holds his nose and walks closer to the charred bodies on the sofa. He looks carefully at the charred gun and the burned hand that's still holding it. He then looks closely at the other victim's charred head, noticing a large hole in the back of the skull. He quickly turns away and walks to the open front door before taking a breath, lurching over like he might vomit.

"You okay, sir?"

"Yes, sorry. You'd think being a homicide detective for over forty years would make me immune to the sight and smell of burned bodies, but frankly, I've never had the stomach for it."

Evan and the photographer smile at each other but say nothing. Reams is one of the best homicide detectives in the LAPD, but he is notorious for his weak stomach and frequently vomits when he first arrives on a crime scene—especially if it involves burned flesh.

Relieved that he won't vomit this time, Reams takes a deep breath and turns to walk back inside the house, and closer to the victims on the sofa.

"So, if that guy with the gun is Reid Garrett, who's the other guy with part of his skull missing?"

"He's likely an attorney named Tony Campanelli. The Rolls-Royce out front is registered to him, and the Russian bodyguard said he drove Mr. Campanelli here and then somebody jumped him. Next thing he knew, he's on the floor of the car, legs out the door, and the paramedics asking him questions."

Reams nods his head. "Do we have an identity on the bodyguard?"

Evan hands Reams the driver's license they took from the Russian's wallet. "Diplomatic driver's license, issued by the State Department."

"A consulate employee? Is he immune from potential prosecution?"

"Called it in to HQ and they are in touch with the State Department. Said they'd get back to us, but to not do anything in the meantime. We can detain him until we know what level diplomat he is."

"Do we have any reason to suspect him in the deaths or the fire?"

"Can't tell. But why is a Russian consulate employee here at a murder scene, and why was he working as someone's driver?"

Reams nods his head. "Coroner on the way?"

"Yep."

Reams asks, "What makes you think the guy with the gun is Garrett and not Campanelli?"

"His height, for one," says Evan. "Both bodies are terribly burned, but this guy is obviously taller. Garrett was very tall. The other guy has some metal pins in his legs." Evan points to some exposed metal parts in his legs. "The driver said he'd just picked him up from the hospital. Someone ran over Campanelli with a car and he can't walk yet. So, that's my guess, boss. I'm sure the guy with the gun is Garrett, and the guy with two bullets through the skull is Campanelli. Want to wager?"

Reams smiles and shakes his head. "The burned gun in Garrett's left hand? Do we know who it belongs to?"

"That is what I wanted to point out to you. Though I'm

sure the guy with the gun is Garrett, the driver out there says Campanelli carried a gun—an Austrian Glock. You can see some of what's left of the shoulder holster on Campanelli's body, even though it burned."

Reams leans in to see what Evan is referring to. "So, the Russian admitted Campanelli carries a Glock?"

"Yep, but he wouldn't discuss much else. We still need to see whether Garrett or Campanelli had a registered gun, but it may be that Garrett pulled the trigger with Campanelli's own gun. It looks like an Austrian Glock, but we haven't touched it. We found two bullets back there, behind the one we think is Campanelli. One is in the wall directly behind him, and the other is just an inch or two below."

Evan continues: "The fire didn't do much damage there. The one we think is Campanelli appears to have two bullet holes in the head and, well, you've seen the backside of his skull. The coroner will have to tell us for sure."

Reams walks a circle around the sofa, staring at both victims, but says nothing. His intense interest in both victims intrigues Evan. He's worked with Reams for years as his assistant, but he hasn't seen this intense victim scrutiny often. After an awkward silence, Evan tells the photographer to take a few more shots outside by the kicked-in front door. After the photographer is outside, Evan walks closer to Reams, who is still staring at both bodies as he continues to circle them. "You okay, detective?"

"Not really. I'm confused. Are there any signs of a struggle elsewhere in this room or the house? Why would Mr. Garrett shoot Mr. Campanelli, who is just sitting here on the sofa?"

"Don't know, sir. No signs of a struggle except for the front door kicked in."

"The firemen didn't kick it in?"

"No, sir. They said smoke was billowing out the front door when they arrived, and the door was lying on the floor right where you see it."

Reams goes to look at the door lying on the floor, and then again at the two bodies sitting across from each other. "Seems odd.

If someone kicks in your front door, you don't invite them to sit down and chat on the sofa."

"It is an odd scene, that's for sure. Perhaps they argued after one of them broke the door down? Tried to reason with the other?"

Reams shakes his head. "No, something makes me think this was a setup. Or at least a deal gone bad. Did you check the house to see if anyone else was here?"

"No one else here that we could see. Did you know that the actress Blair Kilian was here earlier today and phoned in a 911 call on Mr. Garrett?"

Reams nods. "Any idea what that was all about?"

"Apparently she showed up to a scheduled script reading here at Mr. Garrett's house. She said he was drunk or on something when she arrived, so she left and called 911, because he tried to accost her."

Reams rubs his temples with his knuckles and then rubs his eyes. "You spoke with her?"

"Not yet, sir."

"Why don't you let me handle the interview with her."

"Whatever you prefer," Evan replies. "When would you like for us to do that?"

"No need for you to join, Evan. I'll handle it."

Evan frowns. "You sure?"

Reams nods and adjusts his hat.

Evan's cell phone rings, and he picks up the call. "Evan Perry . . . Yes, sir." He listens to the voice on the other end, then hangs up. "Our Russian comrade out there serves as a staff person at the Russian mission in San Francisco. Officially, it's just a facility for visas, but some Russian intelligence operations still take place in San Francisco. It used to be a consulate until the U.S. government shut it down in September 2017—after Russia interfered in our 2016 election. He only has limited immunity, but if we accuse him of anything, we have to clear it with the state department first."

"The paramedic says you spoke with the Russian driver before I arrived. Did he tell you why he was here with Campanelli?"

"No idea," says Evan. "He wouldn't answer many questions. Keeps saying he's a diplomat with immunity. I don't know why he volunteered that Campanelli carried a Glock, unless he wanted to be sure we didn't think the gun was his."

"What do you have on Campanelli?" Reams asks.

"He's a high-powered attorney and part-time private investigator in the entertainment business. Also represents some questionable businesspeople linked to the Russian mob here in L.A."

"Like who?"

"Like Konstantin Raminsky, for one," says Evan. "Sound familiar?"

Reams smiles. "Interesting. You're checking out any connection between our Russian driver outside and Raminsky?"

"Already on it."

"Next of kin notification on Campanelli yet?"

"No, sir. In fact, we won't have a positive ID on him until the coroner confirms it."

"That could take a day or two."

Evan nods his head, but before he can speak, a police officer appears at the entrance to the living room. "Detective Reams! We've got a situation here. Can you come up the driveway to the front gate? It looks urgent."

34

Trouble at the Gate

Reams whispers to Evan, "Situation? What the hell does he mean?" Reams turns around to speak with the officer at the front entry who asked for him. "What's the problem, officer?"

"Detective, please come up to the front gate."

"But what's going on?"

The officer motions for Reams to follow him. It's a long, steep driveway with the gate sitting up at the street level, about seventy feet above the level of the house. As Reams walks toward the gate with the officer, he hears a woman screaming and two police officers trying to calm her down. One of the news cameramen is getting it all on tape for a reporter who's commenting nearby.

Reams stops short of the front gate and asks the officer, "What do you have here? A crazy fan?"

"No sir, she claims to be the executive assistant to a man named Tony Campanelli. Says that's his car, and she knows he came here for a meeting. She wants to see him."

"That won't be pretty. Does she know we have two burned bodies in there?"

"She heard about the fire on the news driving up here. We've said nothing."

"Bring her over to me, but let's get out of earshot of the reporters."

"Yes, sir."

Reams walks back down the driveway about fifty feet and waits as two police officers bring the woman to him. They have her by the arms, and she's struggling and screaming as they walk toward him. He thinks she's extremely attractive; probably late thirties, long dark hair, looks to be Greek or Italian. She's dressed like a model. She's wearing a tight red dress with matching high-heeled shoes, a white coat and a red cape flung across her shoulders. She carries a silver handbag with a Gucci logo. He thinks he recognizes her, but he's not sure.

The police officers stop in front of Reams. One of them addresses the woman. "Ma'am, please calm down. This is Detective Reams. He's investigating the situation and, if you can compose yourself, I'm sure he can answer your questions."

Reams extends his hand, and the woman calms down. The police officers release her arms, and she straightens her coat, wipes her hair out of her face, and shakes his hand. "Marina, my name is Maryna, but my American friends call me "Marina." It's easier."

"Nice to meet you. Do you have a last name?"

"Petrovich. Marina Petrovich."

"Russian?"

"Please, no. Ukrainian. And may I please see Tony now?"

"Who are you in relation to him, and why would you think someone by that name is here?"

"A game?" She looks reams square in the eyes. "We will play games?"

Reams fakes a smile. "You can see we have an emergency here. A fire, people injured. I need to know who you are and why you think your friend Tony is here."

She folds her arms and walks closer to Reams. "Tony Campanelli is my employer. I am his executive assistant. He was to meet me for dinner almost two hours ago and he never showed up. I tried calling him; here's his number." She shows Reams her cell phone call log with multiple calls to a person named Tony. "I remembered him saying he had an appointment with Reid Garrett and then he would meet me for dinner afterwards. Since I couldn't reach him, I drove here. And then I saw all of that." She points up the driveway to the firetrucks, police, and photographers. "And that's his Rolls-Royce down there by the front door.

Is he okay? I need to see him. He should be here with his driver."

"Driver? Would that be a big Russian guy?"

"Yes. He's only driving for him since Tony's accident. He can't drive while he's confined to a wheelchair. May I see them both, please?"

Reams is silent for a moment, then he sees her eyes beginning to tear up. She must expect bad news. "There are two deceased people inside the house. Severely burned. We don't have a positive ID, but we believe one of them may be your employer, Mr. Campanelli."

Bursting into tears, Marina tries to run past Detective Reams. He grabs her and says, "You can't go in there."

"I need to see him. I can tell you if it is him or not."

"There's been a fire. Only the coroner can positively identify the two bodies."

Reams pulls a handkerchief from his suit pocket and hands it to her. "I'm sorry. I hope it's not him, but it's a good possibility it is." He tells the two police officers to return to the gate, "I can handle this from here."

Marina wipes her nose and looks up at Reams. "Is Nicolai here? He must be. I want to see him."

Reams recognizes the name from the State Department driver's license . . the name of the Russian driver for Mr. Campanelli. "You know him?"

"I do. If Tony is here, Nicolai drove him here in the Rolls. Is he dead too?"

"No, he's not. He's injured, but before I can let you speak with him, I have a few questions."

"Questions? Now?" she asks incredulously.

"I'm sorry, ma'am. I need your help before I can help you."

"Detective Reams, you need to understand that I must know if Mr. Campanelli is dead or alive."

"Ms. Petrovich, *you* need to understand that I've got some questions for the driver, and I need for you to do something for me. In return, I promise you a quick answer on Campanelli."

"What do you want with Nicolai? He's just a driver. He knows nothing."

"I'll be the judge of that."

Marina takes a deep breath and looks away from Reams for a moment. "Ok, but you give me what I need, or you will be sorry."

Just a Driver

Marina's statement—that he needs to give her what she wants or he'll be sorry—startles Reams. "Ms. Petrovich, I think we understand each other. Let's start with one thing at a time. I will let you speak with Nicolai, and then you do me a favor."

"Tell me the favor; what is it?"

"I understand Mr. Campanelli worked out of an office at his home. Do you have the alarm code to Mr. Campanelli's home? And a key?"

Marina nods.

"Good. You take me to Mr. Campanelli's home so I can see his office, and in return I will let you talk with the driver. It's getting late, but the coroner should be here soon to take the bodies to the morgue. A positive ID will take a day or two, officially, but I'll get a head up well before then. I will let you speak with the driver and he can verify whether he drove Mr. Campanelli here. He can also tell you what happened after he dropped him off. And I promise to call you as soon as the coroner gives me any clue about the identity of either of the bodies in there."

Marina smiles, but faintly. "Ok, let's start with that. Let me speak with Nicolai."

"Follow me. Oh, and one more condition. You must speak with the driver in English and I must be present. No other conversation with him in any language other than English. At least for now."

Marina is silent.

"Is that a yes or no?"

"His English is poor."

"Then I'll call the LAPD for a Russian-speaking officer who can translate your conversation for me. We will have to wait for one to arrive."

"No, I don't want to wait. English it is. But he will be hard for you to understand."

"Try me."

Reams escorts Marina down the driveway and over to the Rolls-Royce parked in the driveway. The Russian driver, Nicolai, is being interviewed again by Detective Evan Perry. They are both sitting on a bench at the edge of the driveway. As soon as Marina sees Nicolai, she runs over to him before Detective Reams can say a word. Nicolai stands up to embrace Marina. They both start speaking in Russian and Reams cuts them off. "Ms. Petrovich remember our agreement. English only. And Evan, I'm sorry for the late introduction, but this is Ms. Marina Petrovich. She says she is Mr. Campanelli's executive assistant, and she knows Nicolai. I agreed to let the two of them speak so long as it is in English. Then she has agreed to take me to Mr. Campanelli's office. I'd like you to come along."

Evan stands up and nods his head, "Sure, but I got little out of our driver here. His English is poor, or at least he pretends it is. Says he is purely a social acquaintance of Mr. Campanelli and only serving as his driver since he got out of the hospital earlier today. He's vague about what he does at the Russian mission in San Francisco and what Mr. Campanelli wanted with Reid Garrett."

"Well, perhaps Ms. Petrovich can help us out in that regard."

Marina speaks slowly with Nicolai. He confirms to her he picked up Mr. Campanelli from the hospital when they discharged him earlier today. She asks him where else they went and he tells her they went to see Blair Kilian at her apartment, thinking Reid Garrett was with her for a script reading. When they discovered Reid wasn't there, Campanelli tried to reach Reid on his cell phone again, to no avail. They went to Reid's house, hoping he'd be there. When they arrived, Nicolai wheeled Mr.

Campanelli to the front porch in his wheelchair. Someone body-slammed him into the doorjamb and he became unconscious. When he came to, he was halfway on the floor of the Rolls, halfway on the driveway, and firemen were everywhere. He assumes Mr. Campanelli is inside, but his wheelchair is still on the porch so someone would have had to carry him in. Or carried him away. He says he is not sure Mr. Campanelli is inside.

After Marina and Nicolai finish their slow conversation, Reams cuts in. "I'd like to ask Nicolai a few questions if you've finished, Ms. Petrovich."

"I'm done for now, but since Nicolai is not sure Mr. Campanelli is inside, I need for you to let me see for myself."

"We have a deal. I lived up to my end. Now you live up to yours. But before we leave, I'd like to know why Mr. Campanelli was so eager to see Mr. Garrett immediately after they discharged him from the hospital."

Marina looks at Nicolai, "Did you hear what the Detective said?"

Nicolai shakes his head and says a few words in Russian.

"He says he does not know why Mr. Campanelli wanted to see Mr. Garrett. He was just doing him a favor to drive him."

Reams scratches his forehead. "Nicolai, did you kick down the front door?"

Nicolai shakes his head.

"Well, if you didn't do it, do you know who did?"

He shakes his head again.

"You do not know why Mr. Campanelli wanted to see Mr. Garrett?"

Nicolai shrugs his shoulders.

"Let me ask you the same question, Ms. Petrovich. Why was your boss determined to see Mr. Garrett immediately upon release from the hospital? His injuries were serious. What was the rush to see Mr. Garrett?"

"I don't know. They did business together."

"What kind of business?"

"Tony was Reid's attorney, business manager. He looked after his financial affairs. He does that for a lot of celebrities."

"Really? Like who?"

"His clients have confidentiality agreements. I can't tell you."

"Evan, do you have anything else you want to ask?"

"Yes, Nicolai, how is it you know Mr. Campanelli? That was my first question to you and you just shrugged."

Nicolai says nothing and looks to Marina. "Mr. Campanelli has done some work for the Russian ambassador in Washington, DC, and that is how he became acquainted with Nicolai. When the ambassador heard Tony was being released from the hospital and couldn't drive, he asked his driver to come down from the Russian mission in San Francisco and drive for Tony."

Evan is suspicious. "This is Los Angeles. We have thousands of livery drivers and car services. I'm sure Mr. Campanelli has used them many times for business or social events. Why would the Russian ambassador send one of his own employees all the way down here from San Francisco just to be a driver?"

Nicolai and Marina are both silent.

Reams interjects, "Well, Evan, do you have other questions for Nicolai?"

"I have lots of questions, but we aren't getting anywhere with him. I think we should take him to the station. We've got some Russian-speaking officers there and we could get more specific. I'm also waiting for a background check on him."

Marina interrupts, "No, let this man go. He was just doing a favor for Tony. He is not involved in his business."

Reams ignores her. "Have an officer come get him and take him to the station. After we see Campanelli's office, we will go to the station to do a more complete interview. We'll hold him until you get the background check. Come with me now to Campanelli's home and we'll go directly to the station from there."

Marina pulls Reams by the arm and whispers in his ear, "He's a Russian consulate employee. Be careful. I'd let him go, if I were you."

Take the Bait

Detective Reams drives slowly as he approaches the gate to Tony Campanelli's home. Marina has a remote-control application on her phone that opens the front gate, but they see that one gate is closed and the other is partly open and broken. It looks like someone drove through it in a hurry and then couldn't get it fully closed. Reams drives through the opening created by the smashed gate and arrives at the front doorsteps to Tony's home. Marina uses the same cell phone app to enter the security code for the home alarm. After reaching the front porch, Reams, Marina and Evan step up to the front door. Marina opens the door with a key, and they follow her down the hallway to the office. As they enter the office, Marina goes immediately to the desk.

Reams stops her. "I'm sorry, Ms. Petrovich; you must stand back."

"There may be some confidential files on his desk."

"This is a police investigation—a murder investigation. I'm afraid nothing is confidential. I have a warrant if you want to see it. I thought we'd just handle this in a more congenial fashion."

Marina nods.

Reams continues: "I may need your help, so stay close. We will start at the desk first."

The first thing Reams spots is the file in the middle of the desk titled *Sackalow*. He thumbs through it and summons Evan, pointing to a list of cash payments listed like a bank register. "What do you make of that?" he asks.

Evan flips through several pages. "Looks like deposits made

every month for several years. I can't tell for sure, but it looks like payments *from* Sackalow rather than *to* him. All in cash."

Reams looks up at Marina, who is standing against the wall, biting her lower lip. "Ms. Petrovich, do you know who Mr. Sackalow is?"

Startled, she says nothing.

He asks again, "Do you? Do you know who he is?"

"May I see the file?"

"Yes, come on over."

Marina glances at the file. "It's not *Mr.* Sackalow, it's *Ms.* Sackalow. And I thought they stole all the client files. May I look in the file drawer?"

"Please."

Marina goes to the file cabinet behind Tony's desk and opens the file drawers one-by-one. They are all empty. "As I thought. Client files all gone except this one."

Reams leans his head over the open file drawers. "How did you know that someone stole the files?"

"Tony told me."

"Did he know who did it?"

Marina is silent.

"You may as well tell us. We'll find out."

"Reid Garrett. Tony says the security camera caught him breaking in earlier today."

"Where are the security camera recordings?"

Marina takes Reams and Evan to a closet in the hallway and shows them a video recording system installed by the alarm company. It's a common security camera system used by many security companies in the area. Evan knows how to retrieve any video feeds in the past seventy-two hours. He scrolls through footage from inside and outside cameras, only one of which has an episode where a motion sensor activated the camera. He finds the episode from earlier in the day. He sees Reid coming down the hall from Tony's office, some files under his arm, and he flips the bird at the camera. It's a brief clip, and the only recording on any of the interior cameras.

Reams looks at Marina and says, "Okay, so Mr. Garrett was here, but that stack of files under his arm was hardly enough to fill three drawers in the file cabinet. When did he get the other files? Or did someone else take them?"

"I don't know. I just know Tony told me Reid took all the client files."

"Do you know why?"

Marina shakes her head.

"Let's go back into the office. I'll need that Sackalow file and anything else on the desk that can help us." As Reams goes through the other items on the desk, he spots the thick file titled "Reid Garrett Living Trust and Will." He thumbs through the file and looks up at Marina. "This document says Mr. Campanelli is Garrett's trustee and the executor of his estate. Looks like he has a power of attorney for healthcare directives. Is that right?"

"Yes, that's right. They were remarkably close, and Reid had no spouse, children or family."

Evan is scouring through the other items in the office and eyes the trash can. He turns it over and finds a few notes, chewing gum wrappers, and a crumpled note, which he unfolds. He hands it to Reams and remarks, "This is interesting. This note tells Campanelli to bring the Sackalow file to Reid's house and that he owes him a check from the Sackalow payments."

"Ms. Petrovich," Reams asks, "why would Reid Garrett owe Tony payments from this woman, Evelyn Sackalow?"

"Mr. Campanelli got deposits from lots of celebrities and executives to invest for them."

"Was he an investment advisor too?"

Marina shrugs. "I don't know."

"Well, for being his executive secretary, you know surprisingly little about his business. What exactly did you do for Mr. Campanelli?"

"Helped with his appointments, correspondence . . . errands."

"Did you work for him full time?"

"No. Part time."

"And did you know or have any connection with Nicolai Volkov before he started driving for Mr. Campanelli earlier today?"

Marina does not answer at first.

"Must I ask you every question twice?"

"He visited Mr. Campanelli occasionally."

"For what? What business would a Russian diplomatic employee have with your boss?"

"Detective, I really don't know. He just showed up from time to time to drop off packages and pick up packages from Mr. Campanelli. He was friendly, that's all I can tell you."

"How often would he see Mr. Campanelli?"

"Usually only once a month."

"And what was in these packages he picked up?"

"I actually never saw the contents, but they were large and bulky."

"Did he ever ask you to handle any of these packages?"

"Once in a while."

"What did you do with the packages when you handled them?"

"Well, let's see. Once I met Nicolai in a parking lot and we exchanged packages. Another time I left a package at the office of one of Mr. Campanelli's clients."

"Ok, back up. So once you exchanged packages with Mr. Volkov in a parking lot. What was in the package he gave you?"

"I don't know. It was only a letter-sized envelope. It might have contained checks."

"Why would Mr. Volkov be delivering checks to Mr. Campanelli?"

"I told you. Mr. Campanelli invested money for some of his clients."

"And Mr. Volkov is in the investment business?"

"No," Marina replies, "but he does deliveries for one of Mr. Campanelli's clients who invests money."

"Who is this investment person?"

"Someone who works with a man Tony referred to only as 'R'."

"Ok, so Mr. R?" Reams asks. "He's in the investment business?"

"Guess so."

Reams moves closer to Marina. "Could Mr. R be Konstantin Raminsky?"

"I suppose so, but I don't know."

Reams and Evan look at each other with raised eyebrows. Reams then picks up the Sackalow file and the Reid Garrett Will & Trust file and puts them under his arm. "I guess we're done. For now."

Evan objects. "What? We just got here. And this story of hers makes no sense. We need to check the other rooms and have the lab do a full set of prints in the office and around the house." Even reaches for his phone, "I'll call the lab guys to come over here and do a full sweep."

Reams walks down the hallway toward the door. "Put your damn phone away, Evan. We're done here for now. I will let you know if we need the lab guys. Let's go."

"What?" Evan stands in the hallway shaking his head as Reams and Marina walk out the front door. He thinks, *What the fuck is going on here?*

37

Russian Myths and Money

Alton returns to his cottage after leaving Tony Campanelli's house and immediately goes to his surveillance room. After the security pad scans his retina, the door opens, and he runs to the stack of Tony Campanelli's client files he left on the floor of his office. He has around sixty client files, mostly celebrities, but also some business executives, politicians, and even a prominent preacher from a local megachurch.

The celebrity names in the files are easily recognizable, but he's not looking for a celebrity name; he's looking for a Russian name. An employee of the Russian mission in San Francisco was driving Tony Campanelli around town right after his release from the hospital; it intrigues Alton. *What's the connection?* he wonders.

Oksana said she knew nothing about this, and he believes her. The Russian Nicolai Volkov was just one of her sexual escapades. Though she has been out of the KGB for decades, she still circulates with Russian expatriates living in the U.S. At Alton's request, Oksana checked into Nicolai's background through the woman in the Russian consulate who set her up with him for their first date some years ago. She said Nicolai works for the FSB (ФСБ), which is the Russian Federal Security Service and the successor to the former KGB where Oksana had worked. Nicolai is responsible for the security of the Russian mission in San Francisco and reports directly to the Russian Consul General in Seattle. The only other information Oksana could uncover is that Nicolai accompanies one or more staff of the Russian mission in San Francisco to Moscow for a monthly trip. The Russian embassy in Washington, DC, sends a plane from Washington to San Francisco, then to Moscow and returns to San Francisco the following day. After another day in San Francisco, the aircraft travels back to Washington, DC, sometimes with a stop in Seattle on the way. Diplomatic air missions often take sensitive intelligence documents and hard currency back and forth to Russia. Funds wired between U.S. banks and Moscow are easy to trace. Cash and securities taken on diplomatic aircraft escape notice because the flights are immune from inspection by U.S. authorities.

Alton is wondering, *But what's the connection between the Russian mission employee and Campanelli?* Not sure what he's looking for, Alton sets aside every file where the name on it is not famous or recognizable. He's looking for a Russian name but doesn't see one. Two non-celebrity files stand out. One file has a Chinese character on it, but no name. The other one is very thick and titled "R".

The Chinese character on the file is in large red ink: 諜

Alton does not speak Chinese, but from his days at the CIA, he recognizes it as a Chinese character as opposed to Japanese or another Asian language. He scans a picture of the symbol and clicks on the translator application on his phone. A translation appears: "To spy or spying." Alton whispers to himself, "'To spy or spying'? Intriguing."

Opening the file, he finds only two documents. One is a copy of a cash withdrawal slip from HSBC Bank in the amount of seven million Chinese yuan, converted to approximately $500,000 US dollars. The other document is a copy of a Chinese passport with a smaller picture of a man who appears part Asian, part Anglo. The man looks familiar, but Alton can't immediately place him. The writing in the passport, including the man's name, is all in Chinese. Alton will investigate that file later, so he sets it aside.

He then picks up the thickest file, the one titled "R." Alton places the file on his desk and goes through it. The first part of the file is a ledger of deposits with a client name or initials beside each deposit. The names correspond to the names on many of the client files. There are four columns after each name: "Total Amount," "C share," "G share," and "R share." The split varies by client, but in most cases, the "R" column gets a third of the total. The allocation to "C" and "G" varies from client to client. He surmises that "C" stands for Campanelli, and "G" stands for Garrett. But who is "R"?

And then he sees it. At the back of the file is a section several pages long with copies of lots of checks on each page—hundreds of check copies, page after page. About half are payable to Garrett Productions, LLC, and the other half to Paisan Enterprises, which he suspects is a company that Mr. Campanelli might own.

The checks are from a variety of entities: The RR LLC, Kikimora, LLC, Koshchei, LTD, and several others. Curious about the names, Alton does a Google search. Most of the names of the companies are Russian mythical creatures or from Russian folklore. Kikimora is an evil house witch. Koshchei is an immortal Russian figure who cannot die because he hides his soul in objects to protect it. There are other names with similar Russian mythical meaning. The checks are from banks in England, Turkey, and Switzerland.

Alton smiles and shakes his head. Classic money laundering. That's it. Nothing elaborate about it. They give the cash to someone who deposits it overseas or under an unfamiliar name. In return, that individual keeps a third of the money for themselves and writes checks to Tony Campanelli and Reid Garrett for their share.

Typically, checks deposited that total several thousand dollars each month or week draw little attention. But cash deposits, especially larger ones, draw enormous attention. Banks must report cash deposits or withdrawals in any amount over $10,000 to the IRS in a Currency Transaction Report. Such deposits aren't illegal, but a regular series of them in large amounts can show money laundering or tax avoidance. It's a red flag that people like Reid and Tony don't want, because it could draw attention to their extortion scheme. So they have a third partner who takes the cash and gives them a check from an apparently legitimate source in return for holding back a chunk of the cash. Nice and tidy.

It would be so easy for someone like Nicolai to take cash to Moscow every month on the diplomatic flights. He could pass the money off to someone else there, or even make deposits himself into an account owned by someone else. Alton suspects that "R" is someone in the Russian consulate or the embassy in Washington, DC, or someone connected to it.

It could also be Konstantin Raminsky. Alton has run across him before. Konstantin Raminsky is a former Russian ambassador to the European Union who now runs several companies that operate shady businesses in the United States. He's part of the California Russian mob, as they're known, and is a frequent guest for events hosted by the Russian embassy in Washington, D.C. He's a dangerous character and would have access to diplomats in the Russian embassy who could take large amounts of cash from the United States to Russia on diplomatic aircraft. United States dollars are precious in Russia, so the embassy would be very cooperative in transporting them to Moscow—for a fee. The extortion fees collected by Reid and Tony would be chump change to someone like Raminsky, so the question is, why would he do it? Since he probably launders even larger sums of money, it would be easy to include the smaller amounts from Reid and Tony, but why run that risk for such small amounts? A man like Raminsky wouldn't need, or want, chump change partners like Reid and Campanelli. They are small-time crooks. Alton strokes his chin. *Doesn't add up, but it seems a possibility— even if Nicolai was doing it without Raminsky's direct knowledge.*

Alton believes that Reid and Tony likely had Raminsky or someone else launder the money to keep it from being easily traced—In case one of their extortion clients went to the FBI and reported the extortion, they needed to be sure the money wouldn't trace back to them.

To trace cash payments for extortion or blackmail, it would have been common practice for law enforcement to mark or tag the cash in a future payment to see if any of it turned up in the possession of Reid or Tony, or if it turned up in a deposit to a bank account affiliated with either of them. By taking the cash to Russia, it ended up being circulated in Russia or Europe, making it harder to trace once it's out of the US.

Alton smiles and begins duplicating all the pages in the "R" file. He'll make sure it falls into the hands of the LAPD, but he wants to make a slight modification first. The pages listing the payments from extorted celebrities include their name or initials. Since Alton wants to protect the identities of the other victims of Reid and Tony's scheme, he will blank out the names and leave only a letter or two, making it impossible to draw a connection to any of the celebrities. He's careful to wear gloves while he changes the names on the pages and places them in a new file. As soon as he's done, he keeps the original file, and places the revised copy in an envelope. All the other pages remain unaltered except for the pages listing the names and deposits over many years. He places the file in his briefcase and retrieves his car from the garage. It will be up to the LAPD detectives to figure out who "R" is, and it will further deflect attention away from Blair and Cameron.

As he leaves the driveway of the cottage, Alton places a call to Blair. "I'm on my way over. Is anyone there with you?"

"It's Saturday evening, Alton, almost midnight. You think I'm alone, just sitting here by myself in my apartment at this late hour?"

"I know you are. Otherwise, I wouldn't have called."

"Alton, you are so fucking arrogant."

"Must be martini time at the Kilian residence."

"Well, at least I'm not alone."

"Just you and your martini, I presume?" he asks.

"Yes, you presume correctly, asshole."

Alton tells her to stay put, and he will call her from the lobby of her building once he arrives. If she is not alone, she is to say that she is just going out and hang up. Otherwise, he will see her shortly after he phones from the lobby. He's expecting her to be drunk, which she already is.

★

About twenty minutes later, Alton leaves his car with the valet and calls Blair from the lobby. She tells him to come up. When the elevator arrives on Blair's floor, she is standing in the doorway of her apartment with a martini in hand.

Alton smiles at her. "Is that your second or third of the evening?"

"Alton, it's midnight. I've lost track. Why are you here? Hasn't my day been shitty enough?"

"It's about to get better. Fix me a twin to your martini and let's have a chat about this." He points to the thick file under his arm—the "R" file.

Saying nothing, Blair goes to her bar and makes Alton a fresh martini. He sees that she has just poured the last of the Nolet's gin for his martini. He surmises she likely had the rest of the bottle tonight.

"Here you are, my rude, late-night guest. Are you here to tell me Reid is dead?"

"No. I'm not sure of his fate."

"I've been calling Cam, but he won't answer."

"Forget about Cam for now. I have an important acting assignment for you."

"Oh shit, Alton, I can't read a script now. Look at me!"

"You will write your own lines. It's simple. Here's what I want you to do. See this file? I want you to call the LAPD officers who were here earlier today."

"And how will I do that? I don't remember their names, little pricks."

"They left you a card over there on the table." Alton retrieves the card and shows it to Blair. "Here it is. Stan Witkowski, and officer Daniela Salazar. Call her. She'll be more receptive to your call than the male officer."

"What?"

"Blair, all you have to tell her is that you want to give them a file you took from Reid's house. You were afraid to say anything when they were here earlier today, because they accused you of making a false 911 call. But you took a file from the table next to Reid's front door when you left because you were frightened and thought it was the file with the script. It wasn't."

"What? I did no such thing."

"Blair, you are acting. Telling a lie. It's for your own good and it will help focus the attention of the LAPD on Reid and Tony's extortion scheme instead of your sloppy effort to kill or permanently disable Reid."

Blair opens the file and flips through a few pages. "What the hell is all this? Looks like a bank ledger."

"That is pretty much what it is. It's a record of payments from people like you. I know Reid asked you for money, but it looks like you never paid him anything, did you?"

"No. He demanded five thousand dollars when he raped me. That was Friday. I was to bring the money to the set when we film on Monday. But that won't happen now, will it?"

"Unless Reid makes a miraculous recovery, no. If the cops ask you if he was blackmailing you, the answer is no."

"What?"

"You will become a suspect if they think you had a motive to harm him. Just stick to the story: you went to Reid's for a script reading, but he was drunk and belligerent. So you left and called 911 out of concern for him. We later discovered it was just a trick. Stick to that story, but you've got to get that file in the hands of the cops."

"Won't they wonder why I took it?"

"Tell them it was poor judgment on your part. You came over for a script reading, and you thought you put your copy of the script on the side table when you arrived. When you left in a hurry, you grabbed it thinking it was your script file. When you got home, you realized you had your script *and* the file you picked up on the side table. The file you took by mistake ended up being financial gibberish to you, but since it belonged to Reid, you wanted to turn it over to the police."

"Because I'm just stupid?"

"No, because you need them to focus on that file and not you.

I'm leaving, so please make the call."

"It's midnight."

"Make the call and ask them to call you back first thing tomorrow. And get them over here as soon as you can. Get that file out of your hands and into theirs."

"What about Reid? What if he lives?"

"Leave that to me. Make the call."

A Journey Too Far

Early Sunday morning Detective Reams arrives at the Bel Air home of Cameron Haines, who is still in bed. The doorbell goes unanswered, so Reams tries a second time. Then a third. A few moments later, a voice comes over the intercom at the front door. "Yes? Who is it?"

"LAPD. Detective Ed Reams. I need to speak with Cameron Haines."

Cameron clears his throat, "Right now?"

"Yes. If it's too early for you, I can wait in my car until you're up."

"Well, I don't think I can go back to sleep knowing there's a cop sleeping in a car in my driveway. Bel Air is a nosy neighborhood. I'm up now so give me a few minutes and I'll come down to let you in."

Reams stands back from the door to look up at the imposing home. He's impressed that a Hollywood agent lives in such a grand fashion. *No LAPD detectives living in this neighborhood, that's for sure.* Reams has heard of Cameron Haines. It intimidates him to meet him.

He hears the door latch open and turns back to see Cameron standing at the front door in a blue and white bathrobe. "Detective Reams, I presume?"

Reams tips his hat and shows his badge. "Don't take it personally. I never call ahead."

Cameron pulls reading glasses from a pocket in his robe and glances at the badge. "I grew up in South Central L.A., detective.

A cop knocking on your front door at seven in the morning is usually not a good thing. Neither is having a cop waiting in a car in your driveway on a Sunday morning."

"I'm sorry if I've upset you, but I need to speak with you rather urgently."

Without saying a word, Cameron waves Detective Reams into his foyer. "Please make yourself at home in the study to your left. I'll need a cup of coffee before we talk. You like coffee?"

"Yes, if you don't mind. Just a little cream or milk."

Cameron nods and walks toward the kitchen.

Reams enters Cameron's study and is overwhelmed. Paneled walls in mahogany wood with a red hue. The ceiling is extremely high with enormous windows looking out to a courtyard with a fountain. Floor to ceiling bookshelves flank the largest window. Two computer screens sit on the large desk, and a bar at the end of the room looks like it belongs in a classic English gentleman's club. There are celebrity pictures all over the room on walls, bookshelves, and Cameron's large ebony desk. Most include Cameron with Hollywood's rich and famous. Not just actors, but studio owners and producers. *Handsome man, and what a life this must be.* Reams admits to himself that he is envious of a lifestyle much different from his.

A few minutes later Cameron emerges with a tray holding two coffee cups and red porcelain containers for sugar, cream, and sugar substitutes. "Pick either cup, detective. Help yourself . . . cream or whatever else you like."

Reams grabs a cup and pours some cream into his coffee. "South L.A.? That's where you're from?"

"That's right."

"You've done very well for yourself."

"Thank you. I think so. But that's not why you're here, is it?"

"No, no, I'm afraid it's not. I'll get to the point. Reid Garrett is a client of yours, correct?"

Taking a sip of his coffee, Cameron points to a picture on his bookshelf. Reid is holding an Emmy award with Cameron's arm around his shoulders. Both men are in tuxedos and grinning from ear to ear.

"I assume that's a yes," says Reams.

Cameron nods.

"Were you with Reid Garrett yesterday?"

"No."

"You never saw him during the entire day?"

"No."

"Did you speak with him?"

"No, detective. I've not spoken with or seen Reid for a few days."

"You know what's happened?" asks Reams.

"I was about to ask the same question of you. What happened? All I know is what I heard on the news."

"We're trying to figure that out. What about Blair Kilian?" Reams asks. "I understand she is your client as well?"

"Yes, she is my client."

"You see or speak with her in the last couple days?"

"Yes, I have, as a matter of fact. I was with her at her apartment yesterday."

"What time?"

"Early afternoon. We were supposed to discuss a script reading for filming on Monday."

"Ah, was that the script reading with Reid Garrett?"

"Yes, but I guess it never happened."

Reams looks at his notepad and flips through a few pages. "I understand you were with Ms. Kilian when the two LAPD officers interviewed her about the 911 call, right?"

"Yes, I was, but it sounds like you already know that."

"And Mr. Alton Price . . . was he present for part of that discussion?"

"Yes, sir."

"Can you tell me the condition Mr. Garrett was in yesterday?" Reams inquires. "I mean, whether he was drunk or on drugs when Ms. Kilian left his home?"

"No, I can't. Reid was a prankster, so it wouldn't surprise me for him to be taunting her or being playful. He was also was a frequent drug user, so either version of his condition could be true."

"That's quite a mouthful. That saved me a few questions. Then you've no idea what happened?"

"No."

Reams pauses for a moment and looks at the celebrity pictures on the walls and on the bookshelves as he takes a sip of coffee. "Is there a picture of Ms. Kilian here?"

Cameron gets up from his chair and goes to his desk. He picks up a framed picture from the corner of his desk and hands it to Reams.

"Well, are all your clients this good-looking? Like Garrett and this Kilian woman?" Reams grins. "Do you have any ugly clients?"

Cameron smirks. "You pick the ugliest one before you leave, how about that?"

"Mr. Haines, you have what, maybe thirty, forty photographs in this room? The only picture on your desk is Ms. Kilian. Is she your most important client?"

Cameron doesn't like the question. The photographs all around the room make it apparent that he has many more well-known celebrities than Blair. "All my clients are important, detective."

Reams nods. "And you have an office in Beverly Hills, too?"

"I do."

"May I see it?"

"Yes. But you will need an appointment. I don't take walk-ins."

"Ouch."

"Detective, I know it's Sunday morning, but I have some plans today. So unless we've got something else to discuss besides my clients, I'd like to get on with my day." The remark about Blair's picture has upset Cameron. He wonders if that was just curiosity or if Reams knows something about his relationship to Blair.

"Okay, Mr. Haines. I'm almost finished. Did Reid Garrett have any next of kin?"

"There's no family. He's estranged from his parents—if they're still alive."

"Wife? Partner? Anyone else living with him?"

"Not that I know of."

"How long have you been his agent?"

"Over ten years."

"Well then, you must know him pretty well. He must have someone close to him."

Cameron shakes his head. "Reid was a loner. An incredibly famous man, but no close friends that I know of."

"So, there's no one closer to him than you," Reams comments.

Cameron replies, "I didn't say that."

"But if you've been his agent for over ten years and he is a huge star with no friends or partners, you must have a close relationship."

"No one is close to Reid, but as far as that goes, I'm probably closer to him than anyone."

"You his executor? Do you have a power of attorney over his estate?"

"No, to both."

"Well, that's odd, Mr. Haines. There must be someone else he trusted then. Do you know who his executor is?"

Cameron pauses. "I believe it's an attorney named Tony Campanelli."

Reams pretends to be surprised to hear Campanelli named as Reid's executor. "You know him?" he asks.

"Not well, but we're acquainted."

"Interesting. When did you last speak with Mr. Campanelli?"

"Yesterday."

"On the phone or in person?"

"He came by Blair Kilian's apartment after your LAPD officers left."

"Why? Why did Mr. Campanelli come to meet with you and Ms. Kilian?"

"Actually, he wasn't there to see us," Cameron explains. "He was looking for Reid."

"Mr. Garrett? Why would Mr. Campanelli come to Ms. Kilian's apartment to find him? Were they involved?"

"Not romantically involved, but Reid is the new guest star on the mini-series Blair is in. They were to film their first scene together tomorrow morning. They only met a couple days ago."

"*Dark Company?* That mini-series?"

Cameron nods.

"Ok, but why would Campanelli want to see him, and why would he be looking for him at Ms. Kilian's apartment?"

Cameron shrugs. "I don't know why Mr. Campanelli wanted to see Reid. He just showed up at her apartment and insisted that Reid must be there."

"Was Ms. Kilian expecting Mr. Garrett?"

"No. She went to his house for the script reading, as you know. The reading didn't happen at Reid's house, so she came home. Campanelli insisted that Reid had said the script reading was at Blair's and he could meet him there."

"So, Ms. Kilian goes to Mr. Garrett's home for the script reading, but he told Campanelli the reading was at Ms. Kilian's and to meet him there?"

"Apparently."

"A diversion perhaps?" Reams take a breath and quickly exhales from his mouth. "Odd. Anyone with Mr. Campanelli?"

"Yes, a guy Tony said was his driver."

"Description?"

"Big guy, about six feet tall."

"You know his name?"

"No."

Detective Reams answers a call on his cell phone. "Reams here . . . I'm at the Haines residence now . . . Who? . . . Funny, her name just came up . . . Well, that's interesting. Did you get the file from her? I need to see it . . . Call me as soon as you have it . . . Okay. I'm on my way to the office now."

Placing his cell phone back in his pocket, Reams looks at Cameron. "Seems Ms. Kilian just reported taking a file from Mr. Garrett's home yesterday."

"What?"

"She called LAPD Officer Salazar to turn in a file she said she took from Mr. Garrett's house. By mistake."

Cameron recognizes the name of the officer. She was the

Latina woman who accompanied the officer with the Polish last name. He says nothing.

"Know anything about this file, Mr. Haines?"

"No, I don't."

"Were you present the entire time the two LAPD officers interviewed Ms. Kilian yesterday?"

"I was."

"Is that the same meeting where Mr. Campanelli showed up?"

"Afterwards. Mr. Campanelli came over after the officers left."

"Give me your phone number, Mr. Haines. And don't leave town. I may need to speak with you later."

Cameron pulls a business card from the top of his desk and hands it to Detective Reams, who glances at it and places it in his pocket. "A home in Bel Air, a Beverly Hills office—my, you have come a long way, Mr. Haines."

The remark offends Cameron because he thinks Reams is saying a black man doesn't deserve that level of success. "Did I come too far from South L.A.? Farther than a black man should?"

"Oh, no, that wasn't what I was saying."

"Then what were you saying, detective?"

Reams places his coffee cup on Cameron's desk and walks out of his office and down the hallway to the front door. "Thanks for the coffee, Mr. Haines."

Sunday Morning Getaway

Detective Reams leaves the home of Cameron Haines and is back at his desk Sunday morning when Officer Daniela Salazar calls him.

"Sir, Officer Salazar here. I've got the file Ms. Kilian left for you and I'll bring it to you shortly. I'm still at her condominium building. I discovered a few surprises when I arrived to retrieve the file from her. I called for backup."

"You okay? Is Ms. Kilian okay? Why did you need backup?"

Salazar says, "When I arrived at the security desk in the lobby of her building, I asked them to call Ms. Kilian and tell her Officer Salazar was here at her request to pick up a file. The security guard said Ms. Kilian had to leave, but she left an envelope for me. I asked where she went, and he said he didn't know. I missed her by only minutes. She left the building on foot as a couple visitors were on their way up to see her."

"That's odd."

"I know. The guard said she ran out of the elevator shortly after her two guests were on their way up in the other elevator to her apartment."

"Did she leave alone?"

"Apparently so. I also spoke with the doorman. He said Ms. Kilian rushed out the front door on foot and ignored him. She looked a bit disheveled, but he said that wasn't uncommon for her at that hour of the morning."

"The visitors? Did you ask the guard who they were?"

"That's the odd part. I asked to see the names, and at first the security guard was hesitant. When I insisted, he showed me the visitor log. He started sweating and said he may need to take a break. I told him to sit down and don't move. When I looked at the visitor log, it was obvious that this building requires a copy of a driver's license and the license plate of their car or their method of arrival, plus names and signatures of each visitor before they admit them."

"Not unusual for a celebrity-filled building. So what's the problem?"

"No names, no information on these two visitors. That's the problem. When I asked the guard why he made an exception, he said one visitor pulled a gun on him and insisted that he send them both up to Ms. Kilian's apartment right away. They told him if he kept his mouth shut, there'd be a thousand dollars in an envelope for him on the way out."

"Oh, my god. Did he call 911 after the visitors got in the elevator?"

"No. He says he called Ms. Kilian immediately, told her to get in elevator number one and he'd send it up immediately. He says he told her to get in the elevator and come to the lobby right away because there were some intruders on their way up to see her. He told her one of them had a gun. He put the visitors in elevator number two and had it stop a few floors short of Ms. Kilian's floor to give her time to get out of her apartment and into elevator number one. He held the elevator car with the visitors between floors for about a minute before the visitors pushed the call button. The guard told them to sit tight and the car would begin moving shortly. When he saw Ms. Kilian run out of elevator number one in the lobby, he let the other elevator go up to Ms. Kilian's floor. She gave the guard the file to give to me, thanked him for the call, and ran out of the building."

"And even after that he didn't call 911?"

"No, says he panicked. The two men still haven't come down, so they are likely still here in the building. That's why I called for backup."

"How many patrol cars responded?"

"One's here already, two more on the way. We've got the building manager on the phone. The officers are going to Ms. Kilian's unit shortly."

"What about the other residents? Are they safe?"

"The elevators open up directly in the units. We've got both elevators shut down. The only other way out is the stairwell. We've got the ground exits covered. I have to join the officers on the search now, so I'll call you later."

"Damn. I'm on my way down there. See you soon."

Detective Reams arrives at Blair Kilian's condominium building about an hour after his phone conversation with Officer Daniela Salazar. He sees her standing out front with three LAPD patrol cars in the driveway and a crowd of onlookers on the sidewalk. Officer Salazar sees Reams walking over to her and she says, "Sorry you had to come down, detective."

"Did you get the intruders?" Reams asks.

"I'm afraid not, sir."

"What happened?"

"Shortly after I spoke with you, we went up to Ms. Kilian's apartment. No sign of them, but her place was a mess inside. They must have been looking for something, or perhaps thought she was hiding. We were in Ms. Kilian's unit for less than a minute when the building doorman came up the elevator to tell us a resident told the security desk that she saw two men coming out of the emergency exit stairwell downstairs. The guard went to check it out while he asked the doorman to come up to alert us. One officer went down the emergency stairway that opens to the pool area in the back of the building. He spoke with the resident who saw two men in suits carrying a bag run out of the stairway and hop the fence on the side of the building. We lost them, sir. I'm sorry."

"Damn," says Reams. Was it her the intruders were after, or did they want the file she wanted to give to you?"

"I don't know, sir," the officer replies.

"Did you open the envelope?"

"No, sir. I assumed you would want to do that."

"Okay, so let's go into the lobby where we can sit down and have a look."

"Yes, sir. Give me just a moment to find out when we will have fingerprints from the apartment and exit door. Someone is on their way over."

"I assume the officers are taking statements from the guard, doorman, and the resident?"

"Already on it, sir."

"Any need for me to talk with anyone at this point?"

"Leave it to us, sir. We may bring the security guard down to HQ for more questioning and to get a sketch of the visitors."

"Good. I'll meet you in the lobby."

A few minutes later, Officer Salazar joins Detective Reams sitting on a sofa in the lobby of Blair Kilian's condominium building. Reams picks up the unopened envelope, "Tell me again why Ms. Kilian asked you to come get this file?"

"She said that when we interviewed her yesterday, she didn't realize she had this file until after we left. Said she grabbed it from an entry table in Mr. Garrett's house as she was leaving. In her haste to escape Mr. Garrett, she thought it was the file with her copy of the script, so she grabbed it and placed it in her bag. When she went to get her script file from the bag last night, she realized she had picked up this file by mistake. That's when she called me and left a message for me to come get it as soon as possible."

"When did she call?"

"Very early . . . about half past midnight. It went straight to my voicemail until I got the message early this morning. That's when I called you."

Reams opens the file carefully with a pair of gloves, and places it on a coffee table in front of the sofa. He goes through each page of the payment ledger at the front of the file, the pages Alton edited to remove the actual names of the celebrities and business executives being blackmailed. Reams sweats and then squirms as if uncomfortable with what he sees. "Looks like some payment record, and a ledger of who gets what share of the payments. Did she say anything about this?"

"She said it was just financial gibberish to her, and she didn't know what it was."

Reams is silent as he goes through each page. He then comes to the unaltered pages that are copies of thousands of checks issued to Paisan Enterprises and Reid Garrett Productions from various companies. "Interesting."

Officer Salazar leans over and thumbs through several of the pages. "Whoever is being paid, that's a lot of money, sir."

"Yes, it is," Reams says. "And it goes on for years and years. I'll call Captain De La Garza in the Commercial Crimes Division. I specialize in murders and finding people who commit them. I'm not a financial whiz. They have people in their division who can do a forensic financial analysis and tell us what is likely going on here. They can also look up all these companies that are making and receiving payments."

"Why would something like that belong at Reid Garrett's house? He's an actor."

"Exactly my question. And one of our dead victims is a well-known agent and attorney, so what's with this ledger of millions of dollars in financial payments doing in the home of Mr. Garrett?"

"Do you need me for anything else, Detective? If not, I'll rejoin my partner, Officer Witkowski, and wrap things up here."

"Please get back to work, and thank you for retrieving this so quickly for me. Oh, one more thing, Officer Salazar."

"Sure, what is it?"

"Keep looking for Ms. Kilian. I'm worried she is in danger if the story the guard told you is true."

"I'm worried, too. The entire series of events on Saturday just doesn't add up. At first, they dispatch us to interview Ms. Kilian about a false 911 call that turns out to be a prank by Mr. Garrett. Hours later, there's a fire at Mr. Garrett's home. He's now dead, along with another victim. Then this file turns up the following morning and Ms. Kilian must flee two visitors with a gun. We really need to find her."

"I agree. She has no spouse or partner, right?"

"Correct."

"She is pretty well-known, so might be easy for someone to spot. I also interviewed her agent, Cameron Haines, just a few hours ago at his home. I'll notify him of what just happened here and ask him to help locate her."

As Officer Salazar is leaving, Detective Reams phones Cameron Haines, but he doesn't answer. He leaves a message on his voicemail. "Mr. Haines, this is Detective Reams, LAPD. Please call me as soon as you get this message. It's about Ms. Kilian." He then scrolls through the list of contacts on his cell phone, until he comes to the number for Captain De La Garza in the Commercial Crimes Division of the LAPD. Detective Reams stares at the number for a while but does not dial it. He turns his phone off and places the file in his briefcase.

Sunday Afternoon Liaison in the Park

On a hazy Sunday afternoon, Marina Petrovich waits on a park bench in Will Rogers Memorial Park in Beverly Hills. The park is across the street from the Beverly Hills Hotel on Sunset Boulevard. A tall man in a jogging suit with a hoodie runs up to the bench and sits next to Marina. Taking a sip of water from a thermos, he looks at Marina and smiles. "I don't get invited to meet pretty ladies on park benches often."

"Well, from what I hear, Mr. Price, you don't meet many ladies at all, on park benches or otherwise."

"Ouch. Don't believe everything you hear, Ms. Petrovich."

"Your love life, or lack of it, is the least of my worries. It's not why I asked you here."

"Then let's get to the point."

"You stole some things that don't belong to you. I want them back."

"Things that belong to you. What would those be?"

"You know, Mr. Price. They aren't yours and I need them. All of them."

"Well, first off, Ms. Petrovich, I stole nothing from you. If you asked me to meet you here on that kind of ruse, you're wasting my time. I'll be on my way."

"Wait! You liar! The files! You have Tony Campanelli's client files! I was in Tony's office last night with Detective Reams. The security camera showed Reid leaving Tony's office, but he had only a few files under his arm. After seeing Reid on the video,

Reams told me he suspected you took them."

"Suspecting and proving are two different things."

"You were already interfering with his business."

"It's a business built on extortion and blackmail. I love to interfere in criminal activity. I suspect Mr. Campanelli and Reid had a falling out."

"That's not true."

"Really? If things were so great between them, why did Reid go to his house and run him over with his car?"

"I think you're the one who did that, not Reid."

"I've got it on tape and a live witness."

"Look, you've got Tony's files and I want them back. Now."

"Oh my, I misunderstood. I thought you said I stole something from *you*. You don't look like Tony Campanelli to me."

"You know what I mean."

"Why would any of Tony's possessions belong to you? Were you secretly married? A business partner?"

"A business partner."

"I believe you worked for Mr. Campanelli. Part time. Why would anything in his possession belong to you?"

"Because there are other partners besides me."

"Really? Well, Tony's law firm lists him as the sole owner. No other partners. Same for his private investigator's business. I think you're the one trying to steal something that doesn't belong to you."

"You know he had other partners. Reid Garrett, for one. There are others."

"This is a waste of my time. If you, Mr. Garrett, or anyone else wants to stake a claim to the Campanelli estate, I suggest you hire a talented lawyer and have at it."

"You will regret not surrendering those files."

"Ms. Petrovich, what is in those files that is so valuable to you?"

"You know what's in them. Money."

"Really? Money? How could that be?"

"Mr. Price, we know who you are and how you operate. There's no point in playing games."

"You're right, Ms. Petrovich. Don't play games. You've got some serious problems, don't you?"

"What do you mean? I just want the files."

"It's a nice cash business, I'll admit. Stunning, really. I thought we had a snotty movie star who just ran an extortion and blackmail business on the side for a little extra cash. I underestimated him. Some of those celebrities are paying as much as twenty thousand dollars a month to protect their secrets. If you add up all the monthly payments from the celebrities and business executives in those files, it comes to nearly $200,000 a month. That's almost $2.5 million a year. All cash and tax free. Tony and Reid had a very profitable business venture. Illegal, but very profitable."

"You just gave yourself away. You wouldn't know those details without the client files and payment ledgers."

"That is only one of your problems. With Reid and Tony out of the picture, how will those celebrities know who to pay every month? In fact, when those celebrities learn that both of them may be dead, they'll probably celebrate!"

"Not your concern. I know how much each one pays and how they pay it."

"Oh, but that's the least important thing. You need the files with the dirty secrets. Without them, your most important assets just vanish. You can't blackmail someone without the dirt on them."

"I'm prepared to offer you a deal. I'll *buy* the files from you."

"If I sell them to you, then I become an accomplice."

"Mr. Price, I think you need to know that there are more people involved in this than just me, Tony and Reid."

"Thanks for admitting you are an accomplice. I suspected it but wasn't sure until now."

"Your word against mine."

"Not really. I've recorded every word of our conversation. I'll use it if I need to."

"You shit."

Alton stands up and prepares to jog away. "Pick your future

park dates more carefully, Ms. Petrovich."

"Go ahead. Run away. You won't get far. You might feel differently when people close to you go missing."

"I've got no one close to me." Alton places earbuds in his ears and runs away.

Marina pulls a cell phone from her pocket and dials a number. "You were right. He's got the files . . . oh, no, he won't make a deal to hand them over . . . I understand...do what you need to do." She hangs up, places the phone in her pocket, and beings walking out of the park toward Sunset Boulevard.

Thinking they may follow him, Alton jogs on a different path back to the cottage. Will Rogers Park is about two miles from Alton's cottage, and he can jog that distance in less than twenty minutes. He ran along Sunset Boulevard on the way over, but now he jogs through the residential area of Beverly Hills, south of Sunset. Weaving in and out of streets and alleys, he suspects any car he sees. While he is not sure who the other partner is or, if there is one, the connection between Campanelli, the Russian driver, and Marina Petrovich suggests the arrangement may involve Konstantin Raminsky. But this is all chump change to him, so his potential involvement would be odd. Alton tangles with a lot of undesirable characters, but Raminsky is in a different league. Being a pragmatist, Alton will not tangle with Raminsky unless he's being paid well to do it. Since no one is paying, he needs to be sure he doesn't cross paths with Raminsky. He's already planted the payment file with Blair, who should have handed it over to the LAPD by now. When it's in the hands of Detective Reams, he'll make the Raminsky connection and follow that lead. It'll take the focus away from Blair and Cameron. At least, that's Alton's plan.

Rounding the corner two blocks from the cottage, Alton sees a car parked in front. It's a dark van, like the one he has. He pulls his cell phone from his pocket and dials Rob. "Hey, it's me. I'm up the street and see a black van right in front of the cottage. Any idea who it is?"

"No, Alton. I'm home at my place. You need me?" Rob lives in the house directly behind Alton, which Alton owns and lets Rob live in.

"No. I'll disarm the alarm and hop the perimeter fence in the back in my usual spot. I just wanted to be sure I didn't startle you when I came through the backyard of your place to get to mine."

"Call me if you need me. I'm just reading. You want me to help you through the fence?"

"No, hang tight. If I've got a problem with a potential intruder, I'll lock the place up and come back through the fence to your place."

Alton turns around and jogs to the backyard of the house directly behind the cottage. A six-foot wall separates the two properties, with one foot of barbed wire on top, hidden in a hedge that grows tightly to the fence on both sides of the wall. The hedge is over twelve feet tall. There's a small metal door about two feet off the ground that Alton installed as an escape hatch from his place in the event he ever got into trouble. Well hidden, but both Rob and Alton can locate it easily. Disguised as an electrical box on the wall behind the hedge, it is only large enough to crawl through into the back of Alton's pool house. Inside the pool house, he disguised the interior door as a large safe with a combination lock on the front.

Rob spots Alton going through the backyard and through the hedge. Moments later, Alton texts Rob, "I'm in. Call you shortly."

Once inside, Alton checks his phone to be sure that the gate out front and the main house remain armed with the security system. He turns the alarm off and enters the cottage. Checking everything over inside, he goes to the front door. He can't see the van out front because of the wall and hedge in front of his circular driveway. But he sees something else: a pile of clothes is sitting in the driveway, like someone dropped a load of laundry.

Going back down the hall, he scans his retina with the security camera that opens the door to his private surveillance room. He sees the Campanelli files are still on the floor where he left them. Opening a cabinet on the wall, he retrieves the controller for the drone he keeps in the attic over the garage. Releasing a hatch in the roof by remote control, he sends the drone up over the garage and down into the driveway courtyard. He wants to inspect the pile of clothes before venturing outside to investigate. He drops the drone down close to the clothes. There's a note on top of the stack of clothes, but he can't make out the writing. Looking closer, he recognizes two fancy dresses. *Shit, those are Blair's clothes. Damn it.*

41

Dirty Laundry

Alton guides the drone away from the pile of clothes in his driveway and high over the wall separating his driveway courtyard from the street. The black van is still there, but the brake lights come on, and the engine starts. Alton has the drone drop altitude and move behind the van where he snaps a picture of the license plate. He then has the drone gain altitude and hover high above the van until he sees it pull away and drive down San Vicente towards Santa Monica Boulevard. He hits the home button, and the drone returns to its perch in the attic above the garage.

Alton leaves his surveillance room, walks down the hallway, and opens his front door. With a large laundry bag, he dons a pair of gloves and slowly examines the pile of clothes in the driveway. He reads the note first:

Return the files. All of them. And promise you made no copies. We will then return the owner of these clothes. Do it quickly, or the owner won't need clothes for where she is going. And you'll be a dead man.

Shaking his head, Alton slowly places each item of Blair's clothing in the bag. The items appear worn. The scent of cologne is strong. He sees makeup stains, lipstick, and perspiration marks. He's certain they took these clothes from a laundry bag or hamper. Not one item appears unworn. Stealing someone's laundry doesn't mean you have that person in your possession.

He lets out a sigh, temporarily relieved that Blair may be on the run but not kidnapped. Yet.

Once he is back inside, he calls Blair. It rings directly to her voicemail. He then calls Cameron, who answers almost immediately. Before Cameron can say anything, Alton interrupts him. "Cam, when is the last time you spoke with Blair?"

"Last night, why?"

"What time?"

"I dropped her off at the Mondrian Hotel. It was around six or seven o'clock."

"She's not answering her phone."

"Well, it's only Sunday afternoon. That was just last night. Maybe she's still sleeping."

"Maybe. Cam, I need you to do two things for me."

"Sure."

"Where are you?"

"At home. In fact, I just had a visitor. I was going to call you."

"Go on."

"Detective Reams was here asking a lot of questions."

"What time did he come by?"

"Woke me up about seven this morning."

"Cam, it's almost three o'clock. How long were you going to wait to call me?"

"I'm tired, Alton. Detective Reams woke me up from my sleep when he arrived. It embarrassed me. After Reams left, I went to my office to pick up some files. Reams said he may pay me a visit at the office and I, well, you know the files I wanted to get out of my office."

"I can guess. But that's been hours ago."

"When I got home, I lay down in a lounge chair by my pool and fell asleep. I left you a voicemail a couple hours ago to call me. Detective Reams left me a voicemail to call him. About Blair."

"What did he say?"

"I haven't called him back yet. I wanted to talk with you first. He was awfully nosy about Blair when we spoke this morning, so I thought he was going to ask me more questions. Crap, what's going on, Alton? Am I in trouble? Why is Reams asking me questions?"

"I'll get to that later, Cam. For now, I need you to locate Blair and let me know she's okay."

"Why? What's happened?"

"I'll explain later. Go to Blair's apartment and keep calling her while you're on your way. If she doesn't answer her phone by the time you get to her building, ask the security guard to come with you to check on her in her apartment."

"Oh my god, Alton, tell me what's up."

"Cameron, just go see if she's home but not answering her phone. Call me as soon as you're inside her apartment."

"Ok, I'll leave now, but where are you?"

"I'm at the cottage, calling my source at LAPD to see if there are any police reports. Someone dumped a pile of Blair's dirty laundry in my driveway."

"What?"

"Cam, just go! Get in your car and go see if Blair is home and just hiding out. Call me as soon as you get there. I'll see what LAPD has to say and then I'll join you."

42

Who Gets to Die?

After her meeting with Alton at Will Rogers Park, Marina waits in the lobby of the Beverly Hills Hotel. She is expecting to have a business luncheon in the Polo Lounge, but her host never shows. She waits in the lobby for over an hour before two gentlemen in dark suits arrive in the lobby and walk over to her. She recognizes them and becomes worried. They escort her outside the hotel and attempt to put her in a waiting car driven by a third man. She resists and asks to talk at the hotel, not in the car. Before she can cause a commotion at the valet stand, the two men grab her from each side and shove her in the back seat of the black Mercedes. They join her in the back seat, one on each side of her. The car speeds away.

As they leave the driveway of the hotel, the driver turns west on Sunset Boulevard, and then a quick right on Benedict Canyon Road. Marina is uncomfortable as the men on either side of her grip her arm tightly.

"Please," Marina pleads, "you're hurting me. Tell me what you're doing. Why did Alexei stand me up for lunch? He didn't even call."

The man sitting on her right grabs her chin and turns her face toward his. She knows his name to be Sergei, and he's a tough character. Mr. Raminsky hired him from the Russian Intelligence Service, as he did for many of his security employees and bodyguards. Sergei stares intently at her while squeezing her chin. "You greedy bitch!"

Marina tries to push his hand away, but he tightens it even more. "What are you saying? Greedy?"

"Greedy bitch. You were told to make a deal with Mr. Price for just *two* files. He could keep the others as a payment, a courtesy for cooperating. But *you* want them for your own greed. You fucked everything up!"

"I would give both files to you, for Mr. R. You know that. The others were of no use to you, but they were of use to me. I would pay Mr. Price with my money and deliver the payment file and the dragon file to Mr. R."

"But that didn't happen, did it? You deviated from your assignment. We heard every word, and Mr. Price also recorded it. That's very damaging. You've made a fucking mess for us."

"I'll get them. I'll get both files, I promise. Just let me go and I'll get them for you. Today."

"Too late. The payment file is already in the hands of the LAPD, so now you're worthless to us."

"What? That's impossible. Price has all the files. I'm sure of it. He admitted it."

"Shut up!" The conversation ends as the car speeds up Benedict Canyon Road toward Mulholland Boulevard.

Everyone in the car is silent, Marina perspires, and it upsets her stomach.

She pleads, "Let me fix this. I can do it. Please, just let me take care of this for you. I'm sorry."

Both men tighten their grip as the car turns right on Mulholland Boulevard, toward Laurel Canyon Drive. Marina does not know where she is being taken, but she knows it is not good. Just beyond the Mulholland Scenic overlook is a tight bend in the road known as Dead Man's Curve. It has been the scene of hundreds of accidents over many decades.

The driver slows down and pulls to the side of the road. Both men in the back seat pull Marina out of the car and wait on the side of the road. Another man standing across the street and closer to Dead Man's Curve holds his hand up, signaling to wait until he tells them to cross. A few cars go by and then it is silent.

The man across the road drops his hand and waves for them to cross. Sergei pushes Marina into the road, "Go run to him and he'll take you home. Hurry."

It shocks Marina they are letting her go. She runs across the road and a car comes from around the curve at a high speed. She hesitates, thinking the car will stop. It comes even faster, so she tries to run down the road away from the man calling to her. In just seconds, the speeding car hits her and her body flies into the air and lands in the road like a rubber doll. The car swerves after hitting her but does not stop. The man across the road runs to Sergei and the other men with him, standing outside the black Mercedes. They leap into the Mercedes and proceed east on Mulholland, away from the car that just hit Marina. Moments later, several drivers will make that curve and come to a halt to avoid hitting her body lying in the street. The LAPD arrives about fifteen minutes later and they pronounce Marina dead at the scene.

Cameron arrives at Blair's condominium building and leaves his car with the valet. Ahmed is the security guard on duty at the front desk, and he immediately recognizes Cameron. "Good afternoon, Mr. Haines."

"Hi, Ahmed. I didn't expect to see you here this early. Is Jerry on vacation? I need to see Ms. Kilian."

Ahmed bites his lip and turns his head to look at a LAPD officer sitting in the lobby. "I think you need to speak with him."

"What? Something wrong? Is Ms. Kilian ok? Why are the police here?"

"Mr. Haines, I just got here. They sent Jerry down to LAPD headquarters and called me in early to replace him. I was told to direct any inquiries about Ms. Kilian to that police officer standing by the sofa."

The LAPD officer notices the conversation at the security desk and approaches Ahmed and Cameron. "And who do we have here?" the officer asks.

"Officer, I'm Cameron Haines. Blair Kilian is my client. I'm here to see her. Anything wrong?"

"Were you here at all earlier today?"

"No sir, please tell me what's wrong. I've been trying to reach Ms. Kilian on the phone, but she isn't answering."

"And your relationship to her?"

"My relationship? I'm her agent. And friend. What's going on here?"

"Ms. Kilian is missing. Two men came here looking for her a few hours ago. She left the building before they went up to her apartment."

"What? Who was here for her?"

"We don't know. It's under investigation. The security guard tipped her off and sent an elevator up for her. He put the visitors in another elevator going up, so she escaped out the front door before they got into her apartment."

"Oh my god. That's terrible. Any ideas where she went?"

The officer can see that Cameron's eyes are tearing up. "Exactly what I was going to ask you."

Cameron's cell phone rings, and he sees it's his secretary calling. "Faye? Why are you calling me on a Sunday afternoon? Everything ok?"

"Well, I'm not sure," Faye replies.

"What do you mean?"

"Our answering service got a call from a woman who said she was with the Bel Air Patrol and there was some suspicious activity at your home. The alarm was not going off, but they wanted you to meet them there as soon as possible."

"Well, that's very odd. Why would the Bel Air Patrol call the office? For emergencies, they have my cell number and yours."

"Exactly. So, I called them, and they seemed confused. Said they would call the cars on patrol in Bel Air to see if anyone contacted you or the office. They said the alarm was on at your home, but they would send a car over to be sure nothing suspicious was happening."

"They find anything?"

"Don't know, I just called them a few minutes before calling you."

"Okay, thanks Faye. Sorry for ruining your Sunday. I'll see you back in the office tomorrow."

"No bother, Cam. Let me know if there's anything more I can do."

The police officer has been listening to Cameron's end of the conversation. "Everything okay, Mr. Haines?"

Without saying a word, Cameron walks outside to the front of the building and calls Alton. Alton answers immediately. "What's up, Cam? I'm pulling up to Blair's building right now."

"Someone tried to kidnap or kill Blair. The security guard helped her get out of her apartment before the intruders could find her. And . . . "

Alton cuts him off. "Shit, how long ago?"

"A few hours ago."

"And something may be up at my house. I need you with me."

"I'm pulling in the driveway now. Do you see me?"

"Yes, I'll get my car."

"Cam, leave your car there and meet me on Wilshire Boulevard. I'm pulling over now. If you're being followed, I'd rather the valet still have your car in case anyone asks for you. Just walk out front to the curb."

Cameron hangs up and walks to Alton's Bentley, which is waiting at the curb just outside Blair's building. "Thank God you're here, Alton. We need to get to my house right away."

"Okay, I'll get us there fast. What's happening?"

"It seems someone called my office, and it rang over to our weekend answering service. They said it was the Bel Air Patrol reporting some suspicious activity at my home and I should meet them there."

"Hmm. Sounds fishy."

"That's what Faye thought when the answering service called her. So she called Bel Air Patrol, and they knew nothing about it. Said they'd send a car to check everything out at the house, but the alarm was on and everything seemed okay."

Alton is silent for a moment. "Very crafty. That's good, I like it."

"What's crafty? Alton, you aren't making sense."

"It seems someone wants to meet with you in person, but they don't want to call your cell or contact you directly. Either they are afraid of being traced or wire-tapped, or they want to harm you with no record of them contacting you. I've used that trick many times. Usually works."

"Do you have to see a devious intent in practically every-thing, Alton?"

"I see it because it's almost always there. You know that. Buckle up and hold on."

Tantrum in Bel Air

Alton turns down Wilshire Boulevard, then makes a left on Beverly Glen Boulevard, which takes him to the main gates of Bel Air. A few minutes later, he parks a block down the street from Cameron's home. "How well do you know your neighbors, Cam?"

"Are you kidding? You know who lives on either side of me."

"Just kidding. I know I can't go through their yard gates. Here's what we'll do. You wait here in the car for ten minutes. I will go ahead of you, alongside the fence for the estate on the south side of your driveway. I know there's a tall fence with motion sensors, but it hides behind a big string of junipers. I'll hide behind the junipers and watch for you to come up your driveway. Do you have a garage door opener with you?"

"No, it's in my car."

"Ok, then when you get to the driveway, take the walkway to your front door. Don't walk too fast. I'll have my eye on you. Open the door and go inside. I'll be just a few steps behind you. If your little intruder is not hiding somewhere in the yard, then we'll see who shows up."

"Got it."

"Cam, you're trembling. Is there something you want to tell me?"

"Yes, I'm scared."

"Anything other than that?"

Cameron pauses. "No."

"Cam, don't worry. You won't get hurt."

"Not worried for me. I'm worried about Blair."

Alton leaves the car and crosses the street. It's late on Sunday afternoon, so it's still light outside. Alton stays close to the fence and shrubbery in the house next to Cam. At the corner of the property, he ducks behind the junipers to find a spot where he can see the driveway and the steps to the front door of Cameron's house. About ten minutes later, he sees Cameron strolling toward the driveway, hands in his pockets.

As Cameron goes up the driveway and turns toward the walkway to his front door, Alton sees movement to his left, coming from around Cameron's garage. It appears to be a woman wearing a scarf and a bathrobe or lounging pajamas. Cameron doesn't see her. Alton walks up behind her and pulls his gun from the holster. "Hold it, stop right there."

Cameron turns around, and so does the woman.

Alton sees the woman's face. "I'll be damned. It *is* you. I was hoping it would be. Brilliant!"

Alton is pointing his gun at Blair Kilian. Cameron runs over to join them. "Blair, what are you doing here? Is everything okay?"

Blair is angry and disheveled. It is obvious she ran out of her condominium earlier in the day before she could shower or put on any makeup. "Goddamn you both, you really messed this up. I'm furious with you."

Alton puts his gun away, "Save it, Blair, you can yell at us inside. Let's get out of the driveway."

Alton and Cameron usher her inside. Cameron is visibly upset. "Blair, tell me what's wrong. Are you okay?"

"Ask Hollywood's best fixer what's wrong. Let's start there with his big fuck up! And I need a drink . . . now."

Cameron takes Blair's arm, "I'll fix you a drink, let's go into the bar."

Blair pulls free of Cameron's arm, walks into the bar, and takes a seat. She kicks the chair next to her down on the floor and looks at Alton. "Here, asshole, this chair is for you."

Cameron steps behind the bar and makes Blair's martini. He's made hundreds for her over the years, so he knows exactly what to do. His hands are trembling, and he drops some ice cubes on the floor before they reach the martini shaker.

Blair turns her head. "Shit, Cameron. Or should I say, shit, Dad, can't you even do that right?"

Alton is standing at the bar, a few feet from Blair. "Okay, Blair, I get that I upset you. I'm sorry those goons showed up at your building. I did not believe they would implicate you. I don't know how they found out you had the file."

Picking up a silver napkin holder on the bar, Blair throws it at Alton. "Well, you goddamn well should have known, Alton! Looks like this all started out as a way for you to stop Reid from blackmailing me and Cameron. I sort of figured that out, and I know what kind of work you do. But why the fuck did you pick a fight with the Russian mob? Why? Now I'm toast because they think I gave the cops the goods on them. You can't win a fight with them, Alton. You told me to give the LAPD that payment file, so I did. I didn't even know what it was. Now I'm a target, thanks to you."

Alton holds his hands up. "Blair, let's go over all this one thing at a time. You are jumping to conclusions."

"Jumping to conclusions? You fucking kidding me!? The security desk calls me this morning to tell me two guys with guns are on the way up the elevator to see me. He tells me to get in elevator number one while he holds them for a minute between floors in elevator number two. I rush out of the building and leave the file with the security guard to give to Officer Salazar. It is what *you* wanted me to do, but now I know it was a big mistake. I ran away with what you see I'm wearing, and my cell phone. That's it. I ran as far as I could until I couldn't breathe. Then I stopped and ran the voice mail on my cell phone."

Cameron sets the martini he made for Blair in front of her. "Blair, where were you when you stopped running?"

"Some alley behind houses on Ashton Street, I think. A few blocks from my building, below Wilshire Boulevard. I don't know for sure."

"How did you get here, to my house?"

"I walked, that's how. Took me an hour, but I did it. Walked through UCLA in these damn shoes and this ridiculous outfit. Crossed Sunset Boulevard and walked right into Bel Air through the main gate. Got stopped twice by people asking if I was okay, and one who said they were calling the cops. Do you know what it's like walking through Bel Air dressed like this? No fucking sidewalks. Thank God I remembered where your house is, Cam."

"Why didn't you call me? Why the odd message with Bel Air Patrol? I assume that was you?"

"Thank God you got the message and came here with no one but Alton. After I listened to the voicemail, I knew I was toast, and they might track me with my phone or listen to my conversations. I called your answering service with that phony message from Bel Air patrol, then smashed my cell phone with a rock and tossed it in a dumpster behind a building on the UCLA campus. Then I took off running."

Alton moves closer to the bar to address Blair. "You did the smart thing, Blair. Luring us here with the phony Bel Air Patrol call was the perfect thing to do."

"Well, I'm glad one of us did something right today." Blair takes a big gulp from her martini, finishing nearly all of it. "I'll need another of these in just about five minutes, Cam."

"Do you remember what was on the voicemail? The voice, the message?" Alton asks.

"Alton, I'm not an idiot. I remember. Raspy voice, Russian accent so strong I could barely understand him. He was mad I had fled from my building and said to tell my friend Mr. Price to return the file tonight, or else they'll find me, and I'll die. He said you'll die, too. Said they're looking for me, so they must have called a few minutes after finding my apartment empty. Then he said something about how no one lives after crossing the Russian brava or bravado or something like that. It was a word I didn't understand. I think it was a Russian word, but I don't remember it."

"*Bratva?* Was the word 'bratva'?"

"That's it! Now I remember. It had 'bra' in it, but I thought it was 'brava.' But yes, it was 'bratva.' He had a heavy emphasis on the 't' when he spoke. Does it mean mafia?"

"Means 'brotherhood' in Russian, but same thing as mafia or a crime syndicate."

"That's what I thought. Alton, how did they get messed up in this deal with Reid blackmailing Cameron and trying to blackmail me?"

Alton picks up the chair Blair threw on the floor and moves it closer to the bar. He takes a seat while Cameron is making a second martini for Blair. "It was a surprise to me, Blair. And I don't like surprises. I thought we had a conceited pretty-boy actor who liked the thrill of blackmailing a few celebrities. Turns out he was blackmailing about sixty celebrities, producers, business executives, and a very senior minister of a local megachurch. Cameron here was a victim, and you were to be the newest victim. Besides all of that, his agent and attorney, Tony Campanelli, was his accomplice in most of the schemes. That part I already knew, but I did not realize that the blackmail and extortion list included so many people."

Alton continued: "Since all the payments were in cash, Tony and Reid would draw suspicion if they were depositing hundreds of thousands of dollars a month in a bank account. They needed someone to take the cash off their hands and write checks to them from legitimate businesses. Classic money laundering. Simple as that. Nothing glamorous or unusual. Unfortunately, Campanelli selected a prominent member of the California Russian mob to do the money laundering for him . . . or at least that's what I'm thinking. Otherwise, there's no reason for someone like Raminsky to get involved in something this insignificant."

"Why did Tony involve them? Aren't there people that launder money who have a lower profile?"

"Yes, many of them. It's a mystery to me why they brought in Raminsky or one of his minions to handle it. I have a feeling it was to provide insurance that Reid wouldn't try to screw Campanelli, for fear of who's laundering their money. That's my guess, but I'm not sure. We've got a problem. Or, I should say, I've got a problem. My primary goal is to protect you and Cam. Then

I can see how to wrap all of this up."

Blair smirks. "Make it all go away. Isn't that your motto, Alton? That's your reputation. Except in my case. For me, it wasn't making it all go away, but making it worse than it was to begin with."

No one says anything as Cameron and Alton watch Blair quickly down her second martini. She slams her glass down on the bar. "Another."

Before Cameron can pick up the glass, there's a chime from a speaker on the wall. Cameron looks at Alton, "That chime means someone has driven a car or walked across the entry gate at the driveway."

"Do you have a camera at your front door?"

"Yes."

"Show me."

Alton and Cameron walk to the video screen in the hallway that has images from six outdoor cameras. Cameron points to the video feed from the front door camera. Alton looks closely. "Reams. It's Detective Reams. Let me handle this."

44

More Broken Than Fixed

Cameron opens his front door to see Detective Reams standing on his doorstep. It surprises him to see he's alone. "Good Evening, detective. May I help you?"

"I'm counting on it. May I come in?"

"Sure."

Upon entering, Detective Reams sees Alton standing a few feet away in the hallway. Alton extends his hand, "Good afternoon, detective. I'm Alton Price."

Beaming, Detective Reams grasps Alton's hand. "Ah, the enigma emerges."

Alton frowns. "Have we met?"

"No, but I've seen your handiwork, or should I say nasty work, for years. You're a clever man."

Alton smiles.

Reams continues. "May I ask what you are doing here, Mr. Price? What's your connection to Mr. Haines?"

"I think you know the answer to both questions."

Before Detective Reams can reply, Blair yells out, "Where the fuck is my drink, Cam?"

It embarrasses Cameron. "Forgive me, detective, that's my other guest."

"Who is your other guest?"

"Blair Kilian, the actress."

"What a coincidence! That's exactly why I am here to see you, Mr. Haines. I was hoping you could help us find Ms. Kilian, but now it looks like we solved that problem. Where is she?"

"She's down the hallway in the bar off the living room."

Blair yells out again for her drink. Detective Reams smiles. "Sounds like she's thirsty. Who else is here?"

Cameron points down the hallway and closes the front door. "No one else. Why don't you and Mr. Price go to my study? I'll join you after I take care of Ms. Kilian."

"Oh no, I'd like to meet her."

"Detective, she's . . . indisposed."

"Exactly why I want to meet her! Doesn't sound indisposed to me. Sounds like she's having a good time."

Alton and Cameron escort Detective Reams to the bar where Blair is holding up her empty martini glass. "Fix me another one while I meet your guest."

"Ms. Kilian, I'm Detective Ed Reams, LAPD, homicide."

"That's a mouthful," she replies. "Say it again. Slower."

"Name is Ed Reams. I work in homicide for the Los Angeles Police Department."

"That's better. Want a drink?"

"I'd love to, but I'm on the clock. I'm a fan of yours. It's nice to meet you."

Blair smiles, "Well, I knew I really liked you from the moment you walked in!"

"Glad to hear it. I'm surprised, but grateful, to find you here."

"Sorry about the way I look. Not about being drunk, but about the way I'm dressed."

"From what I understand, you had a rough morning."

"That's why I'm drinking."

"Your building manager was a little late calling the police, but LAPD has been over there for the last few hours investigating a report about your kidnapping."

"They tried. But I got away, as you can see."

"Do you know who tried to kidnap you?"

Alton and Cameron look at each other, both worried about what Blair will say. Neither says a word, but Blair notices their glare. "No."

"No suspects at all?"

"No. I never saw them."

Detective Reams scratches his forehead. "Do you think it had anything to do with the file you left for Officer Salazar?"

"I don't know, detective."

Everyone is silent. Blair continues to enjoy her third martini as Alton speaks up. "Gentlemen, I suggest we let Blair relax a bit. She's had a stressful day. Let's go into Cameron's study and resume our discussion."

"Good idea, Mr. Price," responds Reams. "Now that I know Ms. Kilian is safe, I'd like a few words with you. Alone."

Without another word, Alton and Detective Reams walk into Cameron's study and Alton closes the door.

"I'll get to the point, Mr. Price. I'm not through investigating the fire at Mr. Garrett's home and the two deaths. Not sure what was going on, and what your involvement may or may not have been. But for now, we've got something far more serious to contend with. I think you know what I'm talking about."

"Tell me."

"Do I really need to tell you?"

"Yes. I'm not a mind reader."

"Really? I thought you were a miracle worker. Best fixer in town. You can't read minds too?"

Alton is silent.

Reams sits down in a chair opposite Cameron's desk. "Whatever you were up to, I can't imagine you purposely picked a fight with the Russian mob. Am I right?"

"I'm not sure what your definition is of picking a fight, but I would hope that doesn't include exposing a crime?"

"Is that what you call it? That's the reason you arranged for that file to find its way to me? The one Ms. Kilian gave to Officer Salazar? Was it exposing a crime or sent to me as a diversion?"

"If it exposes a crime, what else matters?"

"Mr. Price, from this point on the rest of this conversation never happened."

Alton nods his head.

"Are you wired? Your LAPD file says you record nearly all your conversations. Are you recording this one?"

"I am not."

"Good. I'll take your word for it. Your LAPD file makes for interesting reading, Mr. Price. It was so popular internally that we had to restrict access to it."

"Really? It's secret?"

"Not secret. It was a source of entertainment for many of our law enforcement staff. Like a spy and sex novel. Hard to put down. Now they restrict access so it can't be recreational reading by police officers, detectives and staff."

"I'm flattered."

"Don't be. A career of hiding crime and destructive behavior by spoiled people isn't something I'd be proud of. Here's your problem, Mr. Price. The man you are trying to finger in those money laundering schemes is already under surveillance. By the FBI."

"So? The LAPD works with the FBI on lots of cases."

"True. But not the cases on active supervision by the Department of the Treasury *and* the FBI."

"Treasury is involved because of the money laundering aspect. I get it."

"And other things. The LAPD will assist as needed, but we've had a hands-off policy on Raminsky for almost two years. I can't tell you any more than that."

"You won't do anything with the file I gave you?"

"No. When the Commercial Crimes Unit at LAPD identified the companies controlled by Mr. Raminsky and his affiliates, we delivered the file to the FBI. The money laundering is nothing new and FBI and Treasury are already on it. The minor part you discovered is almost insignificant in the overall scheme of things with Raminsky. I'm sure it will end up on the bottom of the stack of Raminsky misdeeds. Sorry, Mr. Price. You didn't find a blockbuster."

"That's it? You do nothing?"

"Out of my hands, unless *you* care to do something about him."

"Me? Kill Raminsky? I don't do good deeds for free. I get paid for that work. Eliminating him would be a risky and expensive kill."

"Thought that was your specialty. Too bad."

"Nothing you can do to protect the safety of Ms. Kilian?"

"I'm afraid that's your problem, Mr. Price. If something happens, then we would enforce the law. But I hope you won't let it come to that. Don't let her end up like Ms. Petrovich."

Alton thinks for a moment before answering. "You mean Marina Petrovich? I assume that's her full name. Same person?"

"Yes, but she's dead. Hit and run at Dead Man's Curve on Mulholland Drive a few hours ago."

"Shit, I knew she was in over her head."

"Well, Mr. Price, I will be on my way." At that, Reams stands to leave.

"That was a bleak visit, Detective Reams. No good news on anything."

"Oh, I almost forgot. I have one bit of good news for you," says Reams as he returns to his seat.

"I'm all ears."

"The Sackalow file I presume you left for me to discover in Mr. Campanelli's office? The connection between Mr. Garrett and Mr. Campanelli in the blackmail of Ms. Sackalow is clear. The good news is, if either of them ends up alive, we will prosecute. But I doubt that will be the case."

"Then Cameron and Ms. Kilian are in the clear?"

"My team is still wrapping it up. Some questions we'd like answered, but unless there are any surprises, like Mr. Garrett being able to talk, then we're done. You haven't left us much to deal with, have you? But then, I know that's your specialty."

"Campanelli? Was he the other body at Reid's house or not?"

"Oh, come now, Mr. Price, don't be coy. You know everything about the two dead bodies at the morgue. The County Coroner is going to finish his identification tonight or tomorrow morning, but you already know the answers, don't you?"

"I'm not worried about the bodies at the morgue. I'm worried about the safety of Ms. Kilian."

"As well you should. Whatever scheme you cooked up for

Campanelli and Garrett looks like it worked well for you, except for the Raminsky blunder. You didn't need it to throw me off the scent. It was overkill. I've seen your handiwork for years, and all magicians ultimately make a mistake, don't they? If you've made another mistake besides the Raminsky blunder, I'll find it. On this case, or the next one, or the next one after that. Your magic won't last forever, Mr. Price, and when it runs out, I'll be there for your last act."

"Goodbye, Detective Reams. It was nice to meet you after all these years. And don't be too righteous. I assume you're ignoring the murder of Marina Petrovich, so you don't agitate Raminsky over a petty little murder. You and the FBI are waiting for the big stuff. A dead woman is not big stuff, is it, Detective Reams? The victims in my schemes are people who *deserve* punishment. Can you sleep at night knowing you punish the *right* people? I doubt it."

Damn the Files

After Detective Reams departs, Alton joins Cameron and Blair in the bar. Blair is asleep, slumped over the bar with her head resting on her arms. Cameron is sitting in a chair next to her, monitoring Blair so she doesn't fall off her chair. He sees that Alton has returned. Cameron asks, "Everything okay? Is he gone?"

Alton replies, "Yes, to both. He's a liar."

"What? I didn't like him much either, but why do you call him a liar?"

"He's giving me a message to stay away from Raminsky. That everything I gave them is worthless because it's just small stuff. I don't buy it. He's protecting him. Or someone else."

"Alton, what about Blair? Will she be safe now?"

"We'll talk about that in a minute. How long has she been asleep?"

"Just a few minutes."

"Did you make her three or four martinis?"

"Three."

"Only three? Not like her to pass out after just three."

"She's had a stressful day. I doubt she's had that much exercise in years."

Alton grins. "Yep, that trek from Wilshire Boulevard to Bel Air is probably the longest walk she's ever had. Thank God she made it here. Cam, she can't go home, at least not for a while. I'd love to take her to my cottage, but I'm also a target now, so that's out of the question. Can you work from home for a day or two and keep her here?"

"I'd do anything to keep her safe, Alton. She's my daughter. I love her."

"I can send Oksana over here to be sure we protect you."

"Oh Alton, please don't, she's so annoying and obtrusive."

"True, but she's great with a gun, hates corrupt Russians and still has a chip on her shoulder. If anyone tries to harm you or Blair, she's the best protection you can have until the police arrive. Maybe even better than the police."

Cameron shakes his head, "I know you're right, but the thought of her living here for a couple days is dismal."

"I know. Just be sure you have lots of cheap vodka and food. And snacks."

"I know the story, Alton. I'll have my housekeeper take care of that first thing tomorrow morning."

"Great. I'll ask Oksana to come over here tonight after dark. She'll text you something in gibberish. When she does, just meet her at your side garage door. It'll be dark, and she'll have walked over here at least three blocks to avoid having a car in your driveway. Once she's here, let her handle everything. Don't tell anyone Blair is here—not even your housekeeper."

Cameron nods.

"I'm heading off, Cam. Stay safe. I'll be in touch. Keep Blair inside, away from the windows. They must not see her."

Alton walks down the street to his car, careful to keep an eye out for anybody watching him. Once inside his car, Alton places a call to Oksana, giving her instructions about looking after Cameron and Blair. He then places a call to Rob. "Hey Rob, I'll be avoiding the cottage for a bit, but I've got to retrieve something right away."

"Let me get it for you, boss. I can go through the door in the backyard of my house to your pool house."

"Won't work. What I need to give you is in my surveillance room. I have to scan my retina before the door will open."

"Must be important. You never use that room to hide things."

"It is. So, here's the deal. I will park a few blocks away. As soon as the sun goes down, I will go through your backyard to the secret gate to my pool house. You stay put. I'll make a brief trip to my surveillance room, leave through the pool house door to your yard, and set the alarm from there. I'll text you, and then you come into the backyard. You'll find me in the bushes near the metal door in the wall to my pool house. I'll wait there for you."

"Got it, boss."

"Stay there until you hear from me." Alton hangs up before Rob can ask questions.

About thirty minutes later, Alton is crawling through the backyard of Rob's house to the hidden door in the wall separating their two homes. He enters the alarm code, then the combination to the steel door. The door opens to a very narrow and short passage leading to another door at the end. Alton crawls through the passage and opens the second door inside the pool house in his backyard. Walking out of the pool house, he proceeds across the pool patio to the main cottage. It's dark and Alton doesn't want to turn on any lights until he's in the surveillance room. He scans his retina on the scanner outside the steel door to the surveillance room, and the door slides open.

Closing the door behind him, Alton turns on the lights since no windows are in that room. Retrieving a large steel file box from the closet, he uses his phone to photograph the opening pages of twelve of the client files with the blackmail information. He then photographs several pages of the original payment file, the one with the client names and all the payment details. The payment file he gave to Blair for Officer Salazar had all the names of the celebrities eliminated, so the police, or anyone else, couldn't identify the names of the blackmail and extortion victims.

Alton had stored the original file for safekeeping, but now he has a creative idea how to use it since Detective Reams shoved the Raminsky connection under the rug. After he finishes photographing the payment file pages, he places all sixty of the client blackmail files from Campanelli's office inside the steel box and closes the lid. Attached to the lid is another metal box about the size of a battery pack. A square push button combination lock sits on top. The thickness of the smaller metal box conceals an explosive device that detonates if they enter the combination code incorrectly more than twice. He places the original payment file with all the names in a separate envelope.

Alton opens his safe and grabs the file with the Chinese character on it. Taking the metal file box and the envelope and file, he leaves the surveillance room and heads down the hallway to the living room. Checking the iPad on the counter in the living room, he sees that the infrared sensors around his property are not detecting any movement or heat generated by a human body.

Leaving the living room, Alton enters the pool house and uses the combination lock on the metal door leading to the passageway to the backyard of Rob's house. Once through the passageway, he locks the outside metal door on the wall between the two houses and turns on the alarm system for the cottage and pool house. He then texts Rob to meet him where he told him in the backyard. Alton waits about five minutes, but Rob doesn't appear in the backyard. He texts him again. No response. *Shit, what's up with Rob?*

Realizing that something must be wrong, Alton opens the metal door in the wall to the pool house and stashes the metal file box, envelope, and Chinese file just inside the passageway. He closes the door and emerges from the bushes. No one is in sight in the backyard. Some lights are on in Rob's house, but Alton detects no signs of activity.

Alton drifts toward the back of the house. He reaches the back patio and a large sliding door to the living room. The door is ajar and the furniture in the living room shows signs of a struggle. Taking his gun from the shoulder holster, he follows a trail of blood across the carpet to the tile by the front door. He sees a note taped on the back of the front door along with a handprint made from blood. There's a telephone number scrawled in blood next to the bloody handprint. Alton lets out a sigh. *Crap, they've got Rob.*

46

Homage to the Playboy Mansion

Alton rips the bloody note off the front door and runs back to the living room, then to the two bedrooms and bathrooms, and then a quick look at the kitchen. Gun still drawn, he wants to be sure no one is in the house. He sees no signs of any struggle except in the living room and the hallway. They dragged Rob to the front door and left after posting the note. He doesn't smell gunpowder, so he's guessing the blood is from a flesh wound, a knife, or a bloody nose. He suspects the latter, since the nose bleeds so profusely and he's seeing a lot of blood. At least he hopes that's what it's from, and not something more serious.

Before he leaves, Alton opens a drawer in the kitchen and grabs a set of keys and a garage door opener. The house Alton lets Rob live in has a two-car garage. Rob keeps his car in the garage, along with one of Alton's hobby cars, a 1961 Mercedes 300SL Roadster. It's red, with a white interior and red piping. Alton hates the thought of taking it out tonight for a business mission, but he doesn't want to return to his car parked down the street.

With the keys and the garage door opener in hand, he leaves through the sliding door on the back patio and runs around the side of the house to the front corner where the garage is. The street is quiet except for a boyish-looking man walking two dogs. As soon as the man passes the driveway, Alton uses the clicker to open the garage door. Without moving, he watches both directions for anyone approaching. Still quiet, he slowly enters the garage, takes the cover off the Mercedes, and opens the driver's door. It takes a few turns of the key and some gentle pumping of the gas pedal, but then the engine lets out a familiar roar.

Lights off, Alton drives toward the street and closes the garage door before he drives in the opposite direction of where he parked his car. He heads down to Santa Monica Boulevard, then up Doheny to Sunset Boulevard. He stops at the convenience store just east of Doheny on Sunset Boulevard and buys a prepaid phone. Alton is eager to call the phone number scrawled on the note in blood but won't use his own phone for that purpose. A sophisticated criminal like Raminsky or his minions may have tracking capabilities once you make a call to that number from any mobile phone, so the disposable pre-paid phone will be perfect to make the call.

Traveling west on Sunset Boulevard toward Beverly Hills, Alton phones the number on the bloody note. Someone picks up the phone immediately but says nothing. Alton remains silent, and then a raspy voice asks, "Who are you?"

"That's what *I* want to know. Who are *you?*"

"You got our colorful note?"

"The one scrawled in blood? Yes. Where is my friend you kidnapped?"

"You have something that doesn't belong to you."

"I could say the same thing. Get to the point."

"You have a file. We want it—the original. You know which one."

"Who wants it?"

"Doesn't matter. We get the file, or your friend disappears."

"Like what you did to Marina Petrovich? You tell Raminsky I want to meet with him."

"I don't know that name."

"Bullshit. The original file is being held by a lawyer with instructions to take it directly to the FBI if he does not hear from me *and* Rob within three hours. Plus, I've inserted some pictures of the blackmail evidence from six of the client files—the ones that are most damning. I'll show them to Mr. Raminsky when we meet. I'm going to the same bench in Will Rogers Park where I met Ms. Petrovich this morning. I'll be there in forty-five minutes. If Raminsky is not there, these files all go to the FBI."

Alton hangs up, throws the prepaid phone out the window, and keeps driving down Sunset until he takes a left on Charing Cross Road in Holmby Hills. He drives past the former Playboy mansion and thinks back to some wild parties he attended at the mansion years ago. He remembers, *That was a vastly different time.*

Alton turns down Mapleton Drive and then pulls over on a side street behind a very imposing mansion. The side street has access to the service entrance for the tennis courts and an enormous party yard in the back of the property. Originally built by a self-obsessed celebrity, today the neighbors call it the Hermitage. Actually it's the Raminsky estate, but the locals never use his name in public. The Hermitage is a state museum in St. Petersburg, Russia. When Raminsky quietly bought this estate under another name, the Los Angeles press nicknamed it The Hermitage after neighbors reported truckloads of classic art from Russia being unloaded in the large circular driveway. They took the elaborate pieces inside one at a time.

Alton takes a small duffel bag from under his seat. He refers to this duffle bag as his "bag of mischief" because it contains some sophisticated equipment that he "borrowed" from the CIA when he left. He pulls out a device about the size of a cigar, clicks on a button, and points the device toward the gate. He then points it toward the fence, then along the road, and into the tall trees at the back. Several colored lights illuminate at the tip of the device. Alton looks at them closely. *Shit, electric fence, infrared scanners.* Putting the device back in the duffel bag, he whispers to himself, "When they lock up the place like Fort Knox, just use the front door."

Turning his car around, he returns to Mapleton Drive and pulls up to the mammoth metal gates at the driveway. He knows the staff will be armed, but a few of them should be on their way to Will Rogers Park. Alton meant that purely as a diversion, knowing they'd never bring Raminsky to a public place like that on a dark, moonless Sunday night. If Raminsky is in town, he's certain to be home.

A camera on the wall next to the gate turns toward Alton's car and a bright light comes on. A voice comes over the intercom, "Who are you and why are your here?"

"Alton Price. I'm here to meet with the man who wants a file I have."

The silence that follows makes Alton nervous. After about a minute, the voice tells him to get out of his car and leave it there. One of the two mammoth gates opens and three men in suits appear in the driveway about thirty feet away. One of them motions for Alton to walk over, and he points to a spot in the driveway. "Stand there."

Alton walks to the spot, and one man approaches with an empty canvas bag. "Everything in here. Guns, devices, wallet. Everything."

Slowly emptying his pockets and removing his shoulder holster and Beretta pistol, Alton places everything in the bag, including his cufflinks. One is a recording device these guys will be certain to find if Alton keeps it on.

As the man pulls the canvas bag away from him, Alton feels a hood pushed over his head, smells something sweet and passes out.

Risen from the Ashes

A strong whiff of amyl nitrate jolts Alton awake. Nauseated, dizzy, and his vision blurry, he can't make out the male figures staring at him from across a large table. It looks like three men, all in suits. Alton is sitting in a chair, hands cuffed to the armrests. Someone from behind him sets a glass of water on the table and unlocks the cuffs on his right hand. The voice of a man standing behind Alton addresses the others across the table. "We searched his car. No files."

Alton tries to turn his head to see who is speaking, but two hands grab his head from behind and turn it away. He drinks the water and tries to focus his eyes. One man across the table speaks up, but Alton still can't focus. "You just can't take a hint, can you, Mr. Price?"

The voice is familiar to Alton. It sounds like Detective Reams, but Alton tells himself that can't be possible. "I'm sorry, I can hear you, but my vision is not clear enough to recognize you sitting that far away. Who are you?"

The man speaks again, "So maybe the magician is out of tricks? Like Houdini? You too will die from your last illusion, just like him?"

Alton grins, "Houdini didn't die from one of his tricks. That's a myth. He died from a burst appendix. On Halloween. You should know that, Detective Reams."

"I thought you said you couldn't see me?"

"Don't need to. I recognize your voice. It's only been a few hours since we spoke."

"True. Exactly what *are* you doing here, Mr. Price?"

"I ask the same question of you. How is it an LAPD detective is here in the home of Konstantin Raminsky?"

"I just told you a few hours ago to drop this matter. Nothing for you to see, and you need to forget it. And then you barge in here and stir up a bunch of trouble."

"How inconvenient for you. Why do I find you here, and where is Rob? Don't tell me you know nothing about that. And who are your friends? I can see them more clearly now and they don't look like LAPD officers."

"Mr. Price, where are *all* the original files you took from Mr. Campanelli's office?"

"You have the payment file. We just discussed that a few hours ago. You already have it."

"You altered it. It's not the original file. At least not all of it. And you have all the other files we want."

"With Reid Garrett out of the picture, you plan to take over his extortion business?"

"Oh, Mr. Garrett is not out of the picture. Not at all."

"What? He's dead."

"Really? And why would you think he is dead, Mr. Price? Is there something you want to tell me?"

Alton hesitates for a moment. "The fire. You're telling me he survived the fire at his house?"

Reams laughs and takes a cigarette and lighter from his vest pocket. After he lights his cigarette, he leaves the flame burning on his lighter. "Fires are funny things, Mr. Price. When a fire consumes a human body, it makes identification difficult. Sometimes impossible, especially with the drugs and alcohol inside those two bodies on the couch. Completely incinerated beyond recognition."

"Dental records usually do the trick, detective, but you know that."

"True, but that's not a worry here. The coroner will confirm the identities of both bodies at a press conference tomorrow morning. It will thrill Mr. Garrett's fans to know he is alive."

"Alive? Where has he been?"

"Hiding. For his own safety."

"Hiding from who?"

"Perhaps you, Mr. Price. Whoever was trying to kill him. He's very frightened, but very much alive. His fans will rejoice at the news."

"I imagine his blackmail and extortion victims won't be too pleased with that surprise, since they presumed him dead."

"You know the press, always making mistakes. Just like you, Mr. Price."

The news about Reid stuns Alton, but he knows it can't be true. Reid was on the sofa with Campanelli before Alton lit the fire. That's a fact. If Reams has gotten the coroner to declare otherwise, then the fix is in. "What about Campanelli? Is he alive too?"

"Sadly, no. He's dead, as is Reid's brother, Landon. Oh, did you know Reid had a twin brother? I'll just bet you did, didn't you?"

Alton smiles and shakes his head. "Everything works out splendidly for you, Detective Reams."

"Now, about those files. I need them. All of them."

"Exactly. And I finally know why they are so important. How long was I unconscious?"

Reams looks at his watch, "Just long enough to bring you up here and to search your car. About thirty minutes. Why?"

"Because we have only about two hours to make a deal before those files end up at the FBI."

"And how could that be, Mr. Price?"

"My buddy at the CIA knows I was coming here, but he doesn't know why. If I don't show up at my cottage with Rob in a little more than an hour, he's promised to turn over the box of files I gave him to the FBI."

"You're bluffing."

"Try me. You know I used to work at the CIA."

"We know that. Can't say you left under the best of terms."

"Exactly. That's why they know to take me seriously."

"How can I get those files here, immediately?"

"Release me and Rob. Let me drive home in my car. Guarantee our safety and we forget everything. I will deliver all the files to you in a safe setting. The FBI won't ever see them."

"That's it? You refused to give them to Ms. Petrovich, and you don't have them with you now, so why the sudden change?" asks Reams.

"I want Rob back, that's what's changed. I also figured out what you're up to, and I want no part of it. I hadn't figured it out when I met with Ms. Petrovich. But now I know. Returning the files to you turns my stomach, but it's a battle I need not fight."

"You mean one you *can't* fight."

Alton shrugs. "Doesn't matter, does it? You get your files back and I get insurance that you forget all about me and my clients."

"Really? And how will that work?"

"Give me Rob. You can track me to be certain I'm not splitting. I'll deliver all the files to you at the studio."

"What studio?"

"Oh, come now, detective. The studio headed by one of your other victims. I've seen the file. His nickname is Hollywood Rex. A soundstage at the studio is a safe setting for the handoff. And it's more your turf than mine."

Reams is silent for a moment. "Why don't we just kill you now and find the files on our own?"

"Because you can't risk it. You'll never find them before they end up at the FBI. I know what you're up to. I figured it out. It will thrill the FBI to get the files, especially since they not only involve extortion and blackmail, but domestic espionage. I didn't fall for your story about Raminsky. You were just trying to throw me off the trail—*your* trail. All roads now lead to you, detective. Another corrupt cop."

Reams leaps out of his chair. "Enough! You've said enough! Everyone waits here. Nobody leaves." Reams lights another cigarette and steps outside to a balcony where he places a call on his cell phone. Alton cannot make out what Reams is saying, but he is yelling at someone.

Alton feels someone slap the base of his neck and turns his head to see the man standing behind him. "Well, I'll be damned," says Alton.

The man Alton now recognizes punches his face, sending Alton and his chair to the floor.

Pull Back the Curtain

Detective Reams opens the doors from the balcony to step back inside the room. His face is red and perspiring. He sees Alton still lying on the floor with his chair toppled over. "I see you've met Mr. Garrett. Reid, please put Mr. Price upright in his chair."

Two men lift Alton and his chair off the floor and place them at the table. Reid looks on—but it's not Reid. It's Landon posing as Reid. "Creative switch, Detective Reams," Alton says. "Amazing how Mr. Garrett has risen from the dead."

"As I understand it, this was originally your idea," Reams replies. "Brilliant. No one will know the difference."

Alton turns his head to face Landon. "So how long have you been on the other team? From the beginning, or just after Reams offered you a better deal than Reid?"

Landon smirks. "It seems I'm quite popular. I just keep getting better offers."

Alton turns his head back to Reams, who now sits across the table. "So I presume that Reid and Campanelli became a handful to deal with. Or did you just redo the math and figure out how much more of the extortion money you would make with them both out of the picture?"

"I don't think that's any of your business. Let's get back to the files."

"Oh, let's save that for just a minute or two. Maybe it's better we just chat here long enough to run out the clock so my buddy gets the files to the FBI. You're going to kill me anyway because

I know too much, so if that's the case, I'd rather die knowing you'll spend the rest of your life in jail."

"My, aren't we getting dramatic? Do you really think you know *everything?*"

"I know that you are the 'R' in the payment file. Not Raminsky. That was just a bluff."

"That was an easy conclusion."

"Yes, especially since you and Campanelli worked closely together to dig up dirt on celebrities. Your access to police files and arrest records helped a great deal, I'm sure. I also figured out your little spy network at the studio. Blaise Armitage, studio chief. King of Hollywood. Hollywood Rex. What a bullshit cover for a Chinese spy. Damn, it was right there in front of me in those files and I missed it. I was so busy feeling sorry for these spoiled actors and actresses being blackmailed that I assumed the studio head, Blaise Armitage, was just another of your extortion victims. He's been making some hefty payments. How stupid, but now I know.

The Raminsky connection is slim. You're using it as a diversion. I suspect Raminsky is helping you out on laundering the money through Moscow. The Nicolai character makes that clear, although it's such chump change to Raminsky, I think a missing piece is still out there. Otherwise, the smoke screen is brilliant, and it worked, but now I have it all figured out . . . or most of it."

Reams stands up, visibly stunned. "Shut up! Shut your mouth right now. You've already said too much. Bastard! You don't understand what you are saying."

"Oh, yes, I do. Let's start with this place where we are sitting. The Hermitage? An invented name to make it look like Raminsky was the man behind all of this. Armitage is using him. Raminsky, one of the biggest thugs in the California Russian mob, is being used by the real Moscow and China connection. He's a double agent. The studio is owned by a Chinese conglomerate, and they sent Armitage here to look after their interests. And to provide cover for Chinese spies posing as studio employees going back and forth between China and Hollywood."

Alton draws a deep breath and then continues: "But Armitage got greedy. Seems he was doing a little double agent work for the Russians. You figured it out, and now you're blackmailing him, too. You're a clever man, Detective Reams. You look like a rumpled old LAPD detective, but that's just a convenient cover for you, isn't it? I'll bet a closet full of Armani suits is tucked away at home, and a couple fancy houses you own in a phony name or two. So Reid was just a minion; he wasn't clever enough to invent all of this. Just a willing participant driven by greed and his love of bullying people."

Reams walks over toward Alton and points his finger. "You'd better stop right there. You've already said enough for us to kill you."

"But you can't do that, can you? You know I'm not bluffing about the files going to the FBI if I don't return home in about forty-five minutes."

Reams lights another cigarette. "Go. Now. But your buddy isn't going with you. We will swap him out with you when we get the files."

Alton shakes his head no. "No way. Then we just sit here for another forty-five minutes and we don't have to worry about those damn files anymore."

Everyone is silent as Reams paces the floor. A cell phone goes off, and one of the men in suits retrieves it from his pocket. After listening to the caller for a few seconds, he hands the phone off to Reams, who listens for ten seconds before throwing the phone against the wall. "Goddamn you, Price, you killed one of my men!"

"That's quite impossible since I've been sitting here with you."

"The big Russian gal who's apparently guarding the home of Mr. Haines. She just shot and killed the man I sent to retrieve Haines and Kilian."

"Retrieve? You mean *kidnap*? Now you're adding attempted kidnapping and homicide to your extortion and blackmail activities? Stupid move on your part. If your man harmed Blair or Cameron, I will kill you with my bare hands."

"They're not harmed, but now they've left with your Russian

bimbo. This is getting out of hand, Mr. Price."

"Was he a cop? The guy Oksana shot—was he a cop? A crooked cop?"

Reams ignores Alton and points to one of his men. "Get his buddy and put both in Mr. Price's car. Get them out of here now."

The man approaches Alton, releases the handcuffs, and escorts him out of the room. Landon gives Alton a crooked smile.

Reams yells out to Alton, "Arrange that file swap, Mr. Price. You know how to reach me. Let's get this over with as soon as possible. You've seriously fucked this up."

Alton walks down a long stairway and out the front of the house. Reams' men hand him a plastic bag with his phone, cufflinks and pistol. His car is waiting. Rob sits in the passenger seat, his nose bandaged and bloody. Alton gives him a smile. "You had me scared. That won't happen again."

Russian Roulette

As soon as they escort Alton out of the room, Detective Reams motions for the two men in suits and Landon to sit down at the table. He focuses his glare on Alexei. "What the fuck is going on? How is he finding out all this information? We have no choice but to kill him right after we get the files."

Alexei wipes his forehead. "He's got the files, sir. It doesn't take much to put it all together."

Reams lights another cigarette. "I thought we agreed that Ms. Petrovich was the problem. She knew too much about what was going on because Campanelli must have told her. That's why you arranged the unfortunate accident on Mulholland. Are you telling me now that she wasn't the source?"

"During her brief meeting this morning in the park, she told Mr. Price more than she should have about other partners, the value of the files, and the fact the extortion would go on despite Mr. Garrett's death. We've got all that on tape. But she mentioned nothing about Hollywood Rex, Mr. Armitage . . . I don't think she knew about any of that."

"But you think she knew that Nicolai arranged the monthly cash drop to Moscow on the diplomatic flights?"

Alexei pauses. "Yes, she knew that process well and often delivered the cash to Nicolai in person once a month. She also picked up the checks for that cash the following month when she dropped off the new cash. She did that for a few years. That was really all she ever knew. When Reid or someone ran over Campanelli in his driveway, she used his hospital stay to her advantage."

"She snooped through the files?" Reams asks.

"She helped herself to the files while Mr. Campanelli was in the hospital. She figured out where all the cash was coming from. When Campanelli died, well, she just assumed she'd get part of the spoils. If she were truly clever, she would have taken the files before Price got them."

"You had no conversations with her about that?"

Alexei is silent.

"Alexei, your silence tells me you know more than you are saying. I'll find out anyway, so just tell me."

Alexei lets out a sigh. "She confronted me about it Saturday. We met at the Beverly Hills hotel. I told her that if she cooperated, we'd take care of her. That's all. I promised nothing except we'd have lunch at the hotel Sunday afternoon."

"Did your cooperation include having sex with her?"

Alexei turns his head away from Reams and nods.

"Goddamn you, Alexei Raminsky, what would your uncle think of that?"

"He's Russian. He'd be proud of me."

"Even if it resulted in your killing her?"

"Detective, he's Russian. I told you. Let's change the subject. Your ass is sitting in his house, so let's drop it or you might join Ms. Petrovich on that scenic drive."

Reams draws a deep breath. "Just to remind you, Alexei, I'm all that stands between your uncle and an indictment from the FBI and District Attorney. I'm holding them off because they think I'm finishing an investigation assigned to my office. I've slowed that up for months to help your uncle. If you kill or harm me, then nothing stands between your uncle and prison."

"He's already out of the country. You know that."

"I do. But he's got financial interests here that he's still siphoning off. I know he needs more time to get the money and other assets back to Russia. You're one of those assets, Alexei. Need I remind you I'm your ticket out of the country before they decide to arrest you and the others?"

"No need to remind me," Alexei replies. "Just don't lecture me or talk to me about my uncle and what he thinks of me. My role in this is limited, and you know that. My uncle asked me to help you out with the money laundering. That's it. I handled that perfectly. Nicolai did his job every month so you could get your share of that shitty little extortion business. Now you suck me into this petty extortion game and a couple murders. I find your escapades to be boring and the money insignificant."

Reams responds, "Your uncle wanted more time to get his assets out of the country. I obliged by slowing up the FBI and Treasury. And my own office. Reid got greedy and Campanelli couldn't control him. I didn't know the extent of the involvement of Ms. Petrovich. Campanelli never shared that with me."

"Little details, detective. Little details." Alexei stands and says, "Well, I'm done, and you need to get me out of the country. Or I'll tell my uncle how you've messed all this up and he won't be happy. Or I'll just hop a ride on the next diplomatic flight to Moscow."

"Stop bluffing. You can hitch a ride on a diplomatic flight any time you like, but the minute you show up in Moscow, the FBI will assume your uncle did the same thing. Then the gig is up, and they'll freeze all his assets before he can liquidate them. If you try to leave early, you'll be dead on arrival in Moscow. You know that. Alexei, I need you to help me kill Price. And Haines and Kilian. I'll then protect you until your uncle gives the signal to have you extracted."

Alexei rises from his chair and goes to an elaborate bar at the end of the room. He pours himself a glass of vodka. "Then let's drink to that." He downs the vodka in one big gulp and throws the glass toward Reams, just missing him before it smashes against the wall.

Nowhere to Hide

As Alton pulls out of the driveway, he puts his hand on Rob's shoulder. "You okay? I'm so sorry about all of this. Did they hurt you?"

"I'm fine, boss. Sorry they got me. I should have been more careful."

Alton pulls his car to the side of the road and opens his trunk. He retrieves his black bag of mischief from a compartment under the spare tire. He's relieved to see Reams' men didn't discover it at the mansion. "Hang tight, Rob. I'm just going to get my scanner to see if they put a tracker on my car." Stepping back from the car, Alton aims the device that looks like a cigarette lighter at his car. A small screen lights up in two places. "Two trackers. Okay, let's find them."

The lights on the device blink faster as Alton scans an area under the left front wheel well. Removing that tracker, he discovers another tracker inside the right rear fender. He puts both trackers in his pocket, careful to be sure they are both still activated.

Alton gives Rob a pat on the shoulder and reaches for his phone to call Cameron. He sees he already has several calls and voicemails from Cameron and Oksana, all within the past couple hours. He skips the voicemails and calls Cameron, who answers right away. "For God's sake, Alton, where have you been? I've been calling for the past couple hours."

"Sorry, Cam, I'll explain later. Where are you and what

happened at the house? You, Blair and Oksana are okay?"

"You already know about that?"

"Yes. Is Oksana there with you? And where are you, by the way?"

"In the parking lot of the Hotel Bel Air. Oksana drove us here in her car."

"What happened at the house, Cam?"

"A couple hours ago, around 7:00 p.m., the front security chime went off. So I looked at the driveway camera and see two guys jump out of a black van. One goes to the front door, and the other runs around back. Oksana tells me and Blair to go upstairs and lock ourselves in the master bedroom until she comes for us. I put Blair in the bedroom, but I wait at the top of the stairs in case Oksana needs help. The one guy keeps banging on the front door and ringing the doorbell. We hear breaking glass from the kitchen and some guy comes down the hallway pointing a gun at Oksana. She yells for him to drop the gun, but he doesn't. So she shoots him. The other guy at the front door hears the shots and runs back to the van and squeals out of the driveway. Seriously, Alton, it was terrifying!"

Alton pats his friend on the shoulder, then asks, "Is Blair okay?"

"Yes. Very shaken, but she's okay."

"Let me speak with Oksana."

Cameron hands his phone to Oksana, who is eager to speak with Alton. "Hey, my bubee, you okay? Vere have you been?"

"I'm fine, I'll fill you in later. You okay? That guy didn't get a shot off at you, did he?"

"I shoot him first. His gun goes off, but bullet goes in the wall. I get him with only one shot, aiming for shoulder, but he stumbles, and bullet go in heart."

"He's dead?"

"Yes, sorry, boss. He vud have shot me."

"You did the right thing, Oksana. What did you do with the body?"

"Put in two garbage bags and take to garage. Then we leave

right away in my car in case guy come back with more men."

"Did they see your car?"

"No, I park down the street like I alvays do. I get my car and drive them here. Mr. Haines knows manager and vants to get bungalow to hide."

"Okay, let me talk with him. And Oksana, may I ask you to please stay with them until I can get them later?"

"Okay, boss."

Oksana hands the phone back to Cameron. "Alton, what's happening?" Cameron asks.

"I'm on my way over there now. Oksana says you are getting a bungalow at the hotel?"

"Yes. I know the manager well and I just called her at home. It's almost nine o'clock on a Sunday night so she's not on site, but she's arranging a bungalow for me in another name. She will instruct the night manager to leave the key for me under a pot off the lobby."

"Did you tell her what's happening?"

"No, don't worry. I use the hotel for meetings with celebrity clients when we don't want to be seen in a restaurant or at my house or office. The manager gives me a suite under another name, I retrieve the key under a pot and then meet with my client discreetly in the suite. I always have a suite that has an out-side patio entrance to avoid hallways and the lobby. We should be safe there for now. Oksana doesn't think they followed us."

"It's dark out, so if they didn't follow you, there's no one to see you. Text me your suite number when you get the key. I'll meet you there. Rob will be with me."

"Alton, this is getting so out of hand. What is happening?"

"I'll fill you in as soon as I get there. Just sit tight."

Alton arrives back at his cottage but does not open the gate to the driveway. It confuses Rob. "Aren't we retrieving the files?"

"Not just yet. They are expecting us to go get the files and then call Reams for a date and time to make the swap. We will let them think we are picking up the files now. Just bear with me."

After a few minutes, Alton drives up the street to the London Hotel, where he passes the valet and stops down the hill at the driveway exit on Larrabee street. He turns left into the valet parking for the Viper Room, where he waves to the parking lot attendant. "Good evening, Mr. Pappas!"

"Mr. Price, you here with clients tonight?"

"Not tonight, but I have a one hundred dollar bill here that wants to know who your most annoying guest is this evening?"

He smiles, "Well, that's easy. See that black Ferrari? Recognize the license plate?"

Alton nods his head. The actor who owns the car called Alton last month to get him out of a scrape with the police over assaulting his girlfriend in this parking lot. Alton doesn't take domestic abuse cases on behalf of the perpetrator, just the victims. He turned him down. "You still let him park here after he punched his girlfriend and threatened to kill you if you called the police?"

"I don't make the rules, Mr. Price."

Alton hands Mr. Pappas the hundred dollar bill and quietly places the two trackers inside the right rear wheel well of the Ferrari. They both smile at one another as Alton gets back in his car.

As Alton turns up Larrabee Street and then west on Sunset Boulevard, Rob shakes his head. "That was perfect. How did you time that?"

"I love that club and the crowd, but if you ever need to know who the skunks are in this world, just ask the valets at any hotel, club or restaurant. I wanted those trackers on someone else's car since there's a chance the police may go after them, thinking it's me. Someone could get hurt, and I don't want that happening to an innocent person. This guy is a complete jerk. Mission accomplished, as they say."

About twenty minutes later, Alton turns up Stone Canyon Road to the Hotel Bel Air. Cameron has already texted him the suite number. He parks his car at the end of the parking lot to avoid using the valet, and he and Rob go around the side of the hotel to get to the suite without going through the lobby. The suite has a large patio and hot tub, with access from the garden. Oksana is waiting at the gate to let Alton and Rob in while the lights are off in the suite. Once Oksana closes the gate, Cameron turns the lights on.

"Thank God you're here, Alton. The shooting scared Blair to death."

"Where is she?"

"Lying down in the bedroom."

"Go get her and make her a drink. We've got a busy agenda tomorrow and you'll coordinate everything for us, Cameron."

"What?"

"You heard me. We don't have a lot of time."

As Cameron goes to get Blair, the bedroom door flies open and Blair bursts into the room. "What is happening here? Are you trying to drive me crazy?" She throws her cell phone at Cameron. "You told me he was dead."

Cameron picks up the phone from the floor and sees a text from Reid Garrett. "Good evening, my bimbo costar and attempted murderer! See you on the set tomorrow. Hope your weekend was as exciting as mine!"

51

Confessions

Cameron looks like he's about to faint, so Alton grabs him by the shoulders and helps him sit on the couch. Taking the phone from Cameron's hand, he sees the text message from Reid. "So it has begun," Alton says, nodding. "The charade is on. Blair, Cameron, listen to me. Reid is dead. His twin brother, Landon, is posing as him. I guarantee you that *Reid is dead*. I need to tell you what has unfolded and what will happen tomorrow. This will be over soon, I promise."

Blair shakes her head. "This is a fucking nightmare that just keeps getting worse. I don't have the strength to see him on the set tomorrow, whether it's him or someone else."

"Be strong, Blair. We have them trapped if we just play along with the charade on Reid. More on that later." Alton reaches inside his coat pocket and hands a list of names to Cameron. The names on the list are the celebrity names that appear on the client files being blackmailed by Reid and Tony Campanelli. "Cam, how many names on this list do you know personally?"

Cameron scans the list. "Is this a joke, Alton? I know all these names, and ten of them are my clients. You'd know that."

"Exactly. Can you get them to meet us at the studio tomorrow night?"

"Tomorrow night? For what? These are top actors and directors. Most of them will be at work. Some are likely not even in town or filming elsewhere. Most use other agents. I don't want them to think I am poaching them from their current agent."

"You won't be poaching them. Let's just say you will recruit them for a short acting or directing assignment. Can you get maybe a dozen to help us tomorrow night?"

"Where did you get this list?"

"Campanelli's files. Everyone on that list is being blackmailed or extorted by the Reid Garrett—Tony Campanelli partnership. Plus, a third partner I'll tell you about later."

"What?" Cameron asks. "Every name here is paying money to Reid each month just like I am?"

"Well, not to make you feel bad, Cam, but most are paying a lot more than you are."

"Holy crap." Cameron puts the list in his pocket. "Okay, Alton, tell us what's going on. Everything. Don't sugarcoat it. If Blair is right and we're being hunted by Raminsky or the Russian mob, then that's too big a fight for us. You know that."

Alton motions for Cameron, Blair, Rob, and Oksana to sit down. "Get comfy and give me time to explain what's happening. Most of what we have seen so far is an illusion to intimidate anyone from interfering with their little extortion and blackmail scheme. Cameron, since you are the excellent martini maker, why don't you make one for each of us while I start my story?"

Oksana speaks up, "Vodka rocks for me. No martini. Tumbler fine."

Alton nods and smiles at Oksana. "Let me begin. First off, Blair, I want you to know how this all started and how it got off track."

Blair looks at Alton and extends her hand. "Be my guest, Alton. It's about time you explain how we got to this fucked-up state."

"Cameron called me when he learned they cast Reid in your mini-series and gave him the right to fire you if the chemistry wasn't right. Reid also implied to Cameron that he'd hit you up as his latest extortion victim."

"Alton, I know Cam hired you to protect me. But is this how you thought it would turn out? I might have been better off being blackmailed."

"No, this wasn't the plan. When Reid asked Cameron to be sure you were on your balcony last Thursday night, he alerted me that Reid was up to something. It became apparent he was putting on a show for you in the next building, and it didn't take me long to figure out the phony caterers and the apartment Campanelli borrowed for the evening for Reid. My intent was to scare Reid off by making him think he'd killed his stuntman buddy."

"So that wasn't Reid that dove off the balcony? I was sure it was him," Blair said.

"That's what he wanted you to think. Just a little something to torment you, to use against you if he could. That was to be just the beginning. He's the one that left the note in your apartment later that night. Reid knew that by tormenting you, he'd be tormenting Cameron even more."

"Well, he didn't get scared away, did he?"

"No. After the rape in your trailer, I knew he'd never stop and that we couldn't scare him off. Eliminating him was the only answer. And that's what happened, Blair. He's gone for good."

"Well, I took care of that for you, didn't I? I'm the one that killed him, not you."

"You didn't kill him, but you left a sloppy trail of evidence, Blair. Though you just wanted to make him too ill to show up on the set, you overdosed him with illegal drugs. Your crimes are the same as a drug dealer overdosing a client. That's the law in California. And, if he were in a vegetable state or ultimately died, they'd charge you with murder or attempted murder. LAPD homicide detectives see overdose deaths all the time. Had I not cleaned it up for you and changed your story, I'm sure Detective Reams would have booked you by now."

"That's why you started a fire at Reid's that killed him?"

"I didn't say that. All you need to know is that I took care of everything, so nothing points to you."

Cameron interrupts, "But Alton, it looks like your clean-up of Blair's mess at Reid's also included eliminating Campanelli and Reid. You orchestrated that?"

"Cameron, what did I just say? Don't make those kinds of

remarks. The evidence shows Reid Garrett shot Tony Campanelli with his own gun and his cigarette ignited the couch when he passed out. That's what happened."

Cameron and Blair look at each other, but neither says a word.

Oksana shakes her empty glass at Cameron, hinting she needs another tumbler of vodka. Cameron retrieves Oksana's glass from her and walks over to the bar, saying, "Alton, if Landon is going to show up on the set tomorrow posing as Reid, how can he get away with that? I already had a call from the studio head last night. He told me he heard Reid perished in the fire in his home. Won't he question the sudden appearance of Reid on the set?"

"When you say studio head, you mean Mr. Blaise Armitage?"

"Yes, Alton. He runs the whole studio."

"No, Mr. Armitage won't question a thing. The coroner is going to announce that the two dead bodies at Reid's house were Tony Campanelli and Landon Griffith, Reid's twin brother."

"What? How do you know that?"

"More on that in a moment, but you need to know Blaise won't question a thing about Reid's re-emergence. He's part of the blackmail scheme and is, or was, in the pocket of Campanelli and Reid. Now, this leaves just the third partner, but Armitage won't challenge him."

"Blaise Armitage, the studio head representing the Chinese owners is being blackmailed?"

"Yes, Cameron. That's why he gave the contract to Reid to star him in *Dark Company* and gave him creative control over the show. Reid was blackmailing him, too."

"Blackmail? With what?"

"He's using the studio as cover for Chinese Communist Party—or CCP—security agents to operate in the United States as studio employees. And he also made some extra cash as a double agent for a brief gig betraying the CCP for the Russian security services. He's in a heap of trouble, Cam. He'll be dead within a week. The only question is, who kills him first? The Russians or the Chinese?"

Cameron sits down on a stool by the bar. "Holy crap, I don't believe this."

Casting the Parts

Cameron delivers the tumbler of vodka to Oksana and walks over to Alton. "Okay, so Campanelli and Reid are out of the picture, but we've still got the Russian mob to deal with, or whoever is trying to kidnap Blair. And now, maybe me. How do we fight them?"

"It's a smokescreen, Cam. It doesn't involve Raminsky and the Russian mob—at least not in a major way. It's a diversion to intimidate people like us, or Reid, who might go after Campanelli and the third partner, Detective Edward Reams."

"Detective Reams is in on it? I don't believe it."

"Well, believe it, Cam. The payment file showing a third of most blackmail and extortion payments to "R" is not Raminsky, but our old, rumpled detective Edward Reams. You could say the "R" stands for rogue. A rogue cop."

Blair jumps into the conversation: "Wait a minute, just a minute. Then who tried to kidnap me and why the man with the Russian voice on my cell phone? Maybe you botched this up too, Alton."

"Detective Reams has some of Raminsky's security people working with him because Raminsky's nephew, Alexei, plays a small part in the scheme. He's arranged for the cash black-mail payments to go to Moscow every month on a diplomatic flight, and for a series of checks returned the following month from various shell companies. The accounts are in a few differ-ent countries, owned by shell companies named after Russian mythical characters. The phony accounts were likely set up by

Reams and Campanelli as another diversion."

Alton continues: "Raminsky is under investigation by the FBI, Treasury, and the LAPD, and Reams is helping to slow down their indictment of Raminsky to give him time to liquidate his investments in the United States. He's already back in Russia, but the FBI doesn't know that. His nephew is helping to wrap up things here in L.A. for his uncle before his own secret transport back to Moscow. Reams is in on it, and I suspect he will flee to Moscow at some point and leave Landon, posing as Reid, to continue collecting the blackmail payments and keeping the scheme alive. He's cut him in on a share of the payments, but Reams gets a windfall with Reid and Campanelli out of the picture. I think Landon would ultimately screw him, but we will take care of him before that even starts."

Cameron shakes his head, "That's a lot to take in, Alton. I thought we had a spoiled actor with a mean streak, and that was it. I never thought he blackmailed that many people and had other partners. You sure about the Reams involvement?"

"Cam, I went to Raminsky's house in Holmby Hills expecting to confront him about what was happening. Instead, I found Reams there barking out orders to some security goons and a good-looking, blonde guy who looked familiar. And then I recognized him from the background pictures I pulled on Raminsky before I went to his house. Alexei is Raminsky's nephew, his brother's son. A spoiled little son of a Russian oligarch who likes to party more than work for his uncle. I think he finds his work with Reams to be beneath him."

"Excuse me, boss?" Rob asks.

"Sure, what is it, Rob?"

"The work you had me do on this case—I mean, regarding Reid—well, I find it hard to believe he got all the dirt on the celebs on his own. He . . . he just didn't seem that bright, if you'll forgive me for putting it that way."

"Good observation, Rob. Reid wasn't the guy who dug up the dirt most of the time. That was up to Campanelli and Reams. Between the two of them, they had access to police files and private investigators all over the world to dig up dirt on just about anyone they chose. Reid created some extortion opportunities like Evelyn Sackalow, but Reams and Campanelli concocted most of it. Reid was just the front guy to go ask for the money after he showed the victim what dirt he had on them. He was good at that. His mediocre acting skills came in handy, and we all know how threatening he can be."

Cameron agrees. "That is so true. You get a phone call from one of the biggest actors in Hollywood telling you he wants a personal meeting with you. At first, it's flattering. Then this good-looking charmer shows up and throws nasty pictures and other documents in your face. Even though he was my client, it stunned me at how vengeful his presentation of the blackmail material on me and Blair was. He really enjoyed making rich or powerful people squirm."

"Cam, that's exactly why I think you will not have a problem getting a dozen of those celebrities to help us out with our little production tomorrow night. When you tell them it will bring their relationship with Reid Garrett to an end, I think you'll have lots of takers. And Cameron, there is no more sincere guy in Hollywood than you to do the 'ask' for this project. You know that."

"Thanks for the kind words, but what should I tell them?"

"I'm getting to that." Alton reaches inside his briefcase and hands a document to Cameron. "Here's the script for tomorrow night. You need to cast all those parts I have highlighted in yellow."

"What? Alton, I'm a talent agent, not a director or producer."

"Exactly! That's why you need Robert Handley to direct the actors tomorrow night."

"Robert Handley?" Cameron laughs. "And why would one of the biggest directors in Hollywood—who's now filming a movie—want to help me with this little production tomorrow evening? He'll hang up on me."

"No, he won't. He's being blackmailed too. He's one of the biggest payers."

"Impossible. He's a squeaky-clean sort of guy, a popular child-actor turned director, loved by everyone. What could Reid have on him?"

"He's gay, but I think you know that, Cameron."

Cameron laughs again, "Alton, everyone in town knows that. He and Craig have been together for thirty years. I was at their private wedding in Lake Como last year. Why would he pay to keep a secret everybody knows?"

"Well, maybe he's comfortably 'out' here in Hollywood, but he's not out to his ninety-year-old parents in Alabama. When your father leads a Southern Baptist church in rural Alabama, having a gay son is unacceptable. And embarrassing for both parents."

"You're telling me that his parents don't know they have a gay son?"

"Apparently not. They've never visited California; it's too sinful. But they are immensely proud of their famous director son."

"What about Craig? They don't know about him?"

"Robert has told them he has a full-time valet that looks after his household. I know it seems hard to believe in this day and age, Cameron, but you know the rural South. Robert doesn't want his parents to die with the shame of having a gay son in a conservative Southern Baptist Church where they still don't admit blacks, let alone gay people. His parents have both been in ill health, and of course Reid upped the payments two months ago to keep Robert's secret quiet until both parents passed."

"I'm glad Reid is the one who burned to death, Alton. How could one person be so despicable?"

"Exactly. I'll bet Mr. Handley will jump at the chance to get his file back and guarantee his secret is safe from his parents."

"But it will worry him to know that Reid is still alive."

"And that is why you need to tell him we guarantee Reid is dead, and that you will give him his file back at the conclusion of tomorrow night's filming. I wrote everything in the script you have. The whole thing should take less than forty-five minutes."

Cameron scans through the script, shaking his head. "And I need to arrange all of this on Stage 26 tomorrow night by five o'clock, with the filming to start at six?"

"Yep."

"And who will get Reams there?"

"Cameron, I'll take care of that. I will be sure Reams and his men have no weapons, so the actors playing FBI agents at the opening will be my guys—including you, Rob. The rest of the casting is up to you."

Blair objects, "Don't tell me there's a part in this production sham for me too."

Alton nods his head. "Listen, everyone. *We must do this*. Reams will kill all of us tomorrow night if we don't take care of him first. I guarantee it. He knows that I have figured everything out about what he has been doing, and he must kill me. And to be safe, he will need to take care of you three—Rob, Blair, and Cam. Blair, he already tried to kidnap you and failed. He won't fail again. And you, Oksana, you killed one of his men—one of Raminsky's men—so of course he's got to kill you too. The script you are holding there is our key to eliminating Reams and ending the blackmail and extortion scheme for sixty tormented people. Each of you has a part, so let's go over it. If we can't pull this off, then tonight will be our last."

You Won't Sleep at Night

Detective Reams returns to the Raminsky mansion in Holmby Hills less than two hours after setting Alton and Rob free. He drives past the men at the gate, who point to where to park his unmarked police car. Once inside the mansion, another guard points toward the staircase, telling him that Alexei is waiting for him in the usual meeting spot upstairs, Raminsky's elaborate study.

As Reams enters the room, Alexei is sitting in a big, red, overstuffed leather chair, trimmed in gold upholstery studs. He is sipping Cognac from a large snifter with one hand, while holding a cigarette in the other. Landon is sitting across from him on an upholstered bench. They both look up at Reams as he enters the room. Neither man says anything to Reams, but Alexei motions for him to sit in a chair next to Landon.

Feeling nervous, Reams clears his throat and speaks. "So, I'm here. What's the issue, Alexei? Your message was confusing."

"My uncle. He wants to speak with you. We are waiting for him to call on that phone." Waving his cigarette, he points to a black phone sitting on an elaborate desk across the room.

"What does he want? Is something wrong?"

Alexei shrugs his shoulders but says nothing. A few moments later, the black phone rings and Alexei rises from his chair to answer it. He speaks in a soft Russian voice with the person on the other end of the line. After a brief conversation, Alexei motions for Reams to come sit in the chair at the desk. Once Reams is in the chair, Alexei hands the phone to him.

"Reams here . . . yes, sir . . . I know it's not what we planned, I'm . . . I understand . . . Understood, but . . . killing him is best, kidnapping complicates things . . . he's clever, so hiding him won't be easy . . . I agree, but I ask you to reconsider the risk of . . . yes, yes I know . . . but, please . . . no . . . no, that is almost impossible in the United States . . . well, if that is the way you want it to be . . . understood, but . . . but . . . Mr. Garrett just got out of hand . . . Campanelli and I thought we had him out of the picture, and . . . and, yes that is what I am trying to say, but . . . okay, yes . . . I'm sorry this ended up being more involved for Alexei than it should . . . okay, okay . . . understood . . . goodbye."

His forehead is dripping wet, so Reams reaches for a handkerchief in his suit pocket, pulling out a wrinkled cloth that is more yellow than white. He wipes his forehead and his nose, then reaches for a cigarette.

Disgusted at the sight of the crumpled and yellow-stained handkerchief, Alexei reaches inside a drawer on a side table and throws Reams a nice, crisp cocktail napkin. "Detective, throw that rag away and go wash your hands. Then use that cotton napkin if you need to wipe your brow again. It looks like Nicotine coming out from your pores."

Embarrassed, Reams goes to the bathroom down the hall without saying a word. When he returns, he sees Alexei back on the telephone speaking with someone in Russian. Reams sits down next to Landon. "You still in the deal with me?"

Landon shrugs his shoulders, "Why shouldn't I be?"

"They have moved our timeline up. Alexei and I will leave sooner than we had planned. Can I still count on you to collect the payments and keep our business running?"

"Unless I get a better offer." He smiles and reassures Reams, "Just kidding. Yes, I'm in and ready to go. Just a little nervous if I can pull off the Reid impersonation."

"But weren't you planning on doing that for Alton Price? That's what you told me."

"Yes, and I did it. I'm the one that got Blair Kilian on her balcony that night. She thought I was Reid."

"Well, if you fooled her then, you could fool her now."

"It's the acting part I'm not sure of. Too many eyes will be on me. The studio, television. It will be tough to pull all that off without a hitch. Fooling Blair is one thing. But what about the other actors? The director? Fans?"

"We discussed that. If you feel uncomfortable, you just take a medical leave and then don't come back. You retire. Get out of the public eye, but keep up our scheme. You'll live handsomely here in Hollywood."

Alexei finishes his conversation and returns to his chair. "My Uncle. He called back for you, but I told him you had left."

"Anything wrong?"

"He wants to know who else besides Price do we have to worry about? Who else would know anything about my uncle, or my, or Nicolai's involvement? Anyone at all?"

Reams looks at Landon. "You told me that Cameron Haines was in on your scheme with Alton to pose as Reid. Does he know anything about Alexei or Mr. Raminsky? Did you ever hear Cameron Haines discuss anyone else with Alton Price except Reid Garrett?"

"No. I only met Mr. Haines once, at Mr. Price's for a brunch. That was it. We didn't talk about anyone else except Reid."

Alexei nods his head, then looks at Reams. "The Kilian woman. Does she have any idea? Who does she think was trying to abduct her from her apartment?"

Reams lies. "She's clueless."

"She can't connect any of us to the events of the past few days?"

Reams lies again. "No." He suspects Alton Price may have told Cameron and Blair about a possible Raminsky connection, but he is reluctant to irritate his Russian accomplices any further. The phone conversation he just had with Raminsky was unpleasant.

Alexei stares at Reams. "So, it's just Alton Price and his buddy we kidnapped? Rob is his name? Just those two taking a trip with us?"

"Yes, if we must take them with us instead of killing both of them then, yes."

"'If'? Did my uncle use the word 'if'?"

Reams shakes his head, "No. No, he didn't."

"Exactly. When we get the files, my men will take Price and his colleague and hold him here until we all get on the diplomatic flight."

"Yes, but as I told your uncle, when people disappear in the United States, it's not the same as in Russia. Lots of people will ask questions. And someone like Price will have a backup plan to signal to a key contact that something is wrong if he is not home in a day or two. I am certain of it. He's too shrewd to risk being kidnapped without leaving a clue or a signal. The CIA trained him. Don't forget that."

"You want my uncle back on the phone?"

"No! I agreed that you take over as soon as we get the files. Landon knows what he needs to do, and he's met with Nicolai to discuss taking over from Ms. Petrovich on the money drop and check pick up. Once we are out of the country, I will feel better. Getting me, you, Price, and Rob Elliott to the airport and on a diplomatic flight all at once is highly risky. You know that our intelligence community closely monitors your diplomatic flights even though they are immune from search or seizure?"

"I don't need a lecture from you on diplomatic flights. You wanted asylum in Russia so you could receive your income from your little business out of reach of American authorities. My uncle is giving you that in exchange for the time you granted him to wrap up his affairs here. You should consider yourself lucky. Your shitty business was just a little matter for us. A minor inconvenience. Now you make it a big fucked up mess because at least two other people know of our involvement."

"Your uncle made that quite clear. But remember that Ms. Petrovich let the cat out of the bag first, with Price. That's where it started."

"No matter. We have an alternate plan, so you set up last details on file pickup with Mr. Price, and after the transfer, I take over. We meet as planned for the flight to Moscow."

Reams nods his head and stands up to walk out the door of the study. Alexei stands up from his chair. "I'll walk you out, detective." Landon follows along, but Alexei tells him to wait in the study until he returns.

As Reams and Alexei walk down the front doorsteps to the detective's car, Alexei stops and tugs on the back of Ream's jacket. Reams stops halfway down the steps and turns to face Alexei, who is pointing up at the second floor of the mansion. "And you left us with that mess, too."

Reams knows Alexei is referring to Landon, whom Raminsky wants killed and replaced. "I told you we shouldn't have brought him here after he met Nicolai. He didn't need to know about all of this, and to hear the discussions with Alton Price last night. I told you to leave him out of it, but you didn't."

"He has a big mouth. Bragged about his deal with Price, then with you. You didn't tell me everything. We can't trust him. I will find you a more reliable partner."

"But there's got to be the Reid connection, Alexei! Our blackmail victims will be suspicious if Reid is out of the picture. Some may stop paying if a stranger shows up. All it takes is for just one of our blackmail victims to go to the police and we're cooked."

"Sloppy. Sloppy little business. You should have thought of all that. You had things working well for your little scheme, and our involvement was only for laundering the cash. A little pile of cash, really. Then you get greedy, Mr. Campanelli gets greedy, and your movie star gets greedy. Now you have a fucked-up deal. Maybe you should just stay here and handle everything on your own. You can flee to another country instead of Russia. I have a nice connection in Mexico."

"Are you serious?"

Alexei smiles, gives Reams a shove down the steps toward his car, and turns around to walk up the steps. "See you for your file swap, detective."

As he gets into his car, Reams hesitates for a moment, recalling a comment Tony Campanelli made to him years ago when they needed someone to launder their blackmail and extortion payments. "If you make a deal with the Russians, however small, you'll never sleep at night."

54

The Stage Is Set

Alton leaves the others in the suite to discuss the assignments for tomorrow evening, and for Cameron to make his calls to the director and the actors needed to pull off the stunt. He's hoping that Cameron and the director, Robert Handley, have enough clout to book the soundstage tomorrow night and arrange for the film crew and props. It's a long shot, but it only needs to fool Reams for about forty-five minutes.

Reaching for his cell phone, Alton dials Detective Reams, who answers almost immediately. "Okay, Price, I'm listening. Where do we pick up the files?"

"The studio. Soundstage 26, tomorrow night, six pm."

"I don't like it. Why there?"

"Because that's the way it has to be if you want the files. We need a secure place where we can make the swap."

"Swap? What am I swapping? I'm just picking up files that don't belong to you."

"A receipt. For the files."

"What? That's ridiculous."

"Well, we need assurance that you or your goons won't kill us. In return, you have our silence, but a receipt for the files is our insurance that if any of us gets harmed, kidnapped, or killed, your receipt goes to the FBI and the Police Commissioner. And my buddy at the CIA."

"You are in no position to bargain, Mr. Price."

"Neither are you, detective. This is the way it must be. If

I wanted to turn you in, I would have done that already. But I don't want any of these secrets exposed for your sixty victims. There would be no point in returning the files to you if I intended to turn you in. I'm gambling that you'll be a good boy and trust that I won't reveal your secret. I've got nothing to gain by exposing your scheme, and it would only damage my current anonymity, which I depend upon for my business. In return, I need a guarantee that you won't kill me or harm anyone close to me. You've got nothing to worry about unless you're planning to do any of that."

Reams is at a loss for words since the plan is to kidnap Alton and Rob and take them to Moscow, along with him and Alexei. Once in Moscow, he's sure Alton and Rob will disappear forever. That means anything he leaves behind from Reams with Alton may end up with the authorities. While he would be legally unreachable in Russia, it would expose his scheme, probably get Landon arrested, and the money would stop. He'd be penniless in Moscow. And, if the exposure links Raminsky with his scheme, well, he knows he would breathe his last breath in Russia. What a conundrum.

Not hearing a response from Reams, Alton speaks up, "Cat got your tongue, detective?"

"Okay, whatever you say. Will you have something for me to sign when we do the swap?"

"All taken care of. As soon as you sign the receipt, Rob will take care of it. And come alone, detective. The swap should take only a few minutes. You take the files; I get the receipt and you are on your way. If you are bringing any goons with you, leave them outside the studio gate."

"If you try to pull anything, you won't make it out of there, Price."

"You needn't worry, detective. Play it straight and you'll have your files and be on your way."

Reams says nothing and hangs up. He knows he has got to be sure that Rob and Alton are in Alexei's possession before anything he gives Alton is in the hands of someone else for safekeeping. He knows he can't trust anyone. Not Price, Alexei, nor Landon. With Campanelli and Reid out of the picture, Reams is alone. He wonders if Alexei will think he is as expendable as Alton Price, Rob Elliott, and Landon. Maybe Raminsky no longer has a use for Reams and wants everyone out of the picture? His forehead perspires, and he reaches inside his jacket pocket for the cocktail napkin Alexei gave him.

Alton ends his call with Reams and phones Cameron, who picks up after a few rings. "Cam, it's me. We're all set with Reams tomorrow night at 6:00 p.m. as we discussed. How are things on your end?"

"I don't know where to start."

"Start with telling me everything is going according to plan?"

"Well, not perfectly, but enough. Everything is falling in place, but I have called in a lot of favors to make this happen."

"I knew you would, but it'll be worth it."

"Those props and extras and costumes? We are going to have to reimburse the studio, Alton. It's getting pricey."

"No worries. I'll take care of it. Let me know what you need tomorrow night after our performance is over and I'll give you a check."

"On more thing," says Cameron. "Blaise Armitage gave me a bit of a problem earlier."

"How so? He runs the studio, so what's his concern?"

"He just asked a lot of questions. Suspicious, I guess."

"Has he figured out that our special guest is Detective Reams?"

"No. He thinks it's a scene from a pilot, and my actor friends are just helping me out. He insisted that after this little performance, any actual commercial filming must be on union scale and all the usual studio paperwork and overhead. Another favor, as you say."

"Well, he won't have to worry about that, will he?"

"You know how nervous I am, Alton. If this goes wrong, then my career as a top Hollywood agent is over."

"It won't go wrong, Cam. You'll be a hero to your clients

once they realize the blackmail is over."

"My primary concern is Blair. I want her to be safe, I want my friends and the Hollywood community to know she is my daughter, and I want for this treachery started by Reid to be over. For good. If my career ending is a consequence of that, then so be it."

"You're a good man, Cameron. A far better man than me. I wish my motives were as selfless as yours. But you know they aren't."

Alton hangs up, and Cameron stares at his phone for a moment, then whispers to himself, "Alton, I've known you for twenty years, and I really don't know who you are. But I guess that doesn't matter, does it?"

After ending his call with Cameron, Alton drives his car to the Raminsky mansion in Holmby Hills. It is almost dark as he pulls into the entrance and stops at the huge metal gates. Three men with guns appear on the other side of the gate. Just like before, a voice over an intercom asks him why he is there. "I need to see Alexei. My name is Alton Price."

The voice on the intercom replies, "There is no one here by that name."

"Tell him Alton Price needs to see him for just five minutes. That's all. I know he's here. If I can't see him, then I'll have to call his uncle."

After several minutes pass, Alton sees the men at the gate step back as one of the large metal gates opens. As a guard directs Alton where to park his car, he sees Alexei and another man descend the front steps to meet him in the driveway. Alton mumbles to himself, "Here goes."

55

Lights, Camera, Action

It's Monday night, about a quarter to six. Cameron is standing outside soundstage 26 when he sees a tall, burly man with a full beard approach him. He's wearing a butler's uniform and grins at Cameron. "Do I know you, sir?"

"I hope not."

"Well, may I help you? Are you part of the studio crew?"

The man widens his grin. "Cameron, it's me, Alton. I am glad my disguise fooled you. Hopefully, it will fool Reams."

"Ah, so that's why you wouldn't tell me what your disguise would be."

"Exactly. Are we all set inside?"

"Yes, but are you sure Reams will go for everything if he thinks you aren't here?"

"You read the script, right?"

"Yes, I know what happens. Just hope the timing is right."

"No choice, Cam. I can't let that many celebrities in the same room see me and know my name. A lot of what I do depends on anonymity. Some people who hire me never see me. I need to keep it that way."

"Got it."

Alton checks his watch and turns to Cameron. "I hear it was messy on the set this morning."

Cameron nods his head. "I figured you already heard."

"I see you were on set?"

"Yes, but Blair doesn't know that. I came in the back and

stood along the wall with the catering staff. Alton, it was surreal. I would swear Landon was channeling Reid. His mannerisms, his anger, his nasty comments to Blair and the crew. Alton, I would swear it was Reid if I didn't know he incinerated himself on that couch."

"Exactly what I saw."

"You were on set too?"

"No, I was here at the studio and got the entire daily shoot of the episode. At least, all the scenes with Reid and Blair."

"What about the behavior between film shots?"

"Reid's lecture to Blair about being a second-rate actress? That he told her this will be her last episode? Yep, I heard all about it. You know my source."

"I do."

"How is Blair taking it?"

"Not very well, as you would expect," says Cameron. "I thought she did her scenes well, despite Reid trying to trip her up with changed dialogue."

"I agree. You have her here in the soundstage as I asked?"

"Yep. She's not happy about it, but I asked her to trust me until this brief event was over."

"How much has she had to drink?"

"Believe it or not, she doesn't want a drink until this is over."

"She knows what's happening?"

"No. She thinks there's a big meeting to discuss her future on the show. When she sees this room filled with celebrities, she may faint."

"Don't worry. You bring her out when things start and put her in the chair with her name on it. We brought hers over from the set. Tell her to just sit there and watch and say nothing."

"She's got the instructions, Alton."

Alton receives a text from Rob saying, "He's here".

Alton replies, "Is he alone?"

Rob writes back, "Walking in studio gates alone, but two cars waiting for him, with a couple guys in each car."

Alton looks at Cameron. "Showtime, Cam."

Cameron nods and they both enter the soundstage.

Detective Reams shows his identification at Studio Gate 3, and the guard directs him to soundstage 26, about fifty yards from the gate. Reams is meandering as he inspects the surroundings. He sees no one except two studio guards at the entrance to the soundstage. The large soundstage door is open just a few feet. As he approaches, one guard asks for his identification. Reams shows him his LAPD badge and identification card. The guard escorts him into the soundstage, while the other closes the large door behind them. As they step inside, the guard asks Detective Reams to stop for a moment. "Let your eyes adjust to the darkness, detective. Wait here for just a moment. The soundstage filming lights aren't on yet, so I will escort you to the set. It's quite dark."

The soundstage is cavernous but eerily silent. As his eyes adjust, Reams sees a faint glow of light in the center of the soundstage. A huge circular table surrounds the space, with the center left open. It is more like a horseshoe shape, perhaps sixty feet or more across. He squints to make out the details, but he sees that there are many people seated at the table. He counts over twenty people, spaced a few feet apart.

At the open part of the horseshoe-shaped table is a square desk, with a podium and microphone. As he approaches more closely, he can see a stack of files on the desk and a large blank screen behind the podium. Reaching the table, he sees an empty chair in front of him that becomes illuminated with a spotlight from above. A voice from a speaker tells him to sit in the chair at the illuminated spot by the table.

Reams is nervous and sweating as he drags out the chair and has a seat. As soon as he sits in the chair, Alton, dressed as the butler, appears at his side and directs his attention to a piece of paper in front of him on the table. The spotlight is still on, so Reams can easily see the document. "Good evening, detective. Here's the receipt for the files. And those are the original sixty files sitting over there on that desk. Please read this and sign it where you see your name. We will then deliver the files to you shortly."

"Excuse me, but who are you? Where is Mr. Price?"

"He's here. You will see him soon. My task is to retrieve this signed receipt."

Reams takes another long look around the table. It is too dark for him to make out any faces. "First off, who are all these people? I can't make them out, but it looks like there are several people seated at this table. Why?"

"We will get to that. We need them for the file transfer. Please read the document in front of you and sign it. That will get the process started."

Reams reads the single sheet of paper in front of him.

> I, Detective Edward Reams of the LAPD, acknowledge receipt of sixty files with blackmail and extortion on sixty individuals, and one file with a record of extortion payments and disbursements.

Reams seems surprised at the brevity of the statement and that it only acknowledges receipt of the files and not involvement in the scheme. Posing as a butler, Alton hands Reams a pen. "Sufficiently ambiguous, isn't it, detective?"

"I must confess it makes me suspicious. That's it? I sign this and you hang on to it?"

"That's what Mr. Price promised."

"And I get the files?"

"As we agreed."

"Well then, I should have the files *before* I sign this. This document says I have them."

"Ah! Mr. Price thought you would say that!"

Reams appears startled and sits back in his chair.

"Let's get the files in your possession before you have to sign this little piece of paper."

The light over Reams position at the table dims slightly, and the podium and table of files at the head of the horseshoe table becomes illuminated. Cameron Haines is standing at the podium in one of his trademark Christian Dior blue suits, pink shirt, and blue tie. "Let's begin the transfer with file number one. Would the owner of this file come forward to the table and carry the file to Detective Reams?"

A very tall woman with dark hair rises from her chair at the table that remains dimly lit as she comes forward to retrieve the file. Once she is in the bright light at the front of the table, Reams recognizes her instantly. She's wearing a tight black dress with a silver sequined top and is an actress whom they would call a "Hollywood legend."

Reams mumbles under his breath, "Shit."

The woman picks up her file and begins walking from the table at the horseshoe end directly through the center of the ring towards Reams. When she approaches the end of the circular table where Reams sits in his chair, she drops the file practically under his nose. She tells him her name slowly, but loudly, and stares at Reams. "With all the money I have paid you over the years, I'd have thought you would dress a little nicer. I had not expected you to look so utterly ordinary."

Reams says nothing and stands up to greet her properly.

"Don't bother. I want no formal introduction or acknowledgment from you. So I had a beautiful baby girl out of wedlock, who unfortunately is not mentally well. That was eighteen years ago. The studio wanted me to have an abortion, but I didn't do that. When she was born, I wanted to take care of her out of the limelight because of her condition, and because of who her father is. I've cared for her all these years and visit her regularly. Which, of course, is how you discovered my little broken treasure of a child and threatened to have the tabloid paint me as a monster for what you called 'hiding my sin' and locking her away forever."

Reams replies, "I've never met you. I never could have said that to you."

"Didn't have to. You sent your despicable minion to a private birthday party I was having at the care facility for my daughter and a few of her friends that also live there. He barged right in to deliver a mock-up of the headline written for the tabloid if I didn't go along. He insisted on a check before he left."

"Who? Who are you talking about?"

"You know damn well. Here he comes now, your dark messenger."

Reams turns around to see two guards escorting Landon, who is in handcuffs.

She says, "Reid Garrett. Box office star with adoring fans, but poison to so many of his fellow actors. I can't tell you how I have waited for this day."

Landon shouts out, "I'm not Reid, tell them detective! Tell them!"

The guards place a piece of tape over Landon's mouth and move him back into the darkness.

Reams is furious. "Where are you, Alton Price?"

"I'm right here behind you, detective."

Reams cannot see Alton behind him, who is still dressed in a butler uniform. "What is going on, and how did you get Reid here?"

"After filming today, my colleagues and I retrieved him from the set."

"What is this charade? I'm an LAPD detective, investigating this issue, and you bring me here to accuse me of something someone else has done?"

"Detective, you are playing to the wrong audience. We couldn't get all sixty of your victims here tonight, but we have eighteen."

"That wasn't part of the deal," Reams protests. "You lied to me."

"No, no, I didn't. You can keep each file as the victim brings it to you. And you may then walk out of here with those files. Do you think for a minute that any of these eighteen people haven't realized you are not only part of this scheme, but you are the mastermind? And now, you are the sole survivor of the scheme. All your other partners mysteriously eliminated. Except for one incredibly dangerous one."

"They only know because you told them."

"You hid behind your depraved star boy until he was no longer a convenient shield for you. The monster you and Campanelli created turned on you, just like the Frankenstein story."

"So now you're going to have each person deliver their file to me?"

"Yes, for the eighteen victims that are here. Some of the biggest stars in Hollywood are sitting around this table. After each one confronts you, you can keep their file and take all the others with you. And of course, those who choose to no longer pay you have the option of confessing to their secret before you can expose them."

"It's a trick. You tricked me!"

Alton responds, "Not so. You will have all the files, detective. That is what I promised."

"But now you have exposed me to these individuals and lied about my involvement."

"Well, once it's all in the open, you can present your side of each case. But you know your fingerprints are all over this. And your little cozy business relationship with you-know-who won't sit well with them. I doubt you will want to spend your retirement years in Russia as you planned. Once all of this is out, your Russian partners will take care of you before the court system does."

Reams sees a red light flashing on both sides of the table. "These red lights in the darkness. Who are they?"

"Not who, detective, but what. They are cameras."

"What?"

"Yes, we are making a little movie here, a short tragedy film actually, and also broadcasting this event to a very special person you will meet after the file transfer is complete."

Reams reaches inside his jacket to retrieve his gun from his shoulder holster. "Your hands aren't clean in this, Mr. Price. There are the dual murders at Mr. Garrett's home, and I've got Landon to testify about your scheme to replace Reid. This isn't over yet."

"No, it isn't, detective. That's why you're free to walk out that door any time, but you need to see one more thing before you leave and pretend you can just walk away. Sit down for just a moment and then we'll open the soundstage door so you can walk out to your goons in the parking lot, with or without the files. I promise you we won't stop you."

Reams sits down, holding his pistol in his lap. The large blank screen at the horseshoe end of the table slowly illuminates, and a gentleman is sitting at a large desk with the FBI logo behind him.

56

The End You Deserve

The man on the video screen seated in front of the FBI seal does not look familiar to Reams, even though he has dealt with the FBI on investigations for almost forty years. "Good evening, detective. We've never met, but I'm Deputy Director Hunter Malcomb. The Special Agent you have been dealing with, Steven Schloss, reports to me."

Reams squirms in his seat, "Funny, I've never heard your name."

"And you likely won't again. I don't make appearances like this unless we suspect we have a rogue partner or a foreign agent infiltrating one of our investigations."

"So where is Steven? Is he there with you?"

"You won't be hearing from Special Agent Schloss again. I have removed him from assignment for reasons I suspect you have figured out by now."

Reams takes a deep breath and exhales while he wipes his forehead. "What is going on here? Are you really saying all of this in a room full of strangers?"

The Deputy Director smiles. "You know how we love witnesses. And how we love to record evidence for grand jury testimony."

"Good god, is that what's going on here?"

"Enough said, detective. I wanted to see and hear what was going on today, and to be sure they record it. When you leave, be sure to tell your men outside that FBI agents are also out there. The black vans are ours, and if we witness anything inappropriate as you exit the studio, we will act accordingly."

"Are they going to arrest me when I leave?"

"No. But you know the drill, detective. Don't leave the city. Not even on a private charter—if you know what I mean."

The screen goes blank. The light at the podium comes on and Cameron speaks. "Our second file transfer will be . . ."

Reams stands up and interrupts Cameron. "Enough. Enough!"

Alton, still standing in the darkness, calls out to Detective Reams. "Detective, perhaps I can help you out. Will you meet me in that dressing trailer at the back of the soundstage?" A light slowly illuminates the dressing trailer at the far corner.

Reams says nothing but begins walking to the trailer, gun still in hand. Alton follows him several steps back.

As Reams approaches the trailer, the door is open, but he stops before going in. He turns to see if he can locate Alton in the darkness. Alton yells out to Reams, "Put your gun on the table by the steps. Go inside. I promise I am unarmed."

Reams hesitates and looks around. He peers inside the trailer. It is empty except for a big chair in front of a make-up table with bright lights. He puts his gun on the table and steps inside the trailer, looking behind him to see if Alton is following him in.

"Have a seat, detective." Alton sits inside the trailer on a banquette against the wall.

"Shit, you scared the crap out of me. How did you get in here first?"

"An old Houdini illusion."

"You fucked me over, Price. You told the FBI even though you promised you wouldn't."

"I promise you, I have not told the FBI. You've been sloppy."

"What happens now? You said you would help me."

"And that I will."

"So?"

"So, you have several options, detective. First off, you can walk right out of here, with all or with none of the files. That's up to you. I can't forecast what will happen when you step out of the studio gates, but you are free to go and I will guarantee your safety until you are outside Gate 3."

"Shit, that's a lousy option. I can't have any of those files in my possession if the FBI is out there."

"I think your biggest worry is your goons and the FBI. You will need to get a message to your guys before you just pop out of the gate. You don't want to risk one of your guys or the FBI getting trigger-happy."

"That's it? You said there are several options."

"There's still Alexei and your exit to Russia. Alexei is here. I can take you to him and you and Landon can continue with your plan to fly to Moscow."

"I'll be a pauper living in Moscow if Alexei doesn't kill me first. My entire scheme fell apart tonight. Thanks to you, you bastard!"

"I think your scheme fell apart because you got greedy. And vain."

"No matter. Russia is not an option without having a stream of money to live on."

"Okay, you want to go back to the LAPD, turn yourself in and do jail time for extortion, blackmail, and the murder of Marina Petrovich?"

"I didn't murder her."

"Accomplice. You know that word better than I. It's a humiliating way to end your career, that's for sure, but you won't get the death penalty. Just life in prison."

"At my age, that won't be very long."

"Well, detective, there is one more option. And it involves a promise from me."

"A promise? From you? That's fucking worthless."

"Is it? Think about it. I leave you alone here in this trailer. I return your gun to you and close the door. You are a single malt cop, so look over on the make-up table."

Reams walks over to the make-up table to see a bottle of Macallan twenty-five-year-old Sherry Oak single malt scotch. He lets out a big laugh while he picks up the bottle. "I'll be damned. This is a thousand-dollar bottle of scotch. At least. How funny is that? I was going to treat myself to this once I beat you at this game and was on my way to Moscow. And here it is. Now, I get to drink it, but it's because *you* defeated *me*. How ironic! Reams picks up a glass on the table and lifts the bottle. May I?"

"Then you are accepting my offer? That is the option you have chosen?"

"Come now, Mr. Price, this is a Hobson's choice. Among all those options, there really is only one choice. You knew that but thank you for setting me up so nicely." Reams smiles as he opens the bottle and pours himself a glass. "Join me?"

"Of course." Reams pours a glass for Alton and hands it to him.

"Congratulations, Houdini. I really thought the day would come I'd bust one of your schemes. I really did."

"Well, there is one more benefit to this option, detective."

"Besides the Macallan?"

"Yes. If you make this your last drink, or your last bottle and you use your pistol there to end your misery, your reputation will remain intact. Your colleagues will think you died trying to end this scam rather than because you were the ringleader."

Reams finishes his drink and pours another. "Why? Why would you do that?"

"You know my reputation for handing out punishment that I think suits the crime?"

"Like incinerating Reid Garrett and Tony Campanelli?"

"Well, you must admit their crimes justified their end."

"So why do I deserve better?"

"Because for most of your life, as best I can tell, you were a good cop. You got jealous of the lifestyles and wealth of many of the victims and perpetrators of the murders you investigated. You knew an honest cop would never have those material trappings. So, you turned into a corrupt cop because you felt you had earned it. You deserved it."

Reams tears up but tries not to cry. "You pity me as a corrupt cop?"

"I don't pity you. You knew what you were doing, and likely would have gotten away with it, until you let your vanity overcome you. I just don't feel your years as a corrupt cop should overshadow your decades of being a good cop. And your career is really all you ever had. No family. Very few friends. The LAPD was your life."

Reams nods his head and pours himself another drink. "I have one question, Mr. Price. Where did I slip up? I need to know."

"Same as Reid. Your vanity. Your little scheme was unfolding well. You never should have confided in Landon, and never should have been at Raminsky's house when I came there. I really was not expecting to find you there. Once I saw you in that room, barking out orders to Raminsky employees, I knew you were the mastermind and that you'd let your vanity overcome you. You wanted some fame out of it. You relished being the big guy in front of me and the others. You should have stayed in the shadows, overlooked until you were safely on your way out of the country."

Reams says nothing as he sits down in the make-up chair with another drink. He smiles at Alton. "I'm ready for my companion now. This will be the last task for my Beretta."

"I thought the LAPD issued Glocks to their officers?"

"Yes, they have for about eighteen years. I never liked the Glock. I kept my Beretta. Please bring her to me and close the door?"

Alton stands up from the banquette and goes to Reams to shake his hand. Reams smiles, "Congratulations, Mr. Price. Well done."

Alton says nothing as he turns to open the trailer door and retrieves the gun from the table outside. He steps back inside to see Reams finishing his drink and extending his hand to get the gun. As Alton hands him the gun, Reams smiles, winks, and waives Alton away with his hand.

Alton steps outside the trailer and closes the door. He is only five steps from the door before hearing a single gunshot. He stops for a moment, turns to face the trailer while he whispers a prayer:

Never let my pride turn to vanity. Don't let my compassion turn to pity. Spirits, please come forth and retrieve this soul. Now that he has ended the agony of his material life, please redeem him.

Alton turns away from the trailer and walks back to the center of the soundstage.

The Curtain Drops

Alton, still dressed as the butler, returns to the big horseshoe table in the center of the soundstage. He stops short of the light and stands in the darkness behind Blair, who sits in her chair watching her father hand out the last of the files to the victims.

While Alton was with Detective Reams in the trailer, Cameron's job was to thank each of the victims (mostly actors and actresses) for coming and to return their file to each of them. A few victims hung around talking with each other and thanking Cameron. Forty-two files were still left to be returned, which Cameron would begin doing tomorrow morning, in person, since he knows nearly all the victims. Alton offered to have a lawyer do it, or an anonymous person, but Cameron wanted to do it himself. He knew the pain of blackmail and extortion and wanted to look into the eyes of each victim. Alton had ensured that he'd sealed all the files, so only the victims would be able to open them once they received their file.

Blair seemed proud to see her father help end this nightmare in such kind fashion. The crew was wrapping up and Alton was waiting for the last of the celebrities to leave. One of them insisted on thanking Alton personally, but Cameron told them that would not be possible, as he had already left.

As the last celebrity walks away, it is now just Cameron, Blair, and Alton in the soundstage. Alton emerges from the darkness to greet Blair.

"Alton, you startled me! I forgot about your costume. It's

rather silly, you know."

"Well, it did the trick. Thank you for coming. Let's go get your dad."

As Blair and Alton approach Cameron, he beams with joy that the nightmare is over and how much he enjoyed returning the files to the victims. "Thank you for letting me do this, Alton. You missed a lot of tears of joy while you were with the detective."

"As it should be, Cameron. And you were the only one who could pull this off. No one is more trusted. Thank you for setting all of this up. Is the crew gone?"

"Yes, just us here now. The gaffers are coming back later to get the lights. I handed out the cash gratuities to each of them, the camera crew and the studio guards. They were all grateful."

"Any of them suspicious about what really went on?"

"Don't think so. The lighting director asked if Reams was really an LAPD officer, and I told him he did us a favor to add to the reality of the pilot."

"Cam, who was the actor playing the Deputy FBI Director? He was superb. Even I thought he was the real deal!"

"He's a character actor you have likely seen many times, and frankly he wasn't my first choice because I was afraid Reams might recognize him, but apparently he didn't. Name is Ben Nelson. He gave himself more hair and made it darker, otherwise you may have recognized him. Blair likely recognized him right away."

"I did! Great job! All you had to do was fool Reams, and you did that! I think everyone around the table recognized him, but of course said nothing."

"Glad you were happy with the casting, Alton! Ben wanted to meet you. We had him in a sound booth with that FBI logo in the back, but he had to leave while you were with Reams. Where is the detective?" Cameron asks.

Alton puts his hands in his pockets and winks at Cameron.

"Did he turn himself in, like you were hoping?"

"Something like that, Cam."

"Oh no, don't tell me he's another victim."

"He tried to help at the end and the LAPD should view him as a hero."

"What? That nasty schemer who fleeced us all these years. You didn't let him go, did you?"

"Cameron, that doesn't sound like you!"

Blair chimes in. "Well, I agree. He deserves the same end as Reid."

"Well, he's no longer around; that's all you need to know. Just take care of getting all those files to their rightful owners."

"Will there be any charges against Reams or anyone?"

"Cameron, they're all dead. You can't bring charges against three dead men."

"What about Landon, posing as Reid?"

"Stick to the plan. The coroner said Landon died and Reid is alive. He was on the set today. That's it. Just see what unfolds from here, but don't spoil the narrative."

As soon as Alton finishes speaking, he sees two figures enter the soundstage. One is Alexei and the other is a large bodyguard. "Cam and Blair, please excuse me. I have one more detail and then I will meet you at Taix for dinner."

Blair squints to see the visitors. "Who are they?"

"Blair, you don't want to know," Alton says, "so please vanish with your father before this guy gets a good look at you. I am serious. You can't see him, so get going!"

As Cameron and Blair walk out the other soundstage door, Alton walks toward Alexei and his bodyguard. Before Alton can say anything, Alexei stops and stares at him. "Okay, I am here. What do you want?"

"Follow me to that sound booth." Alton points toward a room with a soundproof glass window and escorts them in.

"Thank you for coming. Alexei, I have Landon in the other room with two of my men holding him. I have mildly sedated him. His first public appearance as Reid Garrett went well, but now you need to get him out of the country before he talks."

"I already plan to do that. I told Reams."

Alton shakes his head, "I rather guessed that. He's yours from here on out and I trust you will handle him accordingly."

"We are leaving tonight. Just waiting on Reams. You said he would be here."

"He is, but his traveling days are over."

Alton's statement confuses Alexei. "What the fuck you say?"

"He's dead. You need not take a dead body back to Russia."

"I don't believe you. Are you hiding him?"

"If you don't believe me, go down to the end of the sound-stage where you see that dressing trailer. Look inside. But hurry, the men who are holding Landon have some cleaning up to do in there right away. Go . . . look."

Alexei motions for his bodyguard to go look inside the trailer. As the bodyguard walks away, Alton hands the original payment file to Alexei. "Here, I promised your uncle that you would have the original payment file so there is no record of the money laundering or cash drops. I promise you, I did not make a copy. This is the original."

"You talk with my uncle?"

"Not directly, but we have a mutual contact."

"How you know my uncle? He never mentions you."

"The hedge fund, Global Protocol, in Beverly Hills? The one that was closed up because it was unwittingly laundering money for the Chinese Communist Party?"

"Ah, yes, my uncle, tiny investor. He got his money back. Most didn't."

"Right. Logan and Max Aronheart were my best friends. Logan owned the company with a partner who ended up being used by their largest client. Your uncle had $200 million there disguised as a union pension fund. Before the regulators shut it down, Logan liquidated your uncle's money and transferred it to a Swiss bank account. He asked that I deliver the account codes to your uncle, which I did. He was incredibly grateful."

"I remember. That was the affair known as the Dragon Shroud."

"Exactly. After I saw how upset you were about the Reams

scheme going bad, I knew you and your uncle needed that file."

"Thank you. We will take care of Mr. Garrett."

"I know you will."

The bodyguard approaches Alexei and whispers in his ear. Alexei nods his head. "Okay, looks like you have quite a mess in there. Where is Mr. Garrett?"

Alton leaves the sound booth, goes down the hall and opens a door. He motions for his two men to escort Landon out. They bring him to Alexei and the bodyguard, who then takes Landon by the arm. Alexei extends his hand to Alton. "Thank you, Mr. Price."

"Safe travels, thanks for your understanding. My best to your uncle."

After Alexei and the bodyguard and Landon exit the sound-stage, Alton motions for his men to get Reams body and clean up the trailer. He pulls his cell phone from his pocket and dials the personal cell phone number for the Police Chief for the City of Los Angeles Police Department. "Chief, I'm afraid I have some bad news for you. Can you please dispatch someone to Soundstage 26 at the West Hollywood studio complex? I'm afraid they shot Detective Reams with his own gun while attempting to arrest Reid Garrett. I'll explain everything when your staff gets here."

The Police Chief asks Alton a question about how Reams died.

"He was a hero. Shot with his own gun, and Reid has gotten away . . . at least for now. I'm on it. Get your folks here and I'll give them all the details."

Alton no sooner hangs up with the Police Chief when his cell phone rings. He sees it is the guard calling from Studio Gate 3. "Yes, please let him in and direct him to Soundstage 26."

Alton goes to the soundstage entrance to wait for his visitor to arrive. Minutes later, an attractive younger man with a muscular build walks up to Alton. "Mr. Price, I'm Derek. Derek Christopher."

"My pleasure to meet you, Derek. Thanks for coming on such brief notice."

"This place brings back wonderful memories for me. I did a

lot of stunts filming here. You said you may have a gig for me?"

"Actually, I have a payment for you for a stunt you did last Thursday night."

Derek says nothing.

"Am I confusing you?"

"Well, to be honest, I've had no real stunt work for a while. Just some work as a stunt double, but nothing exciting. See, I have a kid now and I promised my wife there'd be no more risky work. I think I mentioned that to you on the phone."

Alton hands Derek an envelope. "A stunt you did for Reid Garrett, last Thursday. Apparently, he didn't get around to paying you, and he's leaving to shoot a film in Russia tonight. I want to be sure you get paid for your excellent dive. It was quite impressive."

Derek takes the envelope and stares at it. "Really? The last I saw of Reid, he kicked me out of his car in front of my house. I didn't expect to ever receive payment for that stunt. Guess I screwed up the dive. I don't know what happened, but he said I messed it all up. I can't take this money."

Alton smiles. "Your dive was perfect. I was there. You hit the mat dead center and did a perfect tuck and roll. I'm afraid I'm the one who gave you a sedative immediately after you landed. I moved the mat to make it look like you missed. I'm sorry, Derek. I understand Reid promised you fifteen thousand dollars. I put twenty-five thousand in the envelope. Besides the money, I didn't want your self-confidence shaken. You did a perfect dive, and a perfect landing. Didn't want it to haunt you for the rest of your life thinking you didn't do a perfect dive."

"I don't know what to say. Please don't tell my wife."

"Your secret is safe with me, so long as my secret is safe with you."

Derek smiles and nods his head, winking at Alton.

"Now please go home to your wife and child. Delete my number from your phone. This meeting and this payment never happened. Got it?"

"I don't know what to say."

"Goodbye, Mr. Christopher. Go home!"

An hour later, Alton joins Cameron and Blair at Taix restaurant. When he enters the restaurant, he sees them at a table laughing and holding hands. "I hate to break up this love fest, but may I join you for dinner?"

Cameron and Blair both laugh at the comment. Cameron says, "Of course, join us . . . because you're buying!"

Over cocktails they discuss the press conference Blair and Cameron have next week to announce their new production company. And the fact they are father and daughter. Blair's mother has agreed to travel from London to attend the event. It will be the first time that the three of them have been together since Blair was born.

Blair looks at Alton and grabs his hand. "Thank you for everything you did, Alton. I know I was a total bitch, but you knew that anyway, didn't you? I'm sorry. I hope you can attend our press conference next week."

"I'd love to be there, but if I am, you won't recognize me. You know I don't do big events in public. But try to spot me!"

They toast each other with martinis, vowing to keep up with Blair at least for one night.

A Film Titled *Dasvidaniya*

The following evening, a large cocktail party is hosted in Moscow to welcome American movie star Reid Garrett to Russia. The Russian news service says that the American actor will tour Russia scouting out locations for an upcoming movie he will make in St. Petersburg. Many stars of Russian film and theatre are in attendance. Reid seems a bit out of sorts but blames it on jet lag. He adores the attention he is receiving, and a beautiful Russian actress accompanies him and Mr. Alexei Raminsky, who says he will finance Reid's film. The title will be *Dasvidaniya*, which means "goodbye" or "farewell" in Russian. Alexei doesn't let Reid out of his sight.

Two days later, the Russian media announces the untimely death of American actor Reid Garrett in his hotel room in St. Petersburg. The cause of death is unknown. His body was cremated before an autopsy could be performed.

Dasvidaniya.

Also Available

If you enjoyed *Dark Vanity,* you may also enjoy Gregg's previous mystery *Vanquish of the Dragon Shroud,* available wherever great books are sold.

Learn more about the author:
https://gregoryseller.com/
https://www.linkedin.com/in/gregoryseller
https://www.facebook.com/gregory.seller
https://www.goodreads.com/book/
show/36821375-vanquish-of-the-dragon-shroud
https://twitter.com/Gregory
https://www.pinterest.com/authorgregoryseller/
vanquish-of-the-dragon-shroud/

CPSIA information can be obtained
at www.ICGtesting.com
Printed in the USA
BVHW091837140621
609554BV00014B/460